Soulless Ending

ETERNAL FLAME TRILOGY

Blaine Blade

Published by:

FriesenPress
Suite 300 – 852 Fort Street
Victoria, BC, Canada V8W 1H8

www.friesenpress.com

Distributed to the trade by The Ingram Book Company

Acknowledgements

It definitely wasn't hard to decide who should go on this page. First of all, I would like to thank my teacher, mentor, and editor, Jamie Dee. Without her motivation and wisdom, this story would never have blossomed into what it is today.

Thanks to my loving, sometimes annoying, parents; they lit the flame under me. Without their encouragement and powerful life lessons, I would never have become the person to write this novel. I love them both so much.

I would like to say thank you to my girlfriend, Payton. If I had never met her, reading and writing probably would've never become something so dear to me. I love you.

My appreciation and gratitude goes out to the members of the rock band Heaven Below and the songwriter, Patrick Kennison, for granting me permission to include lyrics from their song "When Daylight Dies" in this book. Rock on, guys!

And lastly, thanks to Aaron, Jesse, James, and everyone who suggested ideas and kept asking me: "Can I read your book?" Without friends like them, what would I have done?

To Ms. Trusheim,
Thank you!
Blaine
B laden

To Mom, Drew, and Payton;
I finally did it.

"Still I count the days and nights
Since I survived
This lonely abyss is the place
I've learned to hide
But the memories conflict with
The story I keep in my mind
Then reality comes over me
Like darkness to blind

I can't live without your love
And I can't die
Still I'm standing in the rain
When daylight dies"

- Heaven Below, "When Daylight Dies"

1. Outcast

It's the middle of November. The grass was frosty. Soon, five feet of snow would blanket the state of Iowa, driving off most of nature, rendering our state lifeless. But, so it goes, I suppose.

That day, however, the sun was shining, melting the inconstant frost. We were supposed to have a high of thirty-three degrees. But whether the temperature was thirty-three or seventy five, scorching or relatively cool, I despised sunny days. They brought me no joy and showed how ugly things could be. Besides, there was no chance of getting out of school on a sunny day.

I was a freshman—yeah, a freshman—and being a freshman sucked. Everyone who was one understands. Being a freshman means getting everything last and, more importantly, being degraded by upper classmen. I feel disgusted at how some people could act. Feeling no regret, caring nothing for their prey, these animals act with no reason. I was prey once. I didn't do anything, even though my step-dad said I should've gotten vengeance.

Early in the fall of my freshman year, during an early morning theater rehearsal, a senior girl in the drama club called me to the side. Sultry, round, bouncy...her job of getting my attention was an easy one. After I approached her, another senior, a boy, shoved me down with a thump. Smiling stupidly, the predator spit in my face. Humiliated, confused, and appalled, I took the attack as a sign to continue reserving my

trust. I had been very suspicious of most people years beforehand…
but I'm getting ahead of myself.

Covered in drool and mumbling something from a dream, I had
awakened clumsily from my slumber. A dull, grey light permeated
through my blinds. Darkness so many people associate with fear and
evil. I enjoyed it, and the night. And, secretly, I enjoyed the snow,
which was like a federal crime in Iowa.

Stumbling out of bed and into the hallway, I walked past a mirror,
noticing my haggardness. In my eyes, I saw a teenage, five foot ten,
blackish brown-haired boy. Remnants of dreams swam in his eyes like
fish with names he couldn't remember. His face was round, not yet
matured. Facial hair sprouted in rough patches along his jaw and under
his chin…an average teenage boy.

Sometimes, I didn't consider the figure to be me. It's like when
you listen to a recording of your voice…you wonder what you were
high on.

Black rings were huddled under my eyes, revealing my struggle to
sleep. Panicking about failure, I had been dreading all night about the
mid-term exams. I may not have appeared so, but I did have concern
for my grades, the currency I exchanged for my freedom.

I contemplated feigning sickness, missing the exam days so I could
have more time to study. But, after thinking about it, I decided an
amassed pile of homework wasn't worth the skip.

But the exams weren't solely responsible for scaring off sleep. I had
been having some warped dreams. The visions escaped explanation,
and they seemed to get more and more complicated. Fire…I remembered fire that stretched on forever around a circle of seven crowns.
That was all I could remember, and I had no explanation of what the
visions were, or where they had come from. It's not like I ate anything
before I went to bed, being on a diet.

I walked to the bathroom down the hall to wash my face, to relieve
the tension I had built up overnight. Though, I've been told, I'm tense
all the time.

I wasn't the tallest kid in school, nor was I the biggest. I had strength
and my own distrust to support me, though. Kids knew I could deck
them, but they would still try to pull pranks and take advantage of me.
My cold attitude and hostility towards strangers lost me most potential
friendships. And, some days, it was hard for me to wake up.

"Honey, you're going to be late if you don't hurry!" my mom, a mid-
dle-aged woman with a cloak of chocolate brown hair and fair, freckled
skin, called up from the kitchen, derailing my train of thought.

"I'll be down soon, Mom," I called back, checking my face for acne.

My mom, despite my love for her, was one of the craziest people I knew. One time, I had a huge slash across my cheek. A ghastly scar took its place not long after. Mom said I didn't cry, though. She said I was growing up. I said she was growing silly.

Although I hated it when she fraternized over tiny things like the scar, I knew she couldn't help it. It was in her nature as a mother. I guess it was something I actually adored about her.

"Haydn, get your butt down here!" I heard my step-dad bellow, impatient as always.

"I'm coming, I'm coming," I bellowed back, mocking him as I came down the stairs, my feet, feeling heavy as bricks, stomping against the carpeted, wooden stairs.

"Better shape up your attitude, boy," my step-dad threatened.

Drake, my step-dad, was a huge man in almost every definition of the word. He was about six foot five and weighed about three hundred pounds. He had short brown hair and savage brown eyes. He was very muscular, and never subtle about it or his thoughts. Very blunt, his mind was like a weapon, usually directed at me and my shortcomings.

But I always tried to suppress my anger so I wouldn't blow up in his face. That would be suicide. Anger was my enemy disguised as an ally. Whenever I felt hurt or confused, Anger was there to soothe me, convince me to lash back. And when it came to conversation with Drake, Anger was by my side the whole time.

"Yeah, yeah," I said.

"Now, sit down, eat your breakfast and shut up," he said gruffly, slowly drawing in his coffee as I sat down across from him at our kitchen table.

Breakfast, for me, was a small granola bar and Creatine. I wanted to be a bodybuilder—no not a professional one—and needed to keep a good diet: low fats, plenty of protein and vitamins to build muscle. I lifted weights regularly, considering I had nothing better to do. Even with speculation that I had reached my maximum capacity, Drake thought differently. He said I could push myself harder. But he was letting me take a break to let the muscle repair and build. After that, though, death was certain.

My eyes toured the tiny kitchen like they did every morning, just to see if anything changed. Nothing ever did. The faux wooden table that sat directly in the middle of our kitchen was still there. Along with the four matching, green chairs with green pillows on them. There was also the countertop with a built-in dish washer, which was white. Then a couple feet away from it towards the west was our black stove, right next to the black fridge, which both sat under the white microwave.

I paused at the appliances and chuckled a bit. Looking at them reminded me of my older sister. She graduated a year prior to my inauguration into high school. It drove me nuts how much she could obsess over those two colors. I thought opposites always complimented each other. My older sister, Morgan, always thought differently. She wanted them all to be matching.

I never saw the sense in having everything the same. Black and white had gone together for a long time, so why separate them now? Like nature and animals, they didn't deserve to be separated.

"Morning everyone!" A voice trilled, a high flute tone, from its room only a few feet away off the kitchen.

Out of the corner room emerged a young girl. Only in middle school, yet she was already filled out more than some high school girls. Sometimes, I was scared about how mature she looked.

Her eyes were a creamy baby blue, so innocent, so young. They would seduce any guy. Perceptive individuals could tell her true age. Her eyes didn't reflect the teenage stress of most high school girls. I could tell the difference. My step-sister was the personification of innocence. I couldn't imagine her pressured by the stress I had endured.

It was hard to resist her unnatural, innocent beauty. It was awkward, too, since she lived under the same roof as me. Nevertheless, I reminded myself she was *family*, and that it would be morally wrong to do anything I might accidentally imagine. However…that never stopped *her* from trying.

She had a certain sway to her step, like a cobra hypnotizing its prey as she walked to the table. I just knew, with those swift, elegant, sultry motions, matched with her soft, tween body, that many eyes would turn to watch her pass, bewitched.

Today, she wore a gray cotton sweater with tight "skinny" jeans. Her hair was down, a fountain of gold, to her shoulders. She was definitely pretty and knew it, too. It was easy for her to get big brother to pay attention. I curse teenage hormones.

"So, ready for your tests?" Katria asked, scrutinizing my reaction. She sat down, her long, shimmering blonde hair whispering *Touch me.*

"If you're ready for yours, then I can handle mine, middle schooler," I said, grazing on my granola bar, trying to put her out of my mind. I had stopped getting nervous around her as often as I used to.

Katria ran a hand through her hair, disappointed at my response. She quickly tapped me, her long nail jabbing my forearm.

"What is it?" one eye open, pretending I was uninterested.

"Is high school hard, Haydn?" she asked nervously.

Was she serious? She had another year to go until she should worry. Only a seventh grader, yet she was already worked up over high school?

"Only if you make it that way," I said confidently enough, masking my stress with arrogance. "I honestly have no problem with it. But everyone's different."

"Well, that's great advice," Katria mumbled disdainfully.

"You make yourself what you are," I added. "In high school, you might want to pay more attention to your word choice. Someone might just take it the wrong way. Next thing you know, there's a rumor halfway around the school about how you have a tramp stamp…or how you slept with the class nerd."

Katria gulped. Her eyes were wide with horror.

"Seriously?"

I nodded. "And I haven't even mentioned the classes yet—"

"I've heard enough!" Katria shouted, clasping her hands over her ears. She started making annoying noises to drown me out.

I shook my head, regretting I ever said anything. "Are we leaving soon, Drake?"

"Yeah, we better get heading out," he muttered.

Thank the lord.

*   *   *

My morning routine basically followed that pattern. I got up. Complained to myself about how I looked. I ate breakfast. I tried to ignore family—especially Katria. We loaded into the car. I stayed absolutely quiet while my sister complained about the tiniest things— how'd she get over that scare I gave her? Finally, I got out of the car. And I walked into school and waited for the first bell.

I knew everything that was going to happen in my day. After a few weeks, I couldn't help but get bored. It was hard *not* to get bored with such a repetitive lifestyle. It was easy to wait for the arrival of my senior year, or death, like a gift that no one wants. Or, so it goes, I suppose. And I thought high school was supposed to be difficult.

I shuffled past several other kids and finally leaned against the wall, sighing as I waited for a mob of adolescents to pass. Today felt different, though. I felt a certain energy trickling down my spine, like a honey that made me feel happy. As soon as the crowd cleared, I sighed and trudged towards my locker. It was the same boring locker, with the same boring books and same boring everything. I wished something would happen. I felt like something was going to happen.

How right I was.

When my locker was in sight, my heart skipped a beat. It was then that I was quickly reminded how potentially difficult high school could be. Right next to my locker were the lockers of *them*. Four of the *hottest* girls in the district, and they were called the Gaga Girls. They were beauties that, try as they might, no other girl could beat. It was almost impossible to even get a minute to talk with one of them, which crushed hopes and dreams of desperate boys. Yet, no matter what, they would come back, stuck on their bad romance. Just like that song by Lady Gaga.

They were standing at their lockers. Always together, a word from them to you was like getting a blessing straight from God. Standing there, chatting, those four giggled about something my muscle-headed mind would probably never be able to grasp. It was like stumbling upon a secret civilization.

My immediate plan was to turn tail and run. *I* stood no chance of ever getting noticed by one of *them* and I felt weak and feeble next to them. I felt that I didn't deserve to stand within a five foot radius of them. I felt so ugly. They had too much *class*.

Everyone knew their parents and everyone knew that the Mercedes out front belonged to them. It was just hard to imagine that rich girls like them would even consider going to such a rural and low-grade school like East Klintwood. I couldn't even fathom the idea much less see it with my own eyes. And yet, they were only an arm's length away from me.

I took a deep breath, swallowed hard, and sauntered to my locker and opened it. My arm was only inches away from touching the arm of Rifu Anerex, the leader of the four. Rifu had fiery red hair and daz-zling, large emerald eyes, eyes that could only exist in expression... all the loves songs could not describe their ensnaring radiance. Her face looked so soft and was painstakingly angel-like in any light. She was shorter than me, but not by much, and was also a freshman, as were two other of the Gaga Girls.

I hastily scooped up my P.E. clothes, turned noisily, and fled for the gym. My face heated with embarrassment.

"Hey, you," I heard from behind me. "Come here."

I froze in place and quickly looked around to see if there was anyone there. No one else was present. My anxiety started to culminate, my heart racing like a horse. I could feel the blood leaving my face and rushing back with twice the force. I gulped and took a shaky breath to brace myself.

I turned, discovering that it was one of the Gaga Girls—Jolie Raven—who was calling me back towards the group. Jolie was the oldest of the Gaga Girls and also the second tallest. She was a junior, being two years older than the rest of us, which led me to wonder why she wasn't the leader. Jolie was certainly the perfect one to lead with her more-than-extravagant hair, brown with golden highlights.

But her hair didn't compare to her mesmerizing eyes. Today, though, they seemed lack luster. Any other day, however, her eyes struck me as familiar, but I just figured I had imagined them perfect. I always tried to guess a color. Sometimes, I guessed garnet, then, other times, scarlet.

She curled her finger inwards like she was reeling me in, and I couldn't help but act like the little fish I was and walk over. I felt like I had no control over my body. All four of them were eyeing me, especially Brenda and Neferia.

Brenda, the most developed of the four, with chin length hair dyed blue and golden eyes, stood against the lockers holding her books against her over-developed chest. Neferia, a white-hair-at-ear-length, smoky grey-eyed beauty stood quietly between Brenda and Jolie.

Jolie was staring at me with something I couldn't quite put into words. She seemed slightly interested in me, but I wasn't for sure. Her features were set in a cheerful disposition. My eyes continued to wander helplessly. There was Rifu, a perfect among all of them. She wasn't too developed. However, she and Jolie seemed very identical.

"What's your name?" Rifu asked as my eyes rolled over her. Her voice resembled something from a chorus. A hint of a British accent tinted her tone.

I opened my mouth, but nothing came out. It was as if my voice box had had just exploded. Finally, after silently clearing my throat I managed to get my name out.

"Haydn Ladditz…" I said, my voice cracking at the end. I was an idiot.

Jolie nodded, as if she already knew, smiling as she put her gentle, pale finger tips on the bottom of my chin, tilting it up. She was a few inches taller than me.

"We'll be in touch," she said velvety smooth, just as Rifu had except with more of an old-country accent.

After they left me by myself, my blood rushed through my body. Rifu, leader of the four girls, asked me my name. And Jolie touched me.

And last time I checked, there were guys cooler than me in the school who could never dream of getting that close. But, I wasn't going to look a gift horse in the mouth.

I was on a high and enjoying every single moment of it. But for some reason I felt strange when Jolie put her hand on my chin, something about her touch seemed so weird. Her expression was odd, as if she was dazed, and her eyes looked cloudy.

Maybe, it was just me. I'd never talked to them directly, person-to-person. Of course, being approached by four beautiful girls was a danger, especially when jealousy was concerned. But something just made me shiver about how they stared at me. No, it was just my imagination. Yeah, that had to be it.

*   *   *

We'll be in touch…

The events of the morning weighed on my mind. My body reflected my edginess and anxiety in nervous twitches and quick reactions. I was so hyped.

In my excitement, I memorized every detail I had observed. Their scent, their velvety, flute-like voices, and the soft skin of Jolie's finger tips etched themselves into my head. After some time of reimaging the scene, I couldn't exactly remember what was or wasn't there. I cursed myself for deluding the encounter with my fantasies.

Was Brenda wearing spaghetti strings? That was a pipe dream if I've ever heard of one, but there was something I wasn't sure of. I couldn't quite place it in reality or maybe a strange fantasy that had possessed me, but it appeared to me that Neferia was licking her lips.

Maybe, I didn't imagine it. Maybe, it was just that she didn't have her mind set on me. I mean, what hot girl would?

I sailed through the rest of my day in a blur, unaware of everything happening around me. Even in computer applications, I didn't pay that much attention. I was so staggered from the attention these girls had given me.

Normally, whenever there was a spare moment, I would see the Gaga Girls amongst themselves, but everyone else was watching. Even the eyes of some very green-eyed girls were taking note of their crushing dominance in beauty and popularity. The Gaga Girl's influence was strong, causing me to question the fairness of putting such beautiful and exotic creatures amongst such lowly, wretched, ugly beasts like me.

That day was no exception. I found myself among the many Gaga-junkies carefully admiring these hidden goddesses. Girls gave me small amounts of attention, sometimes upperclassmen girls. But they weren't as vogue as the Gaga Girls. They gave me a reason to keep working out, though. Maybe it was because of muscles that the Gaga Girls noticed me. I was pretty chiseled for my age.

As I watched them, Jolie looked up and saw me. I quickly acted uninterested and looked away. After a second, I glanced back. Jolie was once again engrossed with her conversation.

I left them. If I sat and admired them all day, what would I get done?

*   *   *

After school, I navigated my way through a timber west of town. It was the only way home on foot. I preferred the silence and solitude to a bunch of pestering, bantering, raucous grade school kids that accompanied a bus ride.

In my head, I reviewed the Gaga Girl's behavior. I yearned to breathe in their luscious fragrances again, my skull pounding, head spinning, skin shivering.

Minute details, like what they were wearing, faded from my head. But did that really matter? Knowing what they wore this morning wouldn't get me their numbers. How could I even get their numbers?

Crack.

I turned around, the muffled crack making me jump. Studying the snow-dusted woods carefully, I checked for any signs of another presence. I called out, but received no response.

Sighing, I turned around, ignoring the eerie wind tickling the back of my neck. No one was following me. But, at the same time, I didn't feel alone. I marched forward, leaping over tree roots and ducking low branches, my mind still wandering backwards, towards the school... towards the Gaga Girls.

I took a deep breath. The scents of dormant pines and wintry air mixed together to create a very delicate, yet spicy fragrance that I relished. I hiked up a sloping, barren dirt path which cleared out onto a road. Across the road was my two-story home. The walls were faded blue, so faded that it was hard to tell them from white on bright days. There was a small concrete porch with a sunroof above it, under which a couple of metal chairs rested. I often sat out there and watched the snow and rain.

I trudged across the road, not caring if there was an approaching car or not, and headed for the yard. I slowed to a halt. I turned around to look back into the woods. There was nothing in the clearing except for the echoes of my paranoia.

After turning back around, I walked to the porch sliding door and slid it open. I quickly jumped inside and closed the door. No one was there. If a feather dropped, I would have heard it. Suddenly, I felt glum. I had no homework, but I couldn't remember for sure. I was so preoccupied with my own imagination that everything had felt like a dream. Except the morning, I could almost clearly remember the morning. I knew it happened. I *believed* it happened.

I shifted uncomfortably. I had been resting all my weight on my right leg. Before my leg fell asleep, I went through the living room and quickly ascended the stairs. At the top was my room. I dropped my bag and plopped down on my bed, releasing a large, suppressed sigh, and then a yawn. A few moments later I got back up to turn on my computer. After it groaned to life, I clicked open my e-mail. I sorted through it mechanically, indifferent, finding nothing but junk. I sighed and signed out.

Easing myself onto the floor, I stretched and dug my hands into the soft shag carpeting.

A thought drifted into my mind. That thought then bloomed into a feeling. That feeling burned into a desire. I wanted to be recognized, I realized. I wanted people to know my name. I wanted this because no one knew me. No one cared about me. The Gaga Girls…Jolie, Rifu, Neferia, and Brenda could help me. Perhaps they could raise my popularity.

But, at the same time, I felt like I didn't know what, or who, I wanted to be. Maybe, I just wanted to be normal, to stop being an outcast.

2. Invitation

A few days passed since I had talked to the Gaga Girls. What pleasure did people find in making others feel miserable? I didn't know.

Upon entering the school, my face felt heated … embarrassed, which made me irritable. Everyone could feel it. Especially the kid I darted in the face with a ball during P.E. I just didn't understand why the Gaga Girls would tease me. What had I done to them? They were like a drug. I was so high around them. Then they cut me off, like a druggie from his supply.

The thought of them messing with me was irritating enough. Not being able to do anything about it was even worse. I was ready to cause others pain, but my conscience whispered *No* in my ear.

Lunch rolled around, and I went to my locker to retrieve a protein shake. I had to be missing some inside joke. Sighing, I passed a loving couple huddled against a locker. Dammit, P.D.A. But at least they had each other.

When I looked inside my locker, I found a note taped to the door. My first thought: referral for nailing that poor sap in P.E. on purpose. That was, however, until I got a closer look at the note. The paper was decorated and neatly taped on the edges instead of with a single strip. A light, decadent aroma trailed off the paper.

I carefully pulled it from the locker door, not wanting to tear the bold, gothic designs printed in a shimmering red. On the other side was my name in gold lettering. My heart spiked.

Sweaty, shaky hands opened the envelope slowly, like a surgeon opening up a patient. My eyes scanned the bottom of the note. *Rifu Anerex* was written in a tidy, beautiful script. After fondling the name with my eyes a few moments, I quickly remembered that there was a letter that went before it.

Dear Haydn,

Sorry we didn't get back to you sooner. I wanted to make this card especially for you. We're getting together this Friday evening at my house for some fun. We'd like it if you joined us. Don't worry about getting a ride. I'll have my butler drive you. We'll be waiting.

Rifu Anerex

I wasn't sweating now. Sweating was an understatement. I was *bathing* in sweat and anxiety. The intoxicating aroma of feminine perfume combined with the tantalizing letter lured me under. I *had* to go to this party. It was the first time a girl had asked me to come to *anything*. Most of all, it was the leader of the Gaga Girls asking *me*. I took deep, calm breaths, trying to remain composed. I was invited to Rifu Anerex's house. But, no one cared…yet.

Carefully returning the letter to its envelope, I stashed it away inside my bag. A sigh fluttered from my throat in anticipation of the upcoming Friday. Only two days away. But there was one obstacle in between. How would I convince my parents to let me go?

*   *   *

Getting permission from my parents was my biggest hurdle. Sucking up to them would come shortly afterwards. Drake was old fashioned and a bit sarcastic, but a great guy. He had been with my mother ever since I could remember. He was a father to me. No, he *is* my father. When I started getting overweight, I developed a vicious attitude problem. That's when he decided to stop being so nice to me. That's when I started working out.

After school, I went through the woods again. There were no noises, no strange presences. I was relieved that my imagination may have been toying with me. Clearing the woods, I cut across the road and made my way over the yard. I closed in on the porch door and walked in. Today, Drake was sitting at the kitchen table. Perfect timing.

"Hey, Dwake," I said, drawn out and childlike.

Drake rolled his eyes. He knew I was about to ask something.

"What do you want?"

I shrugged. "Nothin' much, just your permission to go to Rifu Anerex's place this Friday," I mumbled hurriedly.

Drake eyed me. "What was that? Speak louder, boy."

"May I go to Rifu Anerex's place this Friday?"

"Who's she?"

"She's the daughter of the governor, dear! The one who built all the hospitals across Iowa!" Mom chipped in.

Drake nodded. "Oh, well I guess you could go," he replied somberly. "But, what are you going to do in return?"

I saw this coming. What could I do? I felt my stomach curl in nervousness. I bit my lip out of frustration. I was over-thinking this.

Then I remembered something important. The next day we were supposed to get a powerful storm system that would blanket the ground in roughly five inches of snow. Kids at school had been arguing about how we wouldn't have school. Maybe, I could pull something off.

"If it snows bad, like, really bad tomorrow, then I'll shovel the drive and patio!" I blurted.

"That's a wonderful idea," my mom replied approvingly.

My step-dad eyed me warily and then bent in close and said, "Who are you and what have you done with Haydn?"

I masked my nervousness with laughter. "I want to go. That's all there is to it."

My step-dad nodded reluctantly. "If you shovel, then I guess you can go." He patted me on the shoulder. "Just don't do anything I wouldn't do."

"Meaning?"

"If you come back with a huge smile on your face I'll know what happened." His suggestion was obvious, and at the same time very embarrassing.

"You think I would..."

"You're a teen boy. It's only natural you would think like that."

"I'm not going there to have sex…"

"You better not be!" my mom shouted, almost dropping the plate in her hands.

"It's nothing like that, I swear! I don't know anything…except that it's a party," I retorted.

Would something dirty happen? I could only hope, deep inside. But, I was sure they only wanted to talk to me. Maybe play a few games. They're all rich, so I bet they have plenty of entertainment. But two questions, like gnats let in from the outside, buzzed around inside my skull. Why did they invite me? And who else did they invite?

*   *   *

Bull's eye: no school. There was close to seven inches of snow on the ground. After eating breakfast, I got ready to shovel. Drake told me to be careful on my way out, and Mom reminded me to take a break every fifteen minutes. I wouldn't, though. I wanted to be through with shoveling quickly. I did listen to my parents when they said to put on all the necessary garments. However, I considered my winter clothes more like armor.

Stepping into the garage, I was encased in my heavy, chain mail winter coat, my black gauntlet-like gloves, and a grey stocking cap and jeans. I would have worn snow pants, but I refused to feel like a knight in a desert on his way to Jerusalem. I wrapped a gauntlet around the shovel's handle, my sword, lifting it from the wall of the garage. I adjusted my gauntlets one last time and opened the side door of the garage, unsurprised to find a layer of snow blocking the door and sighed.

"Well, this is going to be fun," I grumbled.

I gripped the shovel firmly, pushing the powdery snow out and away from the side door of the garage, into the blowing snow storm. Drake commented beforehand on how the meteorologists predicted we were supposed to have blizzard-like conditions until noon. Maybe, Mom's advice was solid.

After freeing myself from the garage, I scooped my way to the driveway, ready to dive into the white monster. The driveway sat there, glaring at me, silent, like an idle beast waiting, hungry. I set the shovel, my blade, into the snow. I pushed, gliding through the white powder smoothly, carving the white monster. I bent my knees and lifted up, depositing the snow into a drift. This was my battle with the powerful, white monster known as the snowed-in driveway.

As the wind slapped at my face, my face started numbing. It felt as if only ten minutes had expired. The next day would be worth every bit of pain I suffered, though.

After about an hour on the drive, I'd finally gotten to the side of the road. The monster was slain, and I was celebrating in my head; only a day away from seeing Rifu! My daydream was rudely interrupted.

"Haydn! You got a call!" Drake shouted, his head poking out of the patio door.

He proceeded inside and I followed. Standing on the welcome mat, I shook myself free of snow and cold. I took the phone from Drake's outstretched hand.

"Hello?"

"Hey Haydn."

A girl's voice, I thought, and my throat closed up. "W-who is this?"

"It's Rifu. Why do you sound so nervous?"

My heart stopped. Any chill still in my body throbbed. What was the leader of the Gaga Girls calling my house for? How did she get my number? I swallowed my anxiety and gripped the phone tight.

"Hello, Rifu," I mumbled.

I could hear her chuckle on the other end. *"It's okay; you don't have to be nervous."*

"Okay."

"You're probably wondering why I called you."

"Uh-huh."

"Well, there's a change in the plans for Friday."

"Okay."

"Well, it's going to be a slumber party!"

"Cool." *How was I going to get away with this?*

She laughed into the phone again. *"I already spoke to my parents. They said it was all good. That is, of course, as long as you sleep in a room on the other side of the manor."*

Manor?

"Um, yeah, alright then."

"Great!"

A pause. A very, awkward, and seemingly everlasting, pause. "Rifu?"

"Yes?"

"Why did you invite me? Why didn't you invite someone you knew better?" I whispered.

There was a short silence. She erupted in a light, fairy-like laugh, which gave me goose bumps.

"You looked so lonely. And it seemed like you needed someone." A pause, *"Does that help?"* she teased.

"Yeah, thanks." *Not really.*

"Then see you tomorrow night."

And all I heard was the dial tone after that. I hung up the phone.

"Who was that?" Drake asked.

"Rifu Anerex."

"What did she want?"

Even if her parents did approve, how did I know she wasn't lying? My parents were never going to allow anything like that. My step-dad was too traditional. I had to think of something.

"Nothing, she just asked me to bring swimming clothes, that's all. Um, but there is something I forgot to ask you."

"What?"

"Is it okay if I stay the night at a friend's house? He's also going to the party."

"Who?"

"Gerry. Gerry Schneider. He lives right here in town."

"How come I never heard of this Gerry?"

"Because he just transferred." *Because he doesn't exist.*

"I guess, then." *Mission successful!* "Better watch it…that snow's making a comeback."

I turned and saw the snow, indeed recuperating, blowing back into the driveway.

"No!" I shouted and went back outside, secretly filled with glee.

3. Grounds of the Gaga Girls

Amazing. Snow fell all night and all morning and we still had school on Friday! I couldn't believe it when the School Alerts only said 2-Hour Delay. I was ecstatic. Not because I had to go to school, but because I could still go to Rifu's place. I remembered what she said. … *It seemed like you needed someone.* Even if she was lying, I didn't care.

I awoke just as dejected as always, staggered miserably to the bathroom as always, and then back to my room to dress as always. I stopped again to stare at the vile fat that destroyed what could be an almost perfect body. It couldn't be helped, however. There really is nothing perfect in the world.

Rubbing my eyes, I shuffled down the stairs. There was one thing different this morning. Katria was at the table before me. I sat at the breakfast table, beginning to gnaw on my granola bar, when Katria started talking to me like I was an alien.

"Are you okay, bro? You seem…excited."

"Yeah, I'm just thinking about tonight."

"Huh?" Katria obviously was oblivious to my plans.

"Haydn is staying at a friend's house tonight, Katria. Meaning you get the *PlayStation* all to yourself," my mom said, scraping off her plate into the garbage disposal.

I nodded in compliance. "You can even play any of my *Final Fantasy* games. I don't care!"

Then I knew I had everyone's attention. When someone could touch my *PlayStation* while I was gone was decided by my parents. But since I said that Katria could touch my *Final Fantasy* games, they decided there was going to be another blizzard before the day was over. I looked up to see Drake with an open mouth, his coffee mug nearly tipping over.

"Are you sick?"

"Nope, and I wouldn't want to be. Tonight is probably going to be the best night of my life!"

"Whatever you say…dear, better prepare the shotgun. I think we have an alien in our house," Drake called over his shoulder, laughing.

I ignored his comment, disposing of my wrapper and slinging my bag over my shoulder. Waiting for departure, I looked at Drake. As he finished his coffee, Drake stood up and kissed Mom. He put on his work coat and called Katria to get done fast or she'd be left behind.

As I got to school a half an hour later, I noticed that there was a group of guys gathered in front of the school. Were they waiting for me? As I exited Drake's Buick, I couldn't help but eye the number of the guys standing there. It was the entire football team and then some. None of them took their eyes off of me, except for some of the brainless ones.

I sauntered towards the entrance, knowing they would surround me, trapping me within the group. I cross-examined them all, prepared to fend them off. But one advanced towards me and patted me on the back as if we were best friends.

"Hey, man, great job getting invited to Rifu's house! You're so freakin' lucky!" he turned me to everyone with a smile. "I never thought you were cool until I heard about your invitation. No one else was asked to go, man!"

I'm the only one with an invitation?

"I'd say that's pretty unfair," I grumbled.

"Wow, you read my mind! That's why I was going to ask you a favor…"

"What?"

"It's obvious Rifu invited you because she wants to go out with you!" he laughed nervously. "So, why don't you gather us some tips?"

"Look man, I would love to help," I said, aggravated, "But I don't believe in shortcuts."

The guy laughed an idiotic, obnoxious laugh. "Come on, you, Haydn Ladditz, worried about shortcuts? I mean, I'm sure you took plenty of ster—"

Before he could finish, I bonded my knuckles with his upper jaw and nose. He collapsed, his obnoxious laugh becoming a regretful cry. I walked up to him and pulled him up by his shirt collar. Adrenaline and anger laced the veins writhing in my arms and neck.

"Like I said...I don't believe in shortcuts," I shook him, "There are no shortcuts in life. If you wanted their attention...I don't know...go after them yourself. And one last thing...*Don't tell me what to do.*" I dropped him there, turning and glaring at the rest of the nobodies.

As I cut my way through the crowd, I wondered if I had truly done the right thing. I could've gotten suspended for that fight...if you could call it that. No teachers were around, though. And I doubted those imbeciles were going to try me again. But, I felt empty inside. After punching him, was I really different from them? What would they have done in my shoes?

I strode down the hall, the fires of anger in my stomach sizzling down into puffs of smoke. Why did I get so angry? It was stupid. I could have told them to go to hell and left it at that. I shook my head in aggravation.

"Hey, you," a voice said, quick like a bow.

Turning, I came across a boy sitting on a bench near the school entrance. He wore jeans and a denim jacket with a red t-shirt. His skin dark; his voice a heavy accent; his large eyes were light brown and his hair in short black spikes. He sat cross-legged, apparently waiting for me.

"You're Haydn Ladditz, correct?"

"Um, yeah," I mumbled, "Who else has a last name as strange as Ladditz?"

The boy laughed, shaking his head as he turned his round, yet sharp eyes on me. His eyes seemed to pierce into my conscience as he spoke his next words.

"Don't let your anger devour you. And, I'm warning you to stay away," he said, his tone stern and his face the same. His accent, however, made him seem less serious.

"What? Stay away from what?"

"Not, what, but whom; you call them the Gaga Girls. Good things never happen around their kind."

"Yeah, whatever," I chuckled, leaving him behind.

I headed straight for my locker without looking back, anger rekindled. Yeah, now that I look back on it, I got pretty angry a lot. I tried to keep it under control. But with those jerks, I just let it loose.

*　　*　　*

After P.E., I took a shower, thinking about the strange foreigner. I remembered that I had never seen him before. Then, as the bell rang, I determined that he didn't matter. I had to power sprint to my next class, and that's all I focused on as I dashed through the halls half-soaked in sweat. As I drifted around a corner, I, like a pickup truck coming over a hill, slammed into another speeding student, her body smacking against the ground. I stopped to apologize, because I recognized her. Jolie Raven, the eldest of the Gaga Girls.

"Oh, hey there, Haydn," she cooed, as I helped her up, nearly losing her hand because mine were still sweaty.

My heart started beating like a drum in my chest. The coolness of Jolie's fingers sent electricity through my body. I gulped slightly, the anxiety building up once more as I stood there, staring Jolie in the eyes. Her eyes, like crown jewels, sparkled.

"H-hello," I mumbled timidly, "Are you okay?"

"Yeah, I'll be fine," she studied me and smiled toothily. "You excited about tonight?"

I nodded, ecstatic. "It's going to be great."

"That it will be," she stood on her toes and lightly kissed me on the cheek. "Well, see you tonight then, Haydn."

I watched her walk away. Her step, swaying, her hips like a well-timed pendulum, she turned back, smiled, and waved at me as she disappeared around the corner. Despite the sultry display, I was vexed. The way I had plowed into her, she should've been hurt, but walked away as if nothing had happened. I shook my head. If she wasn't hurt, then it wasn't important.

"You aren't going to take my advice?"

I jumped. That boy, the one from earlier, stood behind me. He was almost as tall as me, yet nowhere near as muscular. His dissecting eyes frisked my countenance.

"What advice?"

He sighed impatiently. "I told you. Don't go near those girls. You're tribulation has already begun."

I glared deep into his foreign eyes. "What the hell are you talking about? Now you're just bugging the hell outta me…" I gripped his shoulders. "Leave me alone, or you'll end up like that punk earlier."

My hands on his shoulders didn't affect him. He just looked into my eyes, into me, as if he was doing nothing wrong. This guy was really pissing me off.

"Anger will be your downfall, Haydn. You'll burn for it, and so will everyone else. Not my fault if you don't take my warning. I've done my part." He effortlessly slid out of my grip. "Just don't come crying to me when things go bad." He stopped and turned. "And such a shame too, you're a very attractive young man."

I stared after him, taken aback by his closing comment. Suddenly, I felt exposed and helpless. Anger was boiling from the inside and all the way to my flesh. I tried to calm myself, though. I couldn't let all those years of training and control be washed away by stupidity.

*　　*　　*

After school, I made a beeline for home. When would the butler arrive? I had to make sure I was ready. I didn't want to look stupid. Everything was in my bag: shampoo, deodorant, and an extra set of clothes. I was set. Walking into the bathroom, the lights were off, and darkness, like tar, occupied the room. I shut the door behind me, embracing the darkness.

Suddenly, everything was bright, and before me stood an expanse of grass and a crystal clear sky. Up ahead stood a girl, she turned and smiled. When her mouth moved, however, nothing reached my ears. But, still, I nodded and replied in the same silent speech.

I couldn't see her face. Her hair was in a ponytail behind her head. I couldn't tell the color of her hair. But, perhaps there was no color. I closed my eyes as she walked into my arms.

When I opened my eyes, darkness hung around my shoulders again. I felt around for the light switch. The bathroom lights, strikingly bright, caused me to force my eyes shut momentarily.

"What happened?" I mumbled.

A knock on the bathroom door made me jump.

"Haydn, hurry up!" Katria yelled. "Someone just called saying they'd be here to pick you up in twenty minutes!"

*　　*　　*

"I think tonight will be a blast!" I went to Katria's room after my shower. She seemed irritated by the whole thing. Our relationship was rather tricky. Even if she was family, Katria always tried to push past that barrier.

"Why do you have to go and get a girlfriend?" she asked. "What's wrong with me?"

I sighed, tired of this. Mom and Drake weren't in earshot, so I bent close and whispered, "We went over this once. Your dad and my mom are *married*. We're family."

"Not by blood…"

"I don't care. It wouldn't be right. You're my *sister*."

"If you say so," she murmured.

"Do I look alright?"

She nodded reluctantly.

"Thanks, Katria. Have fun with the *PlayStation*." I kissed her on the forehead.

Staggering to the kitchen table, I sat down, nervousness gnawing on my brain. Mom walked in and stopped, cross-examining me, as if I were a fugitive.

"What? Is there something on my shirt?"

She shook her head. "You're growing up too fast, kid."

"I can't help it."

"I know…"

"But…?"

"I'm just a little worried, that's all."

"*Don't* worry, Mom."

"I just don't want to let you go, I guess."

Silently, I watched her, expecting a tear to escape Mom's eye. But something else escaped her face, this strange expression. But it was only a flash, and she looked back to me, grinning solemnly.

"You remind me of your father."

"I'll never be like him."

"I never said you would be…"

"Mom?"

She pecked me on the cheek. "I think that's your ride, honey."

I turned and saw a very sleek, black Mercedes idling in front of our house. The Gaga Girls rode in that car every morning. It looked expensive, but everyone knew that the Gaga Girls could afford almost anything. I squeezed Mom quickly, gathered my things and headed for the door.

*   *   *

We were out of the small country town in no time. The ride was smooth, but I was uncomfortable. Like another passenger, an eerie silence sat between me and the driver. How could I just sit there with someone I didn't know? And what made things even weirder was the way he had addressed me getting into the vehicle.

"Master Haydn, I will be your chauffeur for this evening."

"Um…can you just call me Haydn?"

"Certainly not; I am of the serving class. It would be very improper."

Old-fashioned… and creepy…

I say creepy because the man was old, stricken with male pattern baldness that left little, greasy wisps of grey hair hanging off the sides of his head. His eyes were beady, constantly moving in their sockets, and I swear he glanced at me every time I looked away.

Peering out the window, my eyes took in the countryside passing by. A few pheasants fluttered about the snow-covered cornfields. That's when the butler's voice made me jump.

"Here we are, young master."

I turned, my jaw dropping to the floorboard. The Anerex Manor was *huge*. It reminded me of a house you would see on MTV Cribs. There was an enormous Greco-Roman courtyard, with a frozen spring and rows of bushes and winter flowers, sandwiched in the center of the large U-shaped drive away. Huge marble pillars stood guard around the mansion and drive.

The house itself was made entirely of stone, maybe marble. It could have been some kind of crystal compound. The house was *so* shiny, like a diamond in the sun. If the clouds weren't out, the house would've been much more radiant.

My heart raced from nervousness. The car came to a smooth stop, and the driver rolled down his window. He spoke into a little black box that was tacked to a steel gate I failed to notice.

"Master Haydn is here."

The gate grated open, obviously rusted.

"This weather isn't kind on the Master's Gate, as you can probably surmise, Young Master."

"Um, yeah," I chuckled.

We pulled up to the front door. I looked and thought it was the doorway to Heaven. We parked, and as the car died down, the butler turned to me.

"Young Master, leave your possessions in my care and I shall relocate them to your room." I nodded in compliance. "Please enjoy your stay, Master Haydn."

I stumbled out of the car and gawked at the beauty and awesomeness of the Manor up-close. Like the Gaga Girls, the manor was a sight I couldn't believe actually existed in Iowa. My heart pounded louder, like a bass drum. I took a much-needed breath, and another, calming breath. I looked up at the steps below the front door. Slowly, I took each step, hesitant to enter. Before I knew it, I was in front of the enormous door. I raised my hand to knock, unsure of what else to do.

"*Come in Master Haydn.*"

I jumped to the moon. Then I noticed the intercoms on both sides of the door. The Anerex family was *very* loaded.

Opening the massive door, I came into a shining palace. Everything was spotless. The entire interior seemed to glimmer like fine metal. I took a few steps forward. An arm flew out across my chest. What a fine greeting.

"Please remove your shoes, Young Master," a young maid said.

I nodded slowly and removed them, setting them down harmlessly on the welcome mat. She smiled approvingly and went back to her business. I walked forward into the shining lobby. To my right were a few plush couches and chairs and a man-sized fire place. To my left there was a large circular table. Spiraling upwards in front of me was a grand staircase. In short, the lobby was Valhalla in size and glory.

I crept towards the fire place, a fire still burning strong. I stood on one knee, watching the wood crackle and spit as it burned.

Imagine celebrating Christmas in front of a fire like this one! Drake always dreamt it. I then saw why he paid five bucks each week to play the lottery. If I won the lottery, I would buy a big house with a fireplace like the one I stood in front of.

Sweat started to drip down my head. The heat was intense. I pulled away, astonished by the amount of heat coming from the large hearth.

"Hey!"

I turned towards the large staircase halfway across the room. Standing at the top, the Gaga Girls were smiling down at me. Smiling at *me*. It must've been Rifu who called me. I stood up and walked towards the stairs. The four came down to meet me.

"You made it," Rifu hummed. Even walking down stairs she was beautiful. I was at the mercy of my hormones.

"Is something the matter?" Jolie asked.

My throat closed up and my mouth was filled with rubber. "N-no… it's just…you all look…so…"

"Cute?" Neferia guessed.

"We're more than that!" Brenda argued playfully.

I couldn't help but stare at them. They were all so extravagant and… Was it illegal to love more than one girl? I wanted to beg them to be my girlfriends.

Knock, knock, Earth to Haydn. That will never happen.

"So, what's the plan?" I finally managed to ask, gaining some self-control.

Rifu smiled impishly. "Glad you asked." The others looked at her with a grin. "We were thinking about a game of hide and seek."

Wait, did she say hide and seek?

"Yeah, I said hide and seek," as if she had read my mind. "It'll be fun though, I promise! There's a whole manor to hide in. Besides, it'll be like your own tour of the place."

I nodded, less interested at a full-mansion hide and seek and more about finding Rifu's room. I felt really dirty. "So, who's it?"

"We are," Brenda grinned.

"Um…all of you?"

"Is that a problem?" Neferia chuckled.

I raised an eyebrow at that. "Um, I thought only one person was usually *it*?"

"Yeah, but we thought it would be more fun this way. I mean, besides, isn't that what every guy wants?"

"What?"

"Four girls chasing after him?"

"Depends," I joked.

"Just play along, Haydn," Jolie giggled. "It'll be different, don't you think?"

"Um, okay," I wasn't going to put up an argument.

"Great! Then start hiding. We'll count to one hundred!" Brenda giggled excitedly.

4. Got'cha

Slowly, I trailed down a long corridor lined with delightful oil paintings and statues of different shapes and sizes. I stopped to look one over. It was Gothic in style, flowing robes and gloomy overall, but rich, none-theless. I couldn't begin to think what it might've cost.

I made my way down the hall only to be given a choice: left or right. I was right-handed, so right seemed a good bet. Down the right hall there was nothing but doors, each individually decorated. I tried opening one, but it didn't budge. Then, I tried almost all of the stupid doors. None of them were unlocked.

Then, the soft whisper of naked feet against the floor tickled my ears. I wheeled around to no one, but I could hear the echoes of their chatter from farther away. The game was still on, so I kept moving.

Down another corridor, hundreds more paintings clogged the walls. Past this hall, I found myself standing at a garden. High above me was a large, frozen sheet of glass, the sun roof. I felt warm, almost tropical.

"Amazing," I breathed. "Mom would love this place."

I stepped forward to look around. Ahead of me was a large hedge. It reminded me of one of those mazes from a story. I think it was the Minotaur. Yes, though I hoped there were no evil beasts lurking within the hedges. I walked around the wall to find a gap between it and another hedge. I saw the two hedges extend farther in and curve off to the right. Maybe it really was like a maze.

"Hello."

I turned around. There, before me, stood a young woman. She had snow-white hair that extended down to the small of her back. Cautious grey eyes seemingly scrutinized my every twitch.

"You're Haydn Ladditz."

"Uh, yeah, and who are you?"

"Forgive me; I've heard *so* much about *you* from my daughter."

After a moment, the resemblance hit me like a truck. The person who stood before me was Rifu's mother.

"I'm sorry, Ma'am," I mumbled, embarrassed.

She waved her hand, grinning. "It's quite alright. It's unusual that my daughter would rave about a boy like she does you."

I blushed. "Seriously?"

"You would think you're a…how do they say…a rock star. The way she writes about you…But, I don't think it'll be good for either of you, honestly." Her face had become sullen and grim, her body stiff.

"Wait, why? Is it because of me?"

She looked at me, her face loosening, a smile, Rifu's smile, emerging from behind her lips.

"No, she's had boy trouble before, that's all."

"Boy trouble?"

She nodded. "Now, tell me, where is my daughter?"

"Oh, we're playing a game of hide and seek." I lifted up my arm to scratch my head, my sleeve falling down, revealing my birthmark.

The woman glanced at my shoulder and that same darkness fell over her face again. She looked towards the entrance.

"Are Rifu's…friends here?"

"The Gaga Girls? Yeah, they're all *it*."

The woman nodded solemnly and then turned towards me, smiling grimly.

"Haydn, can go to my daughter's room? I left a book in there. Please bring it to me. But don't read it."

I was surprised by this sudden request. And what was with her transition from sunny-motherly-love to dark-ominous-doom? I hadn't known her for less than five minutes and already she trusted me enough to enter her daughter's room?

"Um, sure, Mrs. Anerex."

She grinned, shaking her head. "Please, call me Perse."

I turned to leave, and then turned back to Perse. "Where is Rifu's room?"

She pointed to the hedges. "On the other side of the maze."

Knew it wouldn't be simple.

"Ok then," I mumbled. "Oh, wait, what does this thing look like?"

"It's bound with black leather. A red fruit is embedded on the front."

"Cool, I'll be back then."

I entered the maze of hedges. It didn't take long until I was deep inside the confines of lush, green earthiness. The only thing that reminded me I was still inside the manor was the sheet of frozen glass high above my head.

I turned left, right, left again. The number of turns was ridiculous. How would I know when I got out? I could've been making my way straight back toward Perse for all I knew. My heart pounded in my chest. I closed my eyes, wincing at the pain of the sudden pounding.

"I found you!"

I turned, eyes still closed, heart slowing. How had they caught me so fast? One of them placed their hands on my face. Cool and tender, like the hand of a loved-one.

"Why are you crying?"

What? I wasn't crying. But, in fact, I was. I could feel the steamy tears rolling down the side of my face. They burnt my face as my heart pounded, and then my right arm felt strange, as if it were burning as well. I spoke, without willing it.

"I'm so sorry." What was I sorry for? "I've betrayed you. I never loved you."

At the sound of a horrible, death-waking screech, like fine fingernails scraping against a chalkboard, I ripped my eyes open. The pounding had stopped. There were no tears flowing from my eyes. But my arm still felt hot. I ripped up the sleeve to my shoulder, exposing my birthmark to the cool garden air.

"What was that?" I said to myself. "Who was I talking to?"

Then I froze; *Crunch, crunch, crunch.* Someone was climbing the hedges. It wasn't near me, but it was close enough to hear. Then the voices echoed. Perse's voice, mixed with someone else's. Who was she talking to? Then the crunching again; my seekers were closing in fast.

I jerked in the other direction, having almost forgotten about the game. Leave it to a mother to ask you to do something while you're in the middle of something else. This game was a bit odd, but I'm pretty sure it wasn't as odd as the episode I just had. I would just grab the book and give up. Fatigue hung over me, like Death awaiting another victim. Rest felt necessary.

Dead ends and more turns; the crunching was closing in. Then I heard footsteps. I started to sweat. An ice-cold, invisible hand wrapped its fingers around me. From where had such a feeling of dread emerged? I hated to lose. Who doesn't? I was a sore loser, but this feeling went beyond that. Another path, I found an opening. There, right in front of the opening, was a door.

Relief poured over me like sticky, hot syrup, melting the dread away. I hurried, stopping to examine the door. This door was much more decorated and elegant than the others. It was beautiful, and the fact that it was Rifu's door made sense. Then I noticed something else. There was a plate that arched above the door. It read: *Luci's Baby Girl.*

Governor Luci? I shook my head and twisted the doorknob slowly. I looked behind me to see if anyone had caught up with me before pushing the door open and slipping inside.

Then *it* hit me. My nose was flooded with *it*. My mind was being intoxicated, *hypnotized* by *it*. The tantalizing fragrance made me reel. It was Rifu's scent. I now stood in her room.

There were stuffed animals *everywhere*. I hadn't expected Rifu to be a stuffed-animal girl. The only place the fluffy animals didn't occupy was her bed. Her mattress was covered by black silk pillows and sheets. The entire room was black.

A few moments ago, something terrible had its grip on me. Now, I was tempted to hop on Rifu's bed. I wanted to roll around on it. Put my head down on the same pillows she rested her head on. I wanted to breathe in as much of her as I could. Become high off it.

You are such a pervert. I thought you were better than that.

I remembered about what Perse had asked me to do, and began searching for the book. I stood in the middle of the room, glancing around to try and spot this book. I shook my head.

"This place is distracting," I breathed, gripping my head. I stopped, grinned, letting go of my head.

A mahogany desk sat next to the door, complete with everything from a small desk lamp to a clay pencil holder. There was a black square in the middle of the desk. I walked up to it and examined the cover. There, printed on the front, was a red fruit.

"Sweet, now all I have to do is head back to Perse."

I turned for the door, but the book slipped from my hand and fell to the floor.

Butterfingers.

I bent over to retrieve it and noticed the book was opened to a page. Perse told me not to read it, but it was open now. It was a sign. The book wanted me to read it. Yup, sounds like an excuse I would've given my mother.

I picked it up and glanced at the page. It was a passage labeled September 1st. Was this a journal? I shrugged and started reading.

9/1

I've been having some problems with my sister. She's pressuring me into something terrifying. Irritating, that's all my sister is. I wish I were born a single child. Why did we have to be twins? She knows my buttons and when to push them. And for some reason she's been trying to get me interested in this guy. He's one of those lone wolves...kind of boring if you ask me.

Was she talking about me? She thinks I'm a lone wolf? Well, I guess I did make the decision to cut myself away from society.

I've known about him for awhile, but I think I've seen Jolie eyeing him. I don't see much in him. But what's really annoying is that Neferia keeps pestering me to make a move as well. Same with Brenda. Don't they get that I'm not interested? But, there's something about him...he seems familiar, almost.

Well, it's about time to get going. A friend is having a party tonight. A lot of eighth grade guys will be there. I'm getting hungry just thinking about it. Thank goodness there are more guys in the middle school. In my honest opinion, guys are much tastier in their pre-teens. But, then again, they get tastier with age. Sometimes. The lone wolf...I wonder how he would taste? Maybe I'll find out. But...maybe I won't do that. Oh well, a picky soul eater can't be a chooser!

I reread the passage. I flipped to the front and found Rifu's name written in the same script, the same, tidy script imprinted into my invitation. What was the passage talking about? Was it one of those journal-novel things? I would read it.

The door opened. Someone crept closer and closer until they stood right behind me. There was only one person it could be.

"Got'cha," Rifu whispered.

I rotated my head slowly, Rifu's eyes locked onto mine. She stood directly behind me, a cute smile on her face. She put a finger to my lips.

"So, you met my mother?"

"Yeah," I muttered. "Like a mother. She asked me to get this book from your room."

"What book?"

"This one," I brought the open book up so she could see. "I should have listened to her when she said not to read it."

Rifu stared at the book in my hand. "You read it?"

"Well, yeah. I'm sorry I did," I chuckled nervously. "If I had known it was a journal…but this novel you're working on sounds interesting."

"Novel?" Rifu looked up at me, confused.

"You know, the whole soul eater thing? How guys taste good during their pre-teens? Sounds like it could make an interesting book."

Rifu blinked slowly. She chuckled, which erupted into fits of quiet laughter. I stared at her strangely, not catching what was so funny.

"You think I'm writing a book about soul eaters?"

"Yeah?"

Rifu grinned. "Can I tell you a secret?"

"Um…sure."

Rifu leaned towards me and whispered. "That's a journal, a real-life journal. I write in it about the daily occurrences of my life. In other words, I *am* a soul eater."

I looked at her, my eyes wide with confusion. "I don't get it."

Rifu rolled her eyes. "Are you dense? I'm. A. Soul. Eater. A demon. A devil. I eat the souls of humans like *you* so I can survive."

She gripped my collar and flung me onto her bed effortlessly. Before I could think about struggling, she was already on top of me. She wasn't heavy, but she had an immense, *inhuman* strength that I couldn't fight off. It was a power without a face. As she lowered her face down to mine, her emerald gaze drilling into mine, I finally realized what it was. Fear.

"What…what are you?"

She looked my face over, brushing the bangs from her own. She smiled seductively. "I told you. I'm a soul eater, a devil."

"I don't believe you!"

She gripped my arm in one hand, and gripped my neck with the other. It started out as a slight burn, but the pain spread throughout my neck in a blaze of agony. I screamed, shrieked. What was going on?

"Intolerant of pain, are we? Do you believe me now?"

"What are you doing to me?"

"I'm burning you with Hellfire. You can't see it because your human eyes shield you from it. But, I see it perfectly. Don't worry about that, though."

"What are you going to do?"

"What do you think? You're soul is so close…" she trailed off lowering her head down, closer and closer to my face.

"So…you lied to me?" I blurted out.

She stopped, raised herself up a bit and scrutinized me, bewildered. "What do you mean?"

"Why I'm here. You said you invited me because it looked like I needed someone. Or did I mishear you?"

She looked away, as if she had been slapped awake. I felt like I had just beaten a defenseless child and shook my head, already regretting what I was about to say.

"Fine, then," I mumbled. "Eat my soul. I don't care."

She looked down at me, expressionless. "Why?" she whispered, so low it was almost inaudible.

"No one, not even my father cares about me." I looked away, my eyes watering. "I'm just an outcast. People only use me." I glared at her. "Do it!"

For a minute, one agonizing minute, we sat there. Neither of us moved. Rifu just stared deep into my eyes. I felt like I was going to suffocate. It wasn't enough I was shaking from fear. I couldn't tell whether she wasn't going to eat my soul, or if she was just prolonging my suffering. I felt a cool touch. She ran her fingers across the scar on my face. That circular scar I had received in my childhood.

"You're easy," she whispered harshly.

She rolled off me, but I was still shaking. I sat up, looking down at her. She sighed, shook her head. Her red hair tossed and waved like a dancing flame.

"Why did you stop?" I asked, shaken, somewhat insulted, and oddly furious.

She didn't even look at me. "It's hard to explain. And I'm not going to." She stood up and smoothed her dress. She turned to me. "And it wasn't just me. Brenda, Jolie, and Neferia were also in on this. If they had found you, it would have gone the same way. Except…maybe they wouldn't have spared you."

I remained silent.

"We're all demons. We all prey on humans."

I shuddered, and stood up.

"I…think I'll be leaving."

"You can't leave," Rifu said quickly. "If you leave, then I *will* kill you. And if I don't kill you, one of the others will."

"Why? Why kill me then and not now?"

"Because," she looked to the ground, "Because I don't want to kill you."

I stared at her wildly. "What the hell are you talking about? You almost…you tried to…you just threatened you would!"

"I don't know."

"That's damn stupid! I don't believe any of this."

"Where are you going?"

"To my room," I mumbled, walking out the door.

*   *   *

On a bed, I replayed the evening's events; Perse's strange behavior, the voice I had heard, the scream, and the secret behind the Gaga Girls. How would everyone react if they knew their precious Gaga Girls were demons? What would they do if they knew the four were eating humans? I couldn't stomach it, but I wasn't about to just go and spill. Rifu had spared me. Why?

I balled my hands into fists. My anger began to flare again. Had it been a reverse situation, I might've just killed her. But…then again, would I have? Or more importantly, could I have? I guess I'll never know.

A knock at my door brought me out of thought. I didn't respond. No matter who was at the door, I didn't want to talk. I pretended to be asleep. A second, sharper knock came. I knew it was going to annoy me eventually. I sat up, rubbed my eyes and looked towards the door.

"Yes?" I answered, cloaking my irritation.

"Master Haydn, Lady Rifu requests your presence in the Recreational Center." It was the butler.

Could I really go to them? After what had just happened? It could mean my life either way. I started regretting Monday. But, I couldn't change anything. All I could do was move forward. No shortcuts.

"Sir?" he knocked again for good measure.

"Tell her I'll be ready in a moment."

"Excellent, Master Haydn."

His footsteps faded down the hall. I traced his path with my eyes as if I could see through the wall. After his footsteps had faded completely, I let out a deep sigh.

"I'm going to regret this."

I was ready to face my doom, breathing deeply, calmly. I stepped out into the hall. The butler had already returned without a sound.

"Ready, Master Haydn?"

"Lead the way."

"Very well."

I followed him down the hall, turned right, and back into the main lobby. Then we went up the main flight of stairs. I paused a moment, a voice catching my attention. I peered down to the fireplace the furniture was centered around. I could feel the warmth from my spot.

I held out my hands and made a rectangle, as if I had a camera. I noticed a girl sitting in a chair next to the fireplace. She was the voice. I squinted. I could swear it was Rifu, but wasn't she supposed to be in the recreation center?

"Master Haydn?" the butler waited ever so patiently for me.

"Hm? Oh, sorry, I was just admiring the fireplace."

"Ah yes, Master Anerex constructed that fireplace immediately upon the mansion's completion. He wanted to tell tales to his children and even his grandchildren. But, being governor of Iowa, he never did have much time. Sooner than he realized, all of his children were too old to want to gather by the fire."

I nodded, dejected by this heart-shattering reality. Someone getting so lost in something that they forgot what they originally set out to do. I could only think of one person then. My father.

Mom always spoke of him kindly. She didn't fool me, though. I could always sense the bitterness in her voice. Morgan had been kind enough to explain it to me once. I've never looked at my mother the same. I wish I could've been there to comfort her when...

"Shall we continue on, sir?" he said interrupting my thoughts.

"Yeah, let's go," I mumbled.

We continued down the hall, passing many more statues and oil paintings. Those ones seemed different, though, like they were brand new. They didn't seem... aged, but more tragic-looking.

We turned, and there were a pair of steel doors. Above the doors was an alabaster name plate imprinted with *Rec. Area*. The butler held a door open for me. I secretly despised him, even if he was the perfect gentleman.

I emerged into a large, well-lit room full to the corners with different games and even a swimming pool. After minimal searching, I found the four girls sitting around a rock climb machine on lawn chairs. They were deep in conversation. It didn't seem like they were speaking about me. But I really didn't want to find out.

Jolie and Rifu, who sat next to each other, looked disturbed. Like they'd just woken up and didn't know where the hell they were. Their eyes were different. They were still dazzling, as always, but *clear*. They would always be beautiful, it seemed, even when stress pinched their brows.

"This way, Master Haydn," the butler pushed.

Damn him.

I strolled forward slowly, weaving in and around several arcade games. My heart was ready to pop out of its place behind my rib cage. I saw my hand and how red the back of it was. My palm was an oasis of sweat. I could feel the blood draining from my face the closer I got to them. My heart thundered a trumpeting of my approach. Rifu noticed me, and the others turned their attention to me as well.

My heart seemed to stop dead then. An immense chill iced the blood in my veins as I stood there, unable to breathe. I couldn't identify the source of the sound intruding my ears. It was a horrible hissing noise. Maybe I was imagining it.

"Haydn, sit down here," Rifu said, patting the empty chair to her right.

I swallowed hard because the chair was between her and Jolie. Brenda and Neferia sat opposite. They planned this position just in case I tried to make a break for it. But what was I going to do? If I was going to die, then at least it would be at the hands of the Gaga Girls. I kicked myself mentally for thinking like a Gaga-junkie.

I seated myself uncomfortably. My eyes automatically fell to the ground. I could feel all their eyes on me. I was about to be ripped apart. I clenched my fists hard against the steel of the chair, the hollow metal bending at my grasp.

"So… Haydn… can you keep our secret?"

I looked up, not sure who spoke. They all had their eyes on me, a criminal on trial. I couldn't bear anymore, dropping my head again, trying to find the breath to say something, anything.

"Yeah… why would I tell anyone? Really…"

"There are possibilities," Neferia replied, her tone sharp and threatening. "To drive us out, perhaps blackmail?"

"If I even try, you would kill me."

"That's a little harsh, don'cha think? I mean, we're only four innocent girls."

I chuckled. "How many years have you been telling that lie?"

Brenda hummed. "Ever since our parents got their positions in the government, why do you ask?"

I looked up, the blood draining from my face. "Wait, so that means...?"

"All of our parents are demons," Rifu mumbled.

I looked to the ground. "So, I'm screwed, in other words?"

"Pretty much," Jolie murmured.

"We could prolong your fate, though."

"Why would you do that?" I hissed.

"Because I like games," Neferia chuckled. "Hide and seek was my idea."

"What was the point?"

Neferia and Brenda looked at each other. "To have fun?" Brenda laughed.

"How is it fun? Killing someone? Eating someone?"

Jolie shrugged. "It's the circle of life, Haydn. You eat animals all the time. Humans...are...no different to us."

"Then why would you *save* me?"

Neferia shook her head. "Not save you. I have my reasons, Haydn."

"I wasn't talking to you! Why did you spare me, Rifu?" I was standing now. "You're the leader, aren't you? You always make it seem that way!" My anger was boiling over.

Rifu was only sitting there. She hadn't said much. Brenda and Neferia were doing a lot of the talking.

"Calm yourself, Haydn. You want your family to stay safe, don't you?" Brenda grinned.

"I have some relatives that would just love to make your little sister a scrumptious snack," Neferia chuckled.

I turned on Neferia. "Don't you dare put your hands on my little sister!"

Neferia shook her head. I suddenly stopped. The breath was suddenly absent from me. I started coughing, as if something were constricting me. A pressure around my torso became tighter and tighter, until I was close to bursting. I glimpsed down at the large coils wrapped around my waist. They were gray, silky scales that tightened around my body, like a snake's tail. I followed the deathly coils to their source; Neferia.

"W-what the hell are you?"

"I have many names," Neferia stuck out her tongue all the way to my face and retracted it. "Naga. Medusa. Lamia. I prefer the latter. I'm half-snake, half-woman. My favorite meals? Little boys, but mostly teenage ones like you," she licked my face. "And you taste good, Haydn Ladditz. If that is your real name."

"How…do…you…know…?" I coughed.

Rifu sat in a daze. I looked to her, but she didn't look back. Neferia retracted her tongue and giggled.

"The little mouse who wished to run with men, that's what you are. Then you met me, the cat. This game of hide and seek is over. Goodbye."

Tightening, the coils squeezed more and more breath from my lungs. It was impossible to breathe, consciousness drained from my mind like the blood from my face. The squeezing became tighter and tighter. I wanted to scream. I couldn't.

"Let…go…or…" someone said.

I struggled to listen. Who was speaking? What were they speaking about? All I caught were fragments as I faded in and out of consciousness.

"Oh…should…do…can't…"

"Yes…I…peace…parents…"

"…want…war…"

I caught the last two words clearly before I gave up. Darkness engulfed me, and I fell asleep. You know how they say, when you're about to die, that you see your life flash before your eyes? My life didn't. As I lost consciousness, the visions that flooded my mind were of one day. The day that I began to distrust people, the day that I began to feel only I could do things right. It was the day that I went to the Zoo…ten years ago.

5. Before

That day was my Achilles' heel. No other memory had embedded into my skull as deep as that one. The events of that day ultimately lead to my dire mindset.

I ran as fast as my five year-old legs could carry me to my mother's arms. We lovingly, like mother and son, embraced. I was scared about our trip to the zoo in Nebraska. It would be my first time leaving the small town of East Klintwood.

I loved animals. Up to that point, animals had been real to me only through ink in books. The thought of seeing real animals sent a chill up my spine. Mom knew how nervous I was, even though she didn't. Mothers didn't know what you felt, yet they could. That's how it was between Mom and me.

"It's okay, Haydn," my mother cooed. "We're just going to see the fuzzy animals in their cozy little cages."

I sniffled, unconvinced. "Mommy…will they hurt me?"

She laughed, patting me on the head. "It's okay…they can't get to you. Besides, they'd never want to think about hurting you my adorable little monkey," she said lovingly, wiggling my nose.

"I wuv you, Mom," I giggled and hugged her tighter.

"I wuv you too, Haydn," she replied.

Drake came around the corner, frowning a bit.

"Dear, you have a call."

Mom looked up. "Who is it?'

"Who do you think?"

She stood up, patting me on the head. "Everything will be alright, buddy." Mom moved past Drake, taking the phone. My step-dad took one look at me.

"Go change your shirt."

"Why?"

"People don't need to see your birthmark."

I was wearing a tank top for kids. And, yeah, my birthmark was clearly visible on my right shoulder. I didn't understand why I had to change my shirt, but I didn't argue.

"Yay, I'm going to the zoo!" was my response after changing.

"You're so obnoxious."

I turned, and saw my older sister, Morgan, approach me. She was dressed in black. Rather dreary. She would probably be sweating to death by the time we got home. It was supposed to be sunny and extremely hot in Omaha today.

I cheered as I hopped in the car with Katria and Morgan. Morgan, who was twelve, detested going on family trips. She would rather spend the night at a friend's house. I would never understand how she thought.

Morgan's long, curly brown hair represented her perfectly. She was twisted. She would act sweet one moment, and then torture me the next. Her cute games eventually escalated into acts of aggression. We didn't speak much after awhile, but back then we were just brother and sister, normal, mischievous and full of energy.

It was going to take three to four hours to get from our mid-Iowa town to Omaha, Nebraska. We left early in the morning. Mom said I should sleep on the way, but I didn't take her advice.

"Mommy, look at the moon! It's so full!" I cried with glee.

"Yeah…it's nice, isn't it?"

"Almost about as nice as the back of Drake's head," Morgan commented.

Drake laughed sarcastically. "Someone wants to walk to Omaha."

"No, I'll just walk to Laurie's house!"

"See, I'll actually wait until we're halfway there, then I'll make you get out. Where you gonna go then, huh?"

Morgan bit her lip. "Um…I don't know…"

Drake stuck his tongue out. "So be quiet."

Morgan stuck her tongue out back at him before turning to the window to pout. Katria laughed childishly. She enjoyed the sparring matches between Drake and Morgan. I found them funny too, but it got old after a few years, especially when Morgan wouldn't drop it.

It was about nine o'clock. We were still a couple miles out from our destination. My eyes had become heavy. I couldn't resist their unyielding, itching pressure. Darkness wrapped around me like a blanket. A field stood before me. A sense of nostalgia rushed at me, overturning my senses in a barrage of nausea.

A girl came to me, placing her hand on my shoulder. She grinned, the sun bouncing off her teeth. We came together. Our lips met. Then, she was torn from me. A fire was roaring around me. Someone shouted. A tall, shadowy figure gripped my arms and pulled me away from the fire. I kicked and screamed for a reason I didn't possess.

"Stop it, Haydn!"

My eyes ripped wide open. Morgan was punching me, hard and vicious, exuding an anger I had never seen before. Mom was pulling us apart, yelling.

"Why did you punch Morgan, Haydn?"

I didn't recall punching her. As far as I knew, I had been asleep. But, Morgan seemed to think differently.

"Calm down!" Drake barked.

Mom finally restrained Morgan. My arms were sore and bruising. Had I really punched Morgan? In my sleep?

"Are we there yet?" I asked.

"Almost, baby. Just go to sleep."

That was the last thing, I decided, that I wanted to do. So, I waited it out. I watched the clouds, focusing on one, shaped like a cartoon character I liked. Staring at clouds didn't help me stay awake. My attention span had faded away. The visions returned. A fire licked at my ankles. I screamed, threw a fist to beat away the flames. But, instead of hitting the flames, I hit Morgan in the face.

"Haydn!"

"What?!" I cried, surprised.

"Do you want to get paddled? Why would you punch your sister, again?"

"I didn't mean--"

Morgan socked me back, her bony hands smacking against my chubby cheeks. Mom started scorning Morgan, nurturing me in the process. Morgan was grounded for awhile. But, so was I. But, apparently, Morgan's being grounded and my being grounded were two, entirely different things to Morgan.

"If everyone will behave," Drake chimed in, "I'd like to say that we're at the zoo."

"Yay!" Katria cheered in glee.

"Whoopidee-doo-da," Morgan swirled her finger in the air and rolled her eyes.

We pulled into an extremely large parking lot. It was like an African plain to a small five year-old. Cars and other families dotted the horizon of this cemented wilderness, observing the wildlife.

Mom's seat was pulled forward, and I leapt from my cage. Any thoughts about the strange sleep-punching and the strange dreams were erased. I looked left, right. The expanse was vast and grand. It was the perfect place for me to explore. I took off, sprinting like a leopard chasing its prey. The other animals cleared a path for me. I sped blindly past them and their cages, each painted different colors. My prey was the most succulent prey to ever grace my eyes. Huge, arching, and so welcoming, it was the ultimate goal. But another was aiming to take my prey. It was a leopardess, taking the chase at a leisurely gallop. I slowed down, but still crashed into her. I fell to the ground, she stayed standing.

After rubbing my scraped knees, I stared at the girl for a moment. I could tell she was a bit older than I was. She wore a sun hat that kept the sun out of her eyes. Her eyes...they caught mine. They were like shiny gems to a thief.

"You have pretty eyes," I mumbled shyly.

The girl's parents and my parents walked up to us, adoring the scene in front of them. My parents always embarrassed me.

The girl's parents looked like her in a way. They each shared the same eyes as her. The dad, however, had a thick mustache and was a bit taller than Drake. He smiled down on me.

"Your son is such a young gentleman," he had a deep, rich tone, rich like his black hair.

"Why thank you…your daughter is quite lovely," I heard my mother compliment.

"Thank you."

"How old is your son?" asked the girl's mother. She was so flashy, somehow. She wasn't wearing anything glamorous, but she came off as a supermodel. Her hair was flawless.

"He's only five, but we teach him the best we can!" Drake said proudly.

"You've done very well so far, then," replied the girl's father approvingly.

"She's seven years old, only two years apart!" The girl's mother took out a camera and slid the girl and me close together. "Do you mind if I get a picture?"

My mom took out her camera. "Can I take one, too?"

The girl's mother hesitated a bit before shaking her head. "This is a specially-made camera. It prints the pictures right away; much cheaper than a disposable camera."

Mom seemed disappointed to lose that battle, but she didn't argue, either. She just nodded and moved back to allow the girl's mother to get a clear shot.

"Say cheese!"

I don't think I smiled. Back then, I was afraid of cameras. Maybe, it was just because I was so nervous. The woman laughed as the pictures slowly printed.

"What a cute boy. I think they would make a cute couple…" she cooed.

"Yeah…when they get older of course," the girl's father quickly added.

The mother handed a picture to my mom. My mom, keeping her smile, looked at Drake, then back to them. "Where do you live?"

"In Iowa, near Marshalltown," the girl's father replied.

"Well, that's really close to where we live!" Drake remarked, surprised. "So, you must've had to travel for hours as well?"

The girl's father nodded. "Yep, but it's worth it to see little…" I forget her name, "…smile."

"That's nice. At least your little girl appreciates long trips like this." They both laughed. Morgan rolled her eyes. Drake nodded thoughtfully. "Well, maybe we'll see ya later then."

"Maybe, we'll just have to wait and see!" After they shook my parents' hands, they shook my hand with a smile that was different from the one they gave my parents.

"Nice to meet you, boy," the father said to me in a low tone.

The smiles I saw on their faces were like that of a teacher who was aware of you, and not in a good way, either. As she was leaving, the little girl turned and smiled at me, waved, and disappeared into the zoo.

"Come on you three, let's go and see the animals!" Drake said.

I had almost completely forgotten about the zoo. I rushed ahead of my pack to get in first. I wanted a sneak preview. Speeding through the large gate, I came to a plaza laid with granite bricks. Each had been engraved with the names of founders. In the middle of the plaza was a fountain carved to resemble a family of lions. The water spouted from their mouths with littler streams flowing from their backs.

"Let's go see the rainforest!" Katria screeched, having seen a sign fostering a blue parrot perched on a tropical tree.

"What? But, but... I wanna see the giraffes!" I whined.

Drake patted me on the head. "We'll go there after the rainforest, buddy."

"Pwomise?"

"I promise. Now let's go. The faster we get through the rainforest, the faster we get to the giraffes!"

"Yay!"

I ran towards the rainforest. Willingly, I would make any compromise, as long as I got to my giraffes. I saw other kids heading towards the rainforest. They seemed excited, so why couldn't I be? I'm sure they probably were compromising as well. I ran through the crowd, squeezing in, out, and between families and other small crowds of people. That's when I saw *her*, and I stopped.

She was alone, sitting on a stone wall not far from the entrance of the rainforest. It was dangerously high for someone her age to be sitting. I stopped and looked up at her.

"Why are you so high?" I asked.

The girl looked down, her shiny eyes reflecting her smile before her lips moved. She patted the spot beside her. Did she want me to get up there?

"I can't climb up there," I mumbled.

She tilted her head to the side. That smile still tugged at her lips. She held her hand out to me while she mouthed the word 'jump.' I looked at the hand hesitantly, worried if she would be able to support my weight. Gullible, and trustworthy, I jumped for her hand, up and on the wall within a flash. I stared down at the path to the rainforest with wide eyes.

"How did you do that?" I squealed excitedly.

The girl only grinned, running her index finger and thumb across her mouth, as if zipping it shut. I tilted my head.

"Why won't you say anything?"

She pointed to her throat then shook her head. I didn't quite understand what she meant.

"What?"

She scratched her head a moment before opening up her mouth and pointing down her throat, a gurgling noise emanating from within.

"You can't talk?"

She nodded sadly. I stared at her a moment before I put my arms around her. Her eyes turned on me, wide with surprise.

"I'm so sowwy."

The girl didn't respond, she only sat there, until my parents started calling my name.

"Haydn!" I had been away from them for too long.

Her arms wrapped around me gently. She didn't want me to go, that much was obvious. I looked at her and smiled.

"I have to go…"

She nodded slowly. Whatever the reason, this little girl didn't want me to go. I smiled goofily.

"I'll see you again, won't I?"

The girl smiled bitterly and nodded, perhaps because neither of us truly knew. While no one was looking, the girl held me tight and jumped from the top of the wall. The wall was at least ten feet tall. I was only about two feet tall. I was scared. But we landed safely on the ground, the girl letting go and disappearing into the crowd. But, before I lost her in the sea of zoo-walkers, she turned and gave me that smile.

"Haydn?" my mother called out again.

"Mommy!"

"Haydn!"

She came through the crowd to meet me, bringing me into her arms. After scolding me about running off, she kissed me on the forehead.

"Let's go into the rainforest," Drake said, herding us towards the entrance.

The rainforest, in my opinion, was a close replicate of what a real one would be like. Humid, damp, and full of exotic animals you could never find in your backyard. Although I'd never been to a rainforest, I still liked to think I had a pretty good idea what one was like.

There was a wide variety of animals I had only heard of throughout the exhibit. Alligators didn't seem as scary as a lot of people gave them credit for. The monkeys seemed mild compared to what they showed on documentaries. My favorite part was the parrot exhibit. I was a lover of big, colorful birds. All birds made me happy, actually.

What didn't make me happy was the reptile exhibit.

I had never seen any big snakes before. The only snakes I knew were the garter snakes that Mom and Drake killed in the garden and backyard.

This was completely different. This snake was a genuine, breathing, living, Amazon boa constrictor. The cage was opened up for kids who wanted to help feed it. I just so happened to be passing by.

"Hey, little boy," the 'snake-charmer' said, "Why don't you come and say hello to Mr. Snuggles?"

My parents held me back. They were obviously concerned with my safety.

"I'm not letting you put my child anywhere near that man-eater," Mom said.

The man held his hands up in the air like he had been caught red-handed.

"I promise, Ma'am, it is very safe. Besides…" he whispered something in my mother's ears.

"I guess it is okay then," Mom muttered dazedly.

Drake shook his head. "I don't think we should…"

Morgan pushed me inside with the man. "I think he should!" she shouted.

The man smiled. "Welcome aboard the Ferry of Feeding! You're an honorary zookeeper today!"

Mom snapped out of her daze and glared at Morgan before trying to retrieve me from the cage.

"Please, Ma'am," the man said, "If you make any sudden movements, the boa will strike. Stay outside of the cage. Your son is safe, I promise."

I was amazed by the offer I had been given. My mother's concern didn't faze me at all. As soon as I had a rat in my hand, I walked farther into the cage. The zookeeper led me to a nested area with a huge log. There, curled up and staring at us, was the boa. The man stood next to me with a weird looking stick. It was one of those rods like most snake-handlers on T.V. used to pick up snakes.

"Go on, I'm here to help if you need it," he said encouragingly.

I took a confident step forward, holding the rat out. The rat was a bit calm considering it was heading towards certain doom. I also noticed the boa constrictor hadn't moved an inch since I had stepped in the cage. The zookeeper had been keeping his eyes on the boa this whole time as well. But, I never acknowledged anything may go wrong. I was too excited.

A scream split the air. The crowd turned to investigate and the zoo-keeper followed suit. The rat squeaked wildly before sinking its teeth into my tender hands. I reeled in pain, blood streaming from the deep gash. As I sat there gripping my hand, a wheezing breath filtered into my ear. It was nothing I'd heard before. Like thousands of leaves rustling under a strong wind. I felt something start to wrap around me. Before I knew it, I was in the deadly embrace of the boa's coils. I was at the mercy of one of the deadliest constrictors alive.

"My *baby*!" I heard Mom shout.

The zookeeper turned and lost all the color in his face when he saw the boa squeezing the life out of me. Constrictors, as the name implied, waited until their prey stopped struggling to devour them whole. Being as young as I was, I couldn't struggle much. The boa moved its head over mine and began to open its jaw. Wider and wider that cavernous maw opened, ready to accept me. I could only stare into the dark abyss. It was over for me.

As it lowered its jaws over my head, I felt the snake jerk, one of its fangs catching me on the cheek. Everything was silent except for the cries and outraged screams of the crowd. A pressure came from the outside of the snake's body. It was short and repeated. Someone was poking the snake from the outside. After a few more moments, air rushed in. The snake's jaws were lifted from around my head. The zookeeper pulled me out and my parents rushed in, stealing me from him.

"Are you okay?" Mom mumbled, looking me over. When she found the gashes on my arm and face, we left the zoo early.

*   *   *

I was taken to a local hospital with several broken bones and internal bleeding. Without treatment, I was likely to die. The doctors also checked for infection in the gash on my face, washing every inch of my body to make sure any enzymes from the snake were gone. There was a slim silver lining. The zookeeper was fired, and we got a large sum of money for my short, life-threatening ride through hell.

I was transferred from the Omaha hospital to Mercy Hospital in Des Moines. After a week of care and x-rays, I was allowed to go home. My attitude problem followed shortly after.

Katria was also affected. We were intimate playmates. We were buddies, but we couldn't have fun. I was immobilized. There was nothing I could do. Katria became depressed despite her young age. It was the only time I could remember her being sad.

One day, I was lying on the couch—watching Blue's Clues, I think—when Katria came in and sat on the couch with me. She sat close like she always did, and kissed me on the forehead.

"Brother, you feeling better?"

"No. Why'd you kiss me?"

"Well, Mommy always kisses my cuts and bruises and they heal faster."

I was silent a bit, but then I nodded. "I am feeling a wittle bit better." She kissed me on the forehead again. "Get better faster!"

*　　*　　*

It took years to recover. My relationship with Morgan, and nearly every other girl I had yet to meet, had completely changed. I hated her, even though she tried to apologize. After so much rejection, she told me she wished that snake had eaten me. I never trusted her after that. The tension between us made me so uneasy.

Time flew so fast. But what would happen next? Was I dead? Churning in the belly of Neferia? I didn't feel dead, if you could say something like that. Everything felt so dreamy. Maybe, everything was a dream.

6. Oncoming

Sweat and tears. Visions of a dark abyss shaded my mind. A laughing figure coiled around me. I screamed for it to stop.

I sat up, my breaths quick and shallow. Numb pain throbbed in my ribs. I looked around, hoping I was in my own bed, hoping everything that had happened was just a nightmare. My heart sunk as I discovered the stuffed animals and black covers. Then I looked towards the door. Next to it was the mahogany desk.

"No," I breathed. "It wasn't real!"

"It *was* real," a voice whispered.

My head snapped in the voice's direction. I couldn't see the one who had spoke, but I could almost guess who it was.

"Where am I?"

"In my room," the voice mumbled. It was Rifu.

I ran a hand over my body. Nothing was missing, and my skin seemed fine. Obviously, I hadn't been mutilated or scarred, physically, anyways.

"I should be dead."

She tiptoed from the shadows, her eyes set on me. The way she was staring at me made me feel like I was a freak. I noticed something in her hand. At first it looked like a giant square napkin, but I realized it was a drawing pad.

"You're not," Rifu quipped.

"But I should be." I shook my head. "I feel the pain. The pain from Neferia's coils…I remember it clearly."

Rifu tilted her head. "You thought I was going to play the 'I-think-you're-stupid-enough-to-believe-nothing-happened' card, didn't you?"

"I didn't know what you were going to do. Honestly, I don't care."

"Why? I could kill you. I should kill you."

"Then why don't you?"

Rifu shrugged. "I guess there are plenty of reasons. Which one do you want?"

"The one that keeps me alive," I moaned, falling back after a sharp pain pierced my side.

"Healing magic can be so finicky." She sat on the bed, placing her hand on my ribs. "It took a lot of arguing to save you. If Jolie hadn't been on my side then you probably would have been snake food."

I shuddered, and shook my head violently. "Don't say that!" I hissed.

Rifu looked down at me. "What? Save? Jolie? Sna—"

"That last word! Don't say it!"

Rifu stared at me. This was obviously interesting to her. She rubbed my ribs, a melancholy grin on her face.

"They scare you?"

I closed my eyes, the vision from my childhood still burned into my eyelids.

"More than scare."

"I can understand, then. Neferia's assault rocked you to your core."

I swept my hand across my face and kept to the shadows of silence.

"Was it something in your past?"

My eyes shifted back to Rifu. "How…?"

"Devils can't read minds. But we have an ability that is very similar. We possess an insight into your emotions that is unlike any other sense. At any time we know what you want, what you don't want, and what you regret. These things mix into a single image we can see and decipher. That's why we can tempt almost any human."

"Tell me about it."

"You're not just any human, though."

Rifu bent over, placing her forehead against mine. I froze as she stayed there, breathing calmly through her nose. Then she moved away and laid herself down next to me.

"What do you mean?"

"Hm?"

"About…me?"

Rifu was silent then. I shifted uncomfortably. Being next to a girl that I had just found out was a demon freaked me out a little. But just a little. Finally, she spoke, moving her arms through the air.

"You don't seem like the kind of guy who would take advantage of anyone. You seem…loyal…trustworthy…"

"What?"

"I said: you don't seem like the kind of person to take advantage of others."

"That's a shortcut. I don't believe in those."

"Most guys, humans in general, do."

"What about you?"

She shook her head, chuckling. "Humans are selfish. You often compare everything to yourselves. Humanity…that's something generally thought to be possessed exclusively by humans. But, what do demons have? It can't be humanity, can it? Maybe…just maybe…we developed something else. Some argue it was logic…"

"What's your point?"

Rifu turned to me, her eyes drilling into mine. "I'm saying I spared you because it was logical."

I would have started laughing had I been in a better mood and didn't know that she was a demon.

"How is keeping me alive logical?"

"Would you like to die?"

"No, I just want to know what you're thinking."

She made a face. The one people make when they think you are stupid for not getting something so obvious.

"I didn't kill you because you were willing to throw away your life, and I don't like meaningless death. Also," she put her hand on one of mine, "You're just a mystery to me. I want to know more about you. Every time I've walked by you, your true emotions shower me like powdered glass. They're different from your upfront emotions. No, they're not at all like the hot, steel blades of anger. I want to know more about the powdered glass that hides behind the fiery, raging sword."

I stared at her strangely. "You're confusing me."

She chuckled. "Maybe it's better that way. You have more than my words chasing after you."

"What?"

"Neferia and Brenda…they still want you dead."

"Why?"

"Neferia has some sort of affliction against you. It's interesting, but I could only read so much of her emotions."

My stomach started to knot up on the inside and my cheeks twitched. What the hell was up with this? What was I going to do?

"You're struggling."

"Can you please stop doing that?"

Rifu chuckled. "At least I don't know your exact thoughts. Then you would be in trouble."

"Is this the time to joke?"

Rifu shrugged. "Humor can lighten the mood."

"It's not working." Neither of us spoke for a few moments. I thought about how everything was swirling out of control. "What should I do?"

"I don't know, yet."

"That's reassuring."

"First, we have to know what Neferia's problem is. My parents might know something. But, I warn you, there are things more dangerous than Brenda and Neferia."

"Jolie?"

Rifu bonked me on the head. "No. I already said Jolie was on my side in the argument."

"But the way she was talking…" I muttered.

She nodded. "I know, but all of a sudden she started defending you. She didn't want to see you get eaten. She also argued that war might break out considering how far we went with this."

"What's that supposed to mean?"

"Neferia isn't allowed to swallow anyone whole. She can eat people two ways: she can either eat their souls or swallow them. With the soul eating method the victim can walk away alive. The other method, however, is a bit more definite."

"You're telling me." I shuddered.

Rifu started petting my hand gently. Her body was warm. Unconsciously, I scooted closer to her, but she sat up.

"I want to live, and I want my family to be safe," I finally said.

"I can't do both," Rifu mumbled. "You'll have to look out for them by yourself."

"How? I'm only human."

"There's just so much you don't know, Haydn. But don't worry, it'll be alright."

"What the hell is that supposed to mean?"

Then there was a rapid knock on the door.

"Rifu!" a voice whispered.

Rifu looked to the door. She got up and opened the door. On the other side, Jolie and the butler stood. Jolie's face sagged with stress.

"What is it?"

"Neferia and Brenda have left the mansion," the butler said.

"And your sister's gone too," Jolie commented.

Rifu's face went ghost-white. Her eyes dilated. "You've got to be kidding me," she breathed. "Why is she gone?"

"She's off to her Keres..."

Rifu gasped. If whatever Jolie said made Rifu gasp, then it couldn't have been good. I stood up, but stabbing pains in my ribs made me fall back onto the bed. I struggled in pain, shaking my head.

"This is great," I grumbled. "What the hell are Keres?"

Jolie regarded me sharply. "The Keres are basically bodyguards of our world, the world hidden within your human one."

"They are the elite fighters trained solely to hunt down and destroy those who aren't supposed to know about our secrets," Rifu added.

"Me," I muttered.

They both hung their heads.

"How long until they come after me?"

Jolie sighed. "I don't know."

"You're as bad as she is," I growled, jabbing a thumb at Rifu. "Does anyone know anything?"

"If you want to live, then you will shut up," Rifu remarked.

I shook my head. "What do I need to do? I want my family to be safe. If they come after me, my home is obviously the first place they'll check out!"

Rifu and Jolie looked at each other. It was as if they were transferring thoughts by eye contact. I watched them for a few silent moments before they nodded and turned to me.

"We'll do research," Jolie declared.

"You need to get healed," Rifu said. "Tonight, rest. I'll begin the research. Jolie will stay with you for the night."

"What? But, Rifu..." Jolie mumbled.

"Jolie..."

Jolie seemed to understand what Rifu's tone suggested. How were they able to communicate so readily like this? Were they both soul eaters? If so, then they could feel each other's emotions. I seriously doubted they both were devils, though. Neferia had been a lamia. I didn't know what Brenda was. What was Jolie?

"I'm leaving. Goodnight, Haydn," Rifu said before she disappeared with the butler out the door.

Now, it was just Jolie and me. She stood there at the door and I sat there and stared at her. She sighed, and shook out her hair.

"You've caused such uproar," Jolie chuckled. "Really, do you know how?"

"I wouldn't even begin to guess," I droned, falling back on the bed.

"You should get a bath, Haydn. It will help you relax."

"Not while you're in there."

"I won't look, I promise. I'll stay outside the whole time."

"Something tells me you're lying."

"Only fibbing, I swear."

I sighed and stood up, tried to stretch and only regretted it, my ribs protesting with pain. I shook out my arms and limped forward, finding my legs were in pain as well.

"Do you want me to carry you?" Jolie teased.

"Don't even touch me," I muttered.

"That's the girl's line," she giggled.

"Yeah, but I'm not superhuman or whatever you are," I breathed.

"Touché," she replied. "Rifu's private bath isn't far, fortunately for you. But I hate to see you hurt so much."

"I'm sure." I struggled to the door, leaning against the door jam as I caught my breath. Jolie shook her head and rolled her eyes. She got up under me and supported me. "Hey! Stop that!"

"Shut up," she snapped. "I hate macho men. You should know when you've met your limit."

"I have no damn limits!"

"Oh, I'm sure if I punched you in the ribs right now that you would find a limit really quick."

I kept my mouth shut. The threat may not have been real, but I didn't want to find out. She grinned and continued to support me as she walked me to the bath. She was amazingly quick for being weighed down so much. What was she?

The door to Rifu's private bath was a veil of thin satin. It looked like a sheet of mist, so thin and yet so thick to the eye. It felt silky as we passed through and smelled like warm vanilla. Inside was a tiled bath with a tub built into the ground. The interior was a red and black kaleidoscope.

Jolie set me on a bench against a wall. "Stay here, I'll be back."

She disappeared through the curtains at a speed I thought impossible. Sitting down on the bench, I sighed. So much had transpired in the past week. Everything seemed so good. But I guess it's true when they say that nothing is truly what it seems.

"Boo."

I jumped, hurting my ribs in the process. Jolie's eyes were wide with innocence and mischief as she poked her head through the curtain. "Here are your clothes," she said, tossing my bag into the bath. "If you need anything, don't hesitate to call."

"I'll remember not to," I mumbled, picking up my bag.

Jolie frowned, puckering her lip for theatrics. "You're so mean…"

I sighed.

Wasn't she just so down and crap hours ago? What is she, on a freakin' sugar high?

When Jolie's head disappeared from the curtains, I took off my clothes. After stripping down to my underwear, I limped to the fancy diamond-like shower knobs. I turned the hot water all the way and the cold water only halfway.

"So, how's it going in there?" Jolie's voice came from far off.

I kept silent.

"You gonna stay quiet? Do I have to come in there? I will."

"Stop being a freak! Isn't it supposed to be the guy who does this stuff?"

"What stuff?"

"Irritating…"

"You act like a girl," Jolie teased.

"Screw you!"

"I bet you'd like that," she laughed.

After the bathtub filled up all the way, I let my underwear slide off, and I eased myself into the near-scalding water. The place was steamy enough, at least Jolie wouldn't be able to see me if she came inside.

"Are you still alive in there?" Jolie called again.

"Why do you care?"

"Well, I did argue for your life."

I sighed, the melancholia of the situation weighing down on me. Even when Jolie could be so upbeat, I felt like I could only sink down lower and lower. Everything was going downhill. If only I hadn't talked to the Gaga Girls; if only I had kept walking.

"Why did you argue for me?"

This time she was the one to stay silent. It was an enjoyable sound at the moment. I sighed, slid into the bath, and noticed a pair of shining eyes staring down at me.

"What the hell?" I shouted, covering my crotch under the water.

"Am I annoying you?"

"Annoying doesn't even fit the description…"

My heart was a thunderstorm in my chest. She could probably hear it. A lively smile lit up her face. The unique brightness in her eyes subdued me. I wanted to leave. But I was naked and injured. I wasn't leaving that bath.

"What's the matter?"

Looking away, my face turned red. "I can't take a bath with you watching me like this."

"Pretend like … I'm not here."

"Creeper…" I muttered.

"Most vampires are … whoops! Well, you know what I am now."

My eyes widened, and I looked up at Jolie. Her smile was wide, displaying the two fangs pushing out from underneath her upper lip. Sweat built up under my skin. My pulse began to thunder again.

"Vampires aren't myth. But I guess it doesn't surprise you."

I wanted to nod, but my neck muscles seemed to lock up. In truth, all my muscles seemed frozen, rusted. I only stared up at her, pupils dilating. Jolie seemed to notice my trouble, and without another word her pale hands found their way to my neck.

"Your neck is so tense," she murmured caringly, "Let me relieve the pressure."

The only way I knew for relaxing tense muscles was a massage. What was weirder than getting a massage from a vampire? Probably nothing, but I wasn't going to jinx it. And I wasn't going to reject her offer either. If not massage my neck, she could probably snap it, instead.

"S-sure…"

Jolie smiled warily, as if sensing my fear. "It's okay. I'm not going to hurt you. Just let me do this."

I tried to relax, to find peace. But I couldn't. She made me too nervous. Vampires drank blood, usually from the neck. How did I know she wasn't about to suck me dry? I was unaware that she had already begun massaging my tense neck. Sitting there in an awkward silence, I let her work. She hummed, in the meanwhile, and the humming progressed into whispers and then soon into a full chorus.

"*A serpentine*
Her breath too sweet
Succubus in seraphim skin
Forbidden yet fateful
Death trails along
Tugging her tresses
A stigma keen
Infecting innocent eyes

Hearts hear only her lies
Forbidden yet fateful
Succubus in mystic guise
Her words too neat
A serpentine
O devil's descendent..."

Okay, that was a little depressing. It didn't sound like any song I had ever heard before. Had Jolie written it?

"You're definitely tense," Jolie said lightheartedly. "Do I really make you that nervous?"

She moved her hands in a vertical motion. As she did this, she bent over, putting her nose to my jugular, smiled, and sat back up, all the while continuously paying close attention to my neck. After a bit, I could feel my neck relaxing, definitely less tense than before.

"I don't know."

She burst out laughing. "Oh, I'm so sorry! It just caught me off guard." Shaking her head she went back to work.

"This is getting awkward," I stated bluntly, "What the hell am I supposed to do?"

"Um, sit there?"

"No," I rolled my eyes, past irritated. "I mean about this whole damn mess you and Rifu drug me into."

The massage stopped. Her hands were no longer on me neck. A chill went down my spine.

"It is a mess, Haydn," she muttered. "If Rifu hasn't said it already, then I'll say it...I'm sorry. I never wanted anything bad to happen to you. Never, I only wanted you to be safe."

"Then why did you make that comment...?"

"What comment?"

"That one where humans were only animals to eat..."

Jolie was silent. I turned to see her looking off into space, perplexed. She leaned back, started laughing.

"You think I would remember making a comment as serious as that..."

"You mean...?"

She shook her head, grinning. "Nope, I don't remember making any remark like that."

"Oh..."

She tilted her head, her smile shrinking just a bit. "You feel a little better?"

I nodded, but didn't say anything. Jolie cocked her head sideways at me. She lowered her head closer and closer until she was in my neck. She kissed my neck and I almost jumped. She put both of her hands on either of my shoulders. I couldn't move now. My anxiety began to swell.

"But humans like you *are* hard to resist. Vampires…we can lose our cool so easily. Haydn, do you know how crazy you make me? Your blood? Your body? I want them," Jolie murmured breathily. "You don't even know how much." Her mouth opened wide, the two fangs emerging like a pair of pocket knives.

I wrenched my eyes shut, bracing myself for pain. I felt the fangs begin to probe my neck, though they hadn't broken the skin. She never let up, keeping those two blades against my neck. It was as if she were waiting for me to move so her fangs would do the work for her. Her mouth gently closed around my neck, the fangs ready to pierce through. The pain was unbearable.

And, then, it was gone altogether.

Jolie chuckled unevenly. She got up, shook her head as her canines hid perfectly inside her mouth. I opened my eyes, staring up at her in terror. Jolie sat perfectly still, looking down at me expectantly, like she was trying to read my mind.

"You didn't…?"

"No."

"But I thought…?"

"Rifu would agree with me. Right now, you're more important than my own selfish desire."

I stared at her thoughtfully, wondering what she could be talking about. Then she turned and walked out of the bath. She stayed just outside of the doorway. I could see her silhouette through the curtain.

"You're going home tomorrow, Haydn," Jolie called. "Let us do some research, and then we'll get back to you, with better intentions. But you better ready for the oncoming danger."

And she disappeared.

7. Haunted

I woke up, still inside Anerex Manor. My hope that everything was just a dream was crushed. After I threw on a shirt and shorts, I sat back down on the bed, wondering if my parents had figured out I lied to them. I would be screwed worse than I was now if they did. Someone knocked on the door.

"Come in," I shouted.

The butler entered, wheeling in a cart decorated with sausage and eggs. He stopped in front of the bed and gave a little bow.

"Ladies Rifu and Jolie informed me that you will receive a message from them in a few days." He motioned to the cart. "They also requested that I serve you breakfast before turning you over to your parents' care."

I stared at the plate full of food. My stomach was empty, desperately empty. Food hadn't touched my lips since lunch the day before. I nodded and reached for the cart with greedy eyes. The butler nodded, turning to leave. "Wait!" I called. He turned. "Are you sure they didn't say when they would get me the message?"

He shook his head. "There was no cemented time frame."

I hung my head, dissatisfied with his answer. "Thank you."

He bowed again before disappearing through the door, shutting it behind him. I nibbled at the eggs, anxiety dripping into my mind. This week couldn't get any worse. What was I supposed to do? Well, maybe

I could carry on with my normal life until I found something out. I wished everything had been a dream.

After forcing down the complementary breakfast, I looked for my bag. As I opened it to get my jeans, I noticed Rifu's drawing pad. I pulled it out, along with my jeans, and flipped through it as I slipped on my pants.

There were sketches, colorings, shades, tints. There were barely any full pictures. As I flipped through, I came across a fully drawn picture. It depicted a face with a hand up against its left eye. Tears flowed from underneath the hand. On the right side, the eye was absent, but just above the eye socket sprouted a black horn with a crown perched at the horn's base.

I closed my eyes. When I opened them, I was standing alone in a barren wasteland. Ashes fluttered through the air like leaves in a fall breeze. There was something at my lips, but when I tried to speak, all I could do was vomit. I emptied my stomach's contents until I doubled over, dry heaving. The pain was immense, as if an iron claw was cutting up my insides.

My eyes opened. The drawing pad was on the ground. I picked it up again and looked at the picture. I tore it out and stuffed it away in my coat pocket.

"Disturbing…" I muttered, setting the pad on the bed.

I slipped outside my room and walked down the hallway. When I reached the lobby I let out a sigh.

"Something troubling you?"

I whipped around and found Perse standing there, her white hair in a ponytail.

"Um, no," I lied.

Perse shook her head. "I asked my daughter the same thing, and I could tell she was lying when she said no. Neferia tried to kill you."

My mind throbbed from the dire images flashing inside head. I almost shouted back at her, but I tried to remain composed.

"Please, don't mention it."

Perse nodded, and walked forward, running a hand through my hair. "Haydn, you need to combat your fears."

"How did you—"

"I'm a mother, and a daughter. I know many things from experience. Your fear can only lead to destruction. Anger hatches from fear. Anger fuels the beast. The beast will destroy the world."

I turned away from her. "Whatever. Stay out of my business."

Perse sighed and called out for the butler to drive me home. "You're obviously very tired. Your ribs are still causing you trouble."

"How do you...?"

"Stop asking questions and listen. Just go home and rest. Trust my daughter." Her eyes were pleading, and her smile was deceiving. "I don't want you or Rifu to become a slave to your mistakes."

The butler was there momentarily, ready to go. "Are you ready to depart, Master Haydn?"

I looked to Perse, but she was already walking away.

"Yeah. Let's go."

I staggered after the butler and kept looking back down the hall, hoping someone wouldn't sneak up on me again. That's when I heard the stomping of furious feet accompanied by a scream saturated with rage.

"You!"

I turned to see a gold-haired girl glaring at me from the top of the stairs. Her eyes were smoldering, piercing. She glided down the stairs, almost as if she had just jumped from the top. She reached the bottom of the stairs, stopped and glared at me from almost halfway across the room.

As I stopped moving to look at her, I thought it was Rifu for a moment. Her hair was gold, otherwise she looked exactly like Rifu in every way, shape, and form. She had to be the sister Rifu mentioned in her diary. But they were twins? She was in my face now, her eyes burning with hatred. There was another major difference. Rifu was five foot seven, about my height. Her sister was about two inches taller than me. She jabbed me in the chest with one of her nails. Her furious, emerald eyes drilled into my own.

"Where do you think you're going? You belong to my family!"

"W-what?"

"You are Haydn Ladditz, aren't you? I was told by Neferia that you belong to my family. You're *my* slave," she growled, outraged.

"What the hell? I'm a free human! I don't care what or who you are, but you don't own me!"

She grinned. "Oh? Is that so?"

"Yes! Now, get the hell out of my face!"

She backhanded me across the cheek with the scar, sending me into the ground. My ribs screamed from the jolt against the ground. "Do you want to live? Then accept your place!"

The butler only stood there.

"Why aren't you helping?" I coughed.

"I am only a servant…but I serve the members of Anerex before anyone else."

The girl grinned viciously. "Too bad for you; I guess you'll die, if you won't submit."

She stepped towards me, but cringed and fell back, gripping her leg.

"That's enough," a dark voice rung.

A man with silver hair and silvery green eyes stood near the fireplace. He stepped forward and hoisted Rifu's sister to her feet. He was dressed in a suit with a blue tie. His hair was combed back against his youthful skull.

"Governor Luci," I mumbled.

The man's eyes darted to me. "And who are you?"

"A guest of our daughter, Luci." Perse appeared from around the corner. "He was just about to leave when Aria attacked him for no reason."

"Mother!" Aria screamed.

Luci silenced her with a hand. "Don't speak that way to your mother." His eyes trailed back to me. "You must be Haydn Ladditz." He glanced at my right shoulder. "May I see your arm?" Without waiting for my response, the Governor took my right arm and pulled up the sleeve. He carefully studied the birthmark for a moment before turning to Perse. "You are free to leave, Haydn."

"O-okay," I mumbled.

Luci grabbed Aria and looked to the butler, nodding. In return, the butler bowed. He helped me to my feet. In mere moments I was in the Mercedes, going home.

"What was that all about?" I gasped, my jaw and ribs still throbbing.

"Lady Aria, Rifu's twin sister. She left without warning the other night with Neferia and Brenda."

"Does that mean that…?"

"She was most likely lied to. You most certainly are not a slave."

"Some days I wonder."

I sunk back into my seat, grumbling. This wasn't something I needed right now. Where was I going to get arguing with a butler? I kept silent and watched the fields as we passed them, going the other direction this time.

The drive was silent after that. All that was heard was the soft tumbling of gravel under the tires of the Mercedes. I peered out the window, trying to put my focus on something else. I noticed a pheasant again. This one was alone out in the field. It couldn't stand up straight, though. It kept wobbling. Then, with a deafening blast the pheasant fell to the ground. A hunter came to find her prize, holding it up to her face.

"Rifu?" I mumbled hysterically.

I shook my head, turning away from the hunter, and back towards the butler. I didn't know what I was about to do. I figured I would start a gentle conversation with him to relax.

"So…how long have you been—"

I rubbed my eyes. My eyes had to be lying to me. When had Brenda taken the butler's place? She reached out a hand, rubbing it against my chin.

"You can't escape now…are you going to submit?" she asked, a crooked smile on her face.

I shook my head, cringing against the car door. I clenched my eyes shut and prayed she wouldn't hurt me. I gasped and wrenched my eyes open. Now the butler sat there, concerned at my behavior.

"Are you alright? Do you need to see a doctor?"

What just happened?

I shook my head. "No, I'm just…just having an anxiety attack."

"Is that so? Be sure to get plenty of sleep tonight, young master."

"Thanks…"

"You're quite welcome."

We were five blocks from my house when I remembered that I lied to my parents.

"Hey, can you just stop and drop me off here?"

"Are you sure? It's not far."

"Just drop me off here. I can walk."

"If you wish."

The last thing I needed was Drake wondering why Rifu's butler was driving me home. I hurriedly grabbed my belongings, thanked the butler, and headed towards my house. As I rounded the corner, my mood was slightly lifted. There was an old Oldsmobile parked in front of the house. I knew immediately who was home. I rushed inside and there, at the table, was a man with short, blonde hair and green eyes. He was my brother, Chris Ladditz.

"Hey buddy."

"Hey Chris," I replied, breathless, my ribs throbbing again. So was the side of my face.

He looked at me strange. "You okay? You're crying."

I put my hand to my eye, feeling the warm tears, the physical incarnations of my fears. I didn't care that I was crying. "I'm…just so happy to see you."

Katria was also sitting at the table, along with Drake and Mom. While I was scared out my mind, I was glad I could see everyone again. I walked up to Chris and hugged him and then kissed Katria on the forehead.

"Bro, what's wrong?" she asked uneasily.

I shook my head. "I'm just glad to be alive!" It was better to keep what had happened secret. Honestly, who was going to believe me?

"Well, that's a major attitude adjustment!" Drake smiled. "Maybe you should socialize with girls more often."

"I don't think so," Mom interjected.

I chuckled and wished he hadn't brought that up. "Yeah…" I put my stuff on the floor and stood there, rubbing my sides.

"Hey, what's the matter?" Chris asked.

I didn't make eye contact with him for fear that I would let the truth blurt out. "Nothing really, just slept wrong at Garred's…"

"Garred?"

"Yeah. He's a new friend."

"Ah, I see. Well that's good."

I grinned and stretched my arms up behind my back, my shirt pulling up just enough for Katria to see the bruises on my torso. They were dark and angry like storm clouds on the horizon. Luckily, she was the only one who noticed.

"Bro, where'd you get the bruises?"

Drake and Mom looked at me. "What bruises?"

"Um…yeah, what bruises?" I repeated dumbly.

"But, I just saw…"

I yawned loudly, pretending to be sleepy. Which, I actually was.

"I didn't get much sleep at Garred's…the party went pretty late. I think I'm going to head up to bed."

"What about breakfast?" Mom whined. "And you barely get to see your brother!"

Chris grinned at Mom. "I'll be staying all weekend, Mom. I'm sure we'll have time to chat. If he's tired then let him sleep. Goodnight sleepin' beauty."

I laughed a bit. "But really, I am glad that you're here, Chris." I touched my right shoulder. "I really am."

Chris touched his left shoulder. "I thought you would be." He smiled, sipping his Mountain Dew. "Anyways, I'll be in the area until New Year's because I got a personal customer. I figured I'd come by and spend the holidays with you guys, too."

"Well, you know you're always welcome here, Chris," Mom cooed. "You should eat, Haydn, you look hungry," she insisted.

Yeah, I was hungry, even with that large breakfast, but I wanted to sleep. Thoughts of being eaten washed away my appetite...I shuddered in front of everyone. I ignored it at first, and no one seemed to notice. But I remembered the strange happenings from earlier, and shuddered again, more noticeable than before.

"There a cold draft?" Chris asked, looking about.

I shook my head. "Just remembered a bad dream, that's all," or what seemed like a bad dream.

"Food reminded you of a bad dream?" Mom asked apprehensively.

Yes.

"No," I shook my head. "You know me, I think of the most random things at the most random moments."

They all agreed, nodding their heads. "Amen to that," Drake joked.

"So, Chris, who's your customer this time?" I asked, resting myself against a wall.

He sipped his drink again and grinned, his eyes sparkling with excitement. "A good job; I'm going to make a tattoo for Governor Luci's son."

I froze. "Governor Luci? As in, Luci Anerex?"

"Yep," Chris said matter-of-factly.

"Didn't you go to Governor Luci's manor last night?" Mom asked me.

I nodded. "Yeah...it was...fun..." I mumbled.

"Their son, Uron, wanted a tattoo." Chris rolled his eyes. "The guy's one of my best friends, so of course I had to accept the offer."

I stared at Chris in disbelief. "So, you know one of Rifu's siblings?"

He nodded. "Yeah, me and Uron go way back...ever since grade school, I think." He smiled, taking a long sip of his soda.

"A long time," Katria mumbled.

Mom blinked. "I don't remember him."

"That's because I really never told you about him." He put down the glass and turned to Mom with a smile. "Besides, wouldn't have mattered either way. We barely saw each other outside of school, but during school we always had good times." He nodded, as if agreeing with himself.

"So..." I interjected, "What do you know about Rifu, then?"

"Really, Uron always said she was a great girl. If only she were a bit more behaved. She can...be a bit of an enigma, he said." Again, he shrugged. "But I never met her."

I nodded and then shook my head, trying to empty the thoughts out of my head. Those suckers clung tight inside my brain, though. There was no way they were coming out. Fear had been trying to grip me throughout the conversation, the blood drained from my face as I walked in the direction the stairs.

"Hm, what's the matter, Haydn?" Mom asked, vexed at my sudden departure.

I half turned, faking a smile. I looked into my mother's gentle eyes. They were eyes that could only belong to a loving mother. It pained me to have to hide this from her.

"Nothing, Mom," I assured her, "I just need to check my e-mail."

*   *   *

I was on my bed, resting my ribs, my head twisted so I could look out the small octagon window above my desk. My room was standard for a teen. Well for me anyways. It had a computer, a desk, a stereo, and a bed I refused to get out of in the morning. My calendar hung on the wall next to my bed. X's marked a countdown to Christmas. I got up and walked to my calendar, updating it.

"Funny…" I mumbled dejectedly, "It feels like Christmas had just left."

I turned around and eased back into my bed. I gazed back through the window, trying to think of a way out of everything. But my head was too muddled. I couldn't even think of what the next day was, even though it was Sunday. I could only think of Jolie and Rifu. Wasn't it normal to think of girls? Well, Rifu and Jolie weren't normal. And, at that point, neither was my life.

I heard a knock on my door, followed by Katria's voice. "Bro, are you coming down for supper?"

I glanced at my clock, the red digital numbers reading six-thirty. I shook my head. Anxiety had made eight hours fly by like two minutes. The pain in my ribs had numbed, until I stretched. I pulled up my shirt to see the bruises. They were splotches on my side, like a Dalmatian.

I heard the door creak open, and there stood Katria, her innocent eyes huge.

"Bro, are you okay?" she asked, spotting the bruises. "You do have bruises."

I put a finger to my lips. "Don't tell anyone. I was rough-housing last night and got a little aggressive."

"Oh…okay…" she paused and then looked at me. "You coming?"

"Yeah, I'm coming," I assured her.

She came in and put her hand on my face. "Bro, are you okay?" she asked. Concern painted her face and eyes. "You look...like you're scared..." she mumbled.

"I've just been staring at the computer screen too much." I shooed her off downstairs and closed the door behind me as I headed down to the kitchen.

I stopped a moment, looked at the door of my room. I had almost forgotten about the collage I had nailed there. It was a collage of my favorite pro wrestler, Bill Goldberg. I ran my hand across the typed words at the bottom of the collage.

"No shortcuts."

I couldn't remember where the words came from. They may have been from Goldberg. All I knew was that I was going live by those words. Everything had to be done the hard way. No shortcuts. No easy way out.

"Haydn, are you coming?" I heard my mother calling up now.

"I'm coming!"

I came to the table and felt out of place. Visions of when I walked into the Rec. Room flashed through my mind. Now it was my family. They all had their eyes on me. After I sat down, I was somehow able to force a smile.

"Hello family," I muttered uneasily.

Mom and Drake shot glances at each other and then looked to me. They were obviously concerned.

"Haydn, are you okay?" Drake asked, putting down his fork.

"I've been staring at my computer. No big deal."

Drake nodded. He didn't buy it. Silence crept over us. I took a bit of the lasagna, chewing it slowly. My eyes wandered down to see the red, watery sauce leaking out of the pasta. Blood. Jolie. Vampire. I could feel the sweat racing down my face. Mom spoke up.

"Honey, you got a phone call from a girl. I think her name was... um...what was her name...Jolie?" I locked up. "She said to give her a call back at this number." She handed me a sheet of paper.

Thoughts of the previous night continued to haunt me. Pearly white fangs danced around in my head, Jolie's pearly white fangs. Anxiety consumed me from the inside out. I took the sheet of paper, my hand shaking.

"Oh...okay."

"You sure you're okay buddy? You look a little pale," Chris said.

"Yeah...I'll be fine. I think I'll sleep extra hard tonight, though."

Drake nodded and laughed. "At least we know you won't be a virgin forever," he chuckled lightheartedly.

"What's that supposed to mean?" I asked, irritated.

"Well...you get invited to a rich girl's mansion...and now a girl's callin' you. I bet you'll get some...eh?"

I shook my head, trying to hide the chagrin in my eyes. "Shut up!" I shouted. "I don't need to hear this coming from my own parents!" I stood up and walked to the fridge. I took the longest time possible, pretending I couldn't find what I was looking for. The truth was I didn't have a good grip on my anger. I didn't want to snap at anyone.

"Hey, I was only kidding," Drake said gruffly.

I sat back down at the table and sighed. "It won't last."

"What would make you say something like that?" Chris asked, intrigued.

"Trust me...I just know."

I didn't know, and that was why I was so scared.

I ate silently while Katria blabbed about some stupid boy in her stupid middle school that she was concerned about. She went to a party—there were chaperones there, according to her—with this boy she really liked. Sometime during the party, he disappeared. Then, almost five minutes later, the kid reappears, pale as the moon.

"It was weird actually..." she commented, "Because after that, he couldn't stop mumbling about some really beautiful girl."

"Well, what did he say about this girl?" Drake asked curiously.

"I think he said her name was...maybe something with an 'r'? I can't remember that well."

I almost choked on my food when I heard that. My mind instantly flickered back to when I read Rifu's diary. It said she was going to a party. What would stop her from—

"Oh well, so what if this bozo came back sick?" I blurted. "Some things kids do in middle school can make some people sick. The guys in your class are just horrible!" I mumbled, trying to avert my mind from Rifu.

"Well...that's kinda true...but he's a really cool boy. I like him."

"Whatever," I grumbled and got up to dump my plate in the sink. "Now, if you'll excuse me...I gotta go see what Jolie wants."

"Don't stay on the phone all night dear!" Mom called after my retreating figure.

I simply waved at her, as if telling her not to worry. Unknowingly to my mother, or any of the others, I had junked the paper into the trash can while I was dumping my plate. After what had happened in Rifu's bath, Jolie was the last person I wanted to talk to. I decided to play it safe and go to bed nice and early.

I plopped on my bed. My neck muscles were tense again. It was much worse than the other night, though. Rifu and the others used to make me nervous and sweat for good, normal reasons. I never thought I would be nervous of them because they could kill me.

I stood up, retrieved a fresh set of clothes and staggered towards the bathroom, quietly shutting and locking the door behind me. I laid my fresh outfit on the sink and started to slide off my clothes. I jumped when I heard a ringing, my heart in my throat. I calmed when I realized it was the phone and not my head. Just as I was about to turn the faucet handle, I could hear Drake's powerful voice reverberating through the house.

"Haydn! You got a phone call! It's Jolie!"

I shook my head. Was I cursed to be tortured by these people? I wasn't going to do this. I finished stripping down and hopped in the shower. When I didn't hear Drake call again, I sighed in relief. Talking to a vampire wasn't at the top of my to-do list at that moment.

After finishing my shower, I stepped out and dried myself slowly, a headache easing its way into my already sore skull. I gripped my forehead, rubbing it firmly. The pain eased up, but it was still buzzing, nagging at my mind.

Perhaps sleep would wipe my mind clean. When I woke up, I would be living a normal life again. No popular girls, no demons, no anything, just me and my life.

But, did I really want that?

8. The Second Night

Unable to dream, my eyelids replayed everything. The coils, the diary, the visions…everything was flickering through my head like a broken projector. Finally, my eyes ripped themselves open as I gulped for air. My hand swept away the cold bullets speeding down my cheeks. After a few moments, I threw off the covers. My ribs were still tender, but bearable. My neck, still locked up, caused me awkward discomfort. I twisted my head one way, then another, but nothing could relieve the irritating strain.

See what you do? You want the hottest girls, and they turned out to be demons who want to eat your soul. And, to make things worse, you're wanted dead. And, Aria…what did she mean by being her family's slave?

I almost fell out of bed at the tip-tap of a something against glass. My heart punched my ribcage like a boxer. The hairs on the back of my neck stood up, even if they were smashed against the pillow. The tapping persisted. Then there was pure silence except for my fan. Maybe, it had just been my imagination.

Tap, tap, tap.

My eyes rolled in every direction trying to find the tapping's source. After a few more taps, I realized they were coming from my window.

Is someone there? No, that's impossible. I'm on the second floor. But demons exist, so is anything really impossible?

Suddenly, my mind was bogged with thoughts of midnight murders and reports of local teen boy found dead in his room. I shook my head, deciding against submission to paranoia. Maybe it was just an owl or some other annoying creature of the night. I slowly shuffled up to the window behind my computer. My pulse hastened, my breathing followed. I opened the blinds.

I only stared, wide-eyed, at nothing. I shut my blinds and plopped down on my bed. I ran a hand down my face.

What is wrong with me? Even my imagination is against me. I need to get out. I need fresh air.

I reluctantly slipped on some shorts and snatched up a green sweater from my computer chair. With the stealth of a dead cat, I walked downstairs barefoot. I didn't put on my shoes until after reaching the patio doors, unlocked the door, and stepped outside, quietly shutting the door behind me.

I looked out into the night, breathless at the flurry of snowflakes dancing in downward spirals from the pitch black sky. Never conformal, each different, even in their dance to join their brethren on the ground, I always enjoyed watching the snow fall.

"Scathing hatred from a boy
Nothing around gives him joy
Staring at this hateful world
Nothing abound makes him smirk
Down to earth, a crash tonight
Burning light, a past gone by
Scathing hatred from a boy
Nothing around gives him joy…"

She leaned against the wall of the house, watching the snow fall silently to the ground, snowflakes scattered throughout her hair. Each snowflake reflected the moon's light into an array of diamonds. Her scarlet eyes, even in the dark, seemed to glow bright. They seemed brighter than when I had first talked to her. My instant anxiety and fear was replaced with perplexing attraction. She didn't seem dangerous. It was as if I were watching a ferocious tiger; powerful and deadly, yet so painfully beautiful.

"Beautiful night isn't it?" she asked, never looking away from the sky.

I had two choices at this point. I could scream and possibly die. Or, I could deny she was even there and go back inside. But, I was very afraid of what she might be able to do.

"Yeah … I like the snow…even if so many people hate it."

She nodded in return. Her face seemed unscathed by the cold, while mine was getting colder each moment, quivering as a result. We stood there in silence, watching the snow, but then she turned to me. She put her hand on my arm. My heart spiked. I could feel the blood rush to my feet. If Jolie hadn't wrapped her gentle fingers around my wrist, I would have fallen over. Jolie's eyes pierced into mine.

"You didn't return my call," Jolie scolded, scrutinizing my reaction.

"I…I know…I wasn't feeling that great…and…" I trailed off, unable to keep my focus with her eyes on me and my neck knotting worse.

Jolie tilted her head, squinting.

"What's bothering you?"

"Nothing."

"Stop lying," she almost growled. "Tell me what's wrong or…"

I didn't want to hear the "or."

"My neck," I finally admitted, "My neck is locking up so bad…"

The scolding look was replaced by sincerity. She pulled me closer.

"I'm sorry," she whispered, almost matching the quiet wind. "Let me help."

She pulled me to the porch steps and sat us both down, forcing my neck across her soft lap. Her hands found my neck, moving in the same motion as they had before. It felt rushed, though, less thorough. Most of the pain went away, but, in its place, my anxiety returned. After she was done, she looked down at me, lowering her face a bit.

"Look, Haydn, I want to apologize. I came so close to making you a meal." She frowned ashamedly. "I probably seem like such…such a…"

"Blood-sucking monster," I blurted.

"Yes…I wanted your blood so badly. I still do. Rifu scolded me. She told me to apologize, but she didn't need to." Jolie curled a lock of hair around her finger, snowflakes falling to the ground. One fell on my face.

"Is that all you came for?"

"No. I wanted you to know what you're up against. Neferia is a lamia, and a cunning one. Brenda is a succubus. That means she has the ability to invade your dreams and make you hers. You have to be extremely careful. One slip-up and it will cost you your soul."

"Wait…she might be responsible for the visions I've been having…wait…never mind…" I muttered angrily.

"What? What visions are you talking about?"

"Nothing, I was just thinking out loud, my mistake."

Jolie chuckled. "We've made some mistakes, too. Things have gotten complicated."

"Complicated?"

"I can't tell you much. Rifu knows more than I do, but I know everything revolves around Neferia."

"There has to be more to it than that."

"Rifu told me that Aria claimed you were a slave of the Anerex family."

"Yeah, she did. Neferia told her, didn't she?"

She nodded. "We don't know why, though. Aria is usually very skeptical. I have no idea why she would believe something so untrue."

A high-pitch crack whipped the air. Jolie's eyes went wide, and her body became motionless for a second. She pulled me close, her face only centimeters away from mine. Her intoxicating scent made me delirious and almost animalistic in thought.

"It looks like *they're* already here," she breathed. "I was hoping they wouldn't find you so quickly."

"Who?"

"The Keres."

Family Meeting
Rifu

I fell backwards. A loud clatter of pots and pans against tiled floors rang in my sensitive ears. Within moments two maids and a butler had rushed the kitchen to discover the cause of the racket.

"Lady Rifu!" a maid squealed.

"Are you okay, Lady Rifu?" the butler asked me, helping me to my feet.

I brushed off my cotton shirt. "Yeah, I was just trying to find the red wine. Daddy—I mean, Father wanted some."

"He should have told us, Lady Rifu," one of the maids insisted.

"We were talking and he said he wanted some red wine, so I decided to fetch it for him. I thought there was still some in the kitchen."

"No, Lady Rifu," the butler mumbled. "It's in the cellar. Come with us and we'll get the wine for Master Luci. Then you can take it to him."

I nodded, smiling. "Thank you."

*   *   *

Daddy was in his office set down the hall a ways from the Rec. Room. I quietly sauntered in its direction. He had come home so soon. He met Haydn. That's why he wanted to talk to me. If I had known Daddy would be getting home so early, I would have sent Haydn home earlier. Mommy helped Haydn, though. She told Daddy who he was. She told me Daddy seemed shocked. Then he saw Haydn's birthmark and let him leave.

I came to the office door. From inside I could hear the low murmurs of my parents. It was hard to pick up on what they were talking about, and I couldn't sense what they were feeling. Through the doorway, I entered into a carpeted room with papers stacked upon papers on one table. A small fireplace was the only thing that lit this room and next to it was a painting of my grandpa.

My parents sat in chairs next to the table. They dropped their conversation at my approach and turned to me.

"Rifu, how are you, honey?" Daddy said. Mommy took the wine from my hand. Daddy looked down at me, smiling grimly. "Rifu... you're such a young fool."

"Father?"

He sighed and motioned me over to a chair. After seating me, Daddy brandished a glass while Mommy popped the top of the bottle. She poured the red liquor into the glass, filling it full, eyeing him worriedly.

"You know what this does to you."

"I know, Persephone," he mumbled, taking a sip. "I just need to take the edge off my nerves."

"What's the matter?" I asked.

"You know what's wrong," he sighed, taking another sip before setting down his glass. "I don't know how much you know, but I *can* tell you know quite a bit. You brought that boy here."

"But... I kind of like him," I blurted.

"Don't lie. You don't like him. Not the way you're saying it. Maybe you're too young to remember the boy's brother, or the boy's father."

I ran a hand through my hair nervously. "Who are they?"

"More importantly, Rifu, who are we? We are devils; the only family of pure-blood devils remaining in the human world. We have slaves, both human and demon. Our family mark provides us ownership of whoever is branded with it."

"So? His birthmark looks similar, but I don't believe he's our slave."

He grunted. "How much do you know, Rifu?" Daddy turned to the flame of the hearth, sighing. "And what are you thinking about? Your mind is constantly at work, as if you're processing variable after variable, situation after situation... but for what end?"

"I don't understand what you're talking about. But I want to know something."

"Yes," Daddy nodded. "You want to know why I'm so concerned about this. Do you not?"

"I hate our senses."

"There's more to hate than you can love, dear daughter. Remember that while you deal with this mess. You'll be lucky if your grandfather doesn't get involved, somehow."

"I have a plan. And if Grandfather wants to get involved, then let him."

"Watch what you say, niece."

We all turned towards the door. Leaning against the doorway was a man with wispy silver hair and thin, dried lips. He wore a black suit and white undershirt. He was about Daddy's height.

"Who is one boy compared to us? No one would ever remember him after I—"

"Charon," Daddy hissed. "How long have you been there?"

"Not long. Besides, did you forget that our father desires a family meeting?"

"No, I didn't forget."

"Good, be *there* soon."

With that, Uncle Charon disappeared from the doorway. Daddy scratched the top of his white head, sighing. Mommy put her arms around him, kissing his cheek. He nodded and patted her arm. Then he turned to me.

"Rifu," he mumbled, "I know not of what goes on in your head. We cannot read minds, but we can sense doubt, fatigue, fear…I feel all of these things in you. While I do not know the origin of these emotions, I do know they're linked to that boy. Whatever you're thinking about, daughter, I will help you. But no spell or ability that we know, however, is going to aid you in whatever endeavor you plan to undertake. But, there is one book you could try."

"What book?"

"The Tome of Fire; it's a series of higher-class spells. Do anything in your power to end this conflict discreetly. I *will* warn you, however, that Neferia mustn't die."

"What? But—"

Daddy shook his head. "Demons do not slay other demons, the second law of the Hidden World. But, especially, if Neferia were to die…war would ensue."

"Yes, Daddy," I muttered, defeated.

"I will help you, my daughter. I was once stuck within a shell of conflict. But I decided my path. You can make the same decision. You make you, Rifu. Remember that." With a quick hug, Daddy disappeared out the door and down the hall. Mommy stayed behind, putting her arms around me.

"I'll help you search, Rifu."

"Mommy?"

"I'm sure you're confused, but don't lose hope. Don't become a slave to your mistake."

"Like you were?"

She was quiet a moment, before kissing me on the forehead. "That was before I knew I was going to have you, before I *knew* your father."

I nodded. "Where do we start?"

9. Defend Yourself
Haydn

The snow stopped. All was quiet except for the slight crunching of snow beneath feet. Jolie and I stood under the porch roof. She seemed to know exactly what was coming and I didn't, rendering me, for the most part, helpless.

"What are we going to do?" I muttered, shivering from the cold.

"You're going to sit back and stay out of the way. You're only a human. You can't fight them off."

"You'd be surprised what I can do," I growled.

"Just shut up."

There was another crack, similar to the one before. The crunching got louder and louder. More of them were approaching, coming from every direction, the sound of their presence amplified, filtered through the eerie silence. Wind and snow had dominated the atmosphere not too long ago. Had they caused this…emptiness? Were they that powerful?

"Haydn, duck!" Jolie shouted, pushing me to the ground, a dark object zipping over my head and disappearing.

"What the hell was that?"

"A Hades' Bolt, something you definitely don't want hitting you. If one does, you won't be able to tell until it's too late."

"Great," I mumbled.

"Move!" she shouted, wrapping her arms around my waist, hoisting me up while she practically glided along the snow away from the porch.

"Where the hell are we going?"

"Away from your potential killers!"

Zip. Zip. Zip. More dark arrows flew through the air, barely missing us.

"What about you? What if a Bolt hits you?"

"It doesn't affect demons; only humans and other Keres!"

"Great!"

We ran across the street. There, an abandoned school building stood, decaying to dust. We hid on the other side. I was taking huge gulps of air, even though I had done very little running. Jolie didn't even seem winded.

"Are all vampires this tireless?"

"Some more than others."

I bent over, my ribs burning. I always thought my body was resistant to pain, but I felt so fragile, like a vase, but not as pretty. Jolie peeked around the corner of the building. Her glowing eyes looked off towards my house.

"What do Keres look like?"

Jolie shot a weird look at me then went back to watching. "Why does that matter? Do you really care about what your hunters look like?"

"It might help."

"The only thing that could help you now is…" she rolled her eyes, smacking her forehead with her palm. "Why didn't I think of that?"

She turned and grabbed my wrist, bringing it to her mouth. I ripped it away, somehow escaping her powerful grip.

"What are you doing?"

"Give me your hand!"

I put my hands behind my back defiantly. "Not until you tell me what you're going to do."

Dark lighting-like cracks zipped above our heads. My eyes went wide and my heart stomped in my chest. Jolie grabbed my arm and started pulling me along, almost ripping my arm out in the process.

"Keep moving!" Jolie screamed.

More darting bolts; some disappeared off into the distance while others fell to the ground.

"Can't you negotiate with them?"

"If they were mine, but they're not, so we keep running!"

We were already halfway down the highway next to the abandoned school building, perfectly in open range for any shooters. They probably could've hit me easily enough if Jolie weren't dragging me along.

"What happens if a Bolt hits a demon?"

"Nothing, like I said," she shouted, still pulling me along.

"I'm not running and you know how exhausted I am?" My legs were ready to give out.

"Do you want to die?"

"No…"

"Then try your best to stay upright!"

Only a few yards down the highway rested another timber that could shield us from the onslaught of these mysterious assailants. It seemed to be Jolie's eventual goal. My energy was giving out, and I could feel myself begin to slump. Jolie wrapped her arms around me, hugging me to her as she leapt from the highway and into the timber. We rolled, down and down a hill, my already bruised body cried out in agony.

Even after going so far, Jolie was still latched to me. She looked up, gasping, obviously worried. I stared at her, my vision blurred from dizziness.

"Why are you doing this?"

Jolie didn't look at me. She only watched above, moving away to examine our surroundings. When she deemed the coast clear she came back to me.

"I…We want you to be safe."

"Who's 'we?'"

"Rifu and I," she mumbled.

"Why are you doing it?"

"I have my reasons. Just trust me."

"Rifu almost killed me! You almost sucked my blood!"

"Yes," Jolie shook her head, "And I regret it."

I shook my head, sat up. A scowl disfigured my face, made my eyes gleam dangerously. They turned on Jolie, shooting knives at her.

"Quit that, you're freaking me out," she mumbled.

"You're one to talk. The way you were talking before Neferia tried to eat me…"

Jolie sighed, pinching the bridge of her nose. "I didn't say anything. If I did, I don't remember."

"How do you not remember? They were *your* words!"

"I guess," Jolie turned and gripped my wrist. "But I also said that I wanted to protect you. Having you dead would be counterproductive. Now, hold still."

"What the—"

Jolie opened her mouth, and the fangs, two pearly-white needles of death, emerged, and sank into my wrist. I screamed, expecting weakness to overwhelm me, for dizziness and sleepiness to cover me. But that didn't happen. I felt the same as I had a moment before; bruised and cold. Jolie withdrew her fangs and closed her mouth, wiping my wrist, giving it back to me. She wiped the excess blood from her mouth.

"That was so hard to do," Jolie breathed.

"What *did* you do?" I quivered, staring at the two holes in my wrist.

"Normally, vampires only take blood. But, they can *give* blood, too. My blood will temporarily gift you with a vampire's abilities. However, you can only use it by drinking your own blood. And it does run out."

I stared at my wrist, then at Jolie. "You, put your blood in me? Weird..."

"Rifu suggested it. I like it about as much as you do."

"You and Rifu...seem close."

"Rifu and I have been friends ever since we were born. We trust each other, which is more than what I can say for you."

"What the hell is that supposed to mean?"

"Forget it. It's not your concern anyways."

"Could you please not treat me like a baby?"

"It's necessary, Haydn. You're necessary, okay? If you die, terrible things might happen."

"This is the first time I've heard about it."

Jolie chuckled and shook her head. "I've spoke too much. Rifu wants you to stay alert. Keep your ears open for her."

"For what? And why? She can, like, read minds...why the hell would she need me?"

"Everybody makes mistakes." She placed a pale hand on mine, grimacing. "But we're going to help you. Then we'll leave your life forever."

Wait, so, after this nightmare was over, I would be free? I didn't want to be stuck in this nightmare forever, but Rifu and Jolie were going to leave, just like that?

"That seems extreme."

"It's necessary. We can't endanger you. Too much rides on your safety." She sighed, the wind snapping up a lock of her golden hair. "We don't have much time. Can you promise your cooperation, if not for either Rifu or me, then for your family?"

I was silent, thoughts drifting through my mind, an open field. My thoughts were fluffs from flowers, events in my life. Each had a respectable name; Regret, Anger, Sorrow, and Hopelessness. There was one tiny ball of fluff—tinier than the rest—that floated alongside the bigger ones, though. He was much lighter than his siblings. His name was Hope. He had a twin brother that floated close by called Gratitude. Rifu and Jolie were doing so much, but Anger and Sorrow screamed *It's their fault!* over and over inside my head. Then Hope whispered *Maybe, they're trying to help you.*

Jolie sighed, taking me away from that calm, grassy field. "Haydn, I know a lot has happened…and I am sorry. You know…it may seem like Rifu and I enjoy doing what we do, what we are. But we don't enjoy hurting innocent lives, even if death is our reputation."

"What about Rifu's journal? She said she enjoyed boys in their pre-teens."

"She only feeds on those who deserve it."

"I didn't deserve it."

"Drop it. Will you just cooperate?"

I nodded slowly. "Fine, I can defend myself. I've been in death's embrace once. Death doesn't scare me."

Jolie mumbled to herself.

"What?"

"Nothing, it's nothing. I want you to stay low, Haydn. We're about to have company."

Her garnet eyes drilled intensely into mine, gazing into my soul. Then her hand shot up, gripping a black arrow that had been aimed for my head.

"They've found us!" she hissed, got to her feet and then shoved me flat against the earth.

Dark arrows showered us. Jolie, agile, graceful, blocked a majority of the arrows. With fluid motion, and deadly accuracy, she snatched each one out of the air, as if catching flies, and threw them back, maybe even harder than they had been shot at us. Suddenly, the assault stopped.

"They're coming," Jolie huffed, standing her ground over me.

Through the trees emerged six figures. Humanoid in shape, their frames were wrapped under black cloaks. One stepped forward, the others halting.

"By helping him, you are labeling yourself as Lady Neferia's enemy. You will become an enemy of the Lamia Family."

"Then so be it, I couldn't dissuade you, anyways. You have to follow Neferia's orders."

"Indeed, but you could have spared yourself from the pain we will inflict upon you."

Jolie chuckled. "Keres have no power over me. I am *your* superior."

She was standing in front of the ghostly servant the next moment. Arching forwards, Jolie crossed her arms. Before the Keres could respond, Jolie flung her arms up, her hands meeting at the Keres' neck.

But the ghostly figure, like a fleeting snowflake, danced away from Jolie. It threw a punch aimed for Jolie's larynx. Jolie side-stepped the creature and responded with a pirouette-like kick into the side of the Keres. Jolie's adversary landed against a tree nearly ten yards away.

I nearly started cheering for Jolie, but I noticed the other Keres looking towards me. Their eyes were hidden behind their hoods, but I could feel them. The malice that emanated from those ghost-like creatures drove an icy spike into my spine.

One of the hooded assailants raised its arm. From within the sleeve emerged a crossbow. A bolt shot at me, grazing my right shoulder. I crumpled to the ground, the pain intense, like snake venom deteriorating my flesh.

Jolie caught the Keres who shot me with a wild haymaker, sending it crashing to the forest floor, a sickening crack. The other four, plus the first monster she had immobilized, converged on her. She ducked low, thrusting her leg like a spear into the throat of one of the Keres, a cruel snap. With swiftness unmatched by any natural predator, she then caught another Keres with a series of rib-cracking punches, one open-fisted blow crushing against the monster's solar plexus.

The remaining three agents of Neferia had her surrounded, unmoving. But, like a majestic eagle, Jolie seemingly took flight. When she returned to the ground, she landed a fatal kick to the head of a Keres.

With their numbers dwindling, it seemed like Jolie would finish this battle easily. But the whizzing of arrows convinced me that we were far out of danger. We both looked to the sky at the cloud of arrows descending upon us.

Jolie didn't take more than half a second to decide what to do. She scooped me up, my arm still burning, and put me on her back. We ducked around and between trees. Were we going to make it? I heard the whiz of Hades' Bolts, but, luckily, Jolie was one step ahead of them.

"Once I get you home, stay inside. I know how to drive them off," she gasped, pulling me up a sudden slope of dirt and slushy snow.

"Why my house? Isn't that the last place I want to go?"

We were out on the highway again, closer to the abandoned school. She dashed, her feet barely touching the ground. More arrows were aimed for us, but they never came close.

"If we left completely, your family would be dead. Besides, I never meant to leave your house. The Keres just arrived sooner than I expected!"

In only seconds we were on the other side of the school, then on the front porch. After Jolie let me down, I hobbled to the garage. Next to it was a pot that contained a key. I retrieved it and unlocked the garage, motioning Jolie in. I knew the porch door was unlocked, but I needed to talk to Jolie some more.

"Get inside," Jolie growled.

"I was grazed by an arrow… It's your fault for dragging me out there! You owe me at least five more minutes of conversation!"

Jolie winced, but quickly filed into the garage, me following. I locked the door and closed it. Jolie stood there as I fell back against a wall, pain and cold racking my body. She, noticing the wound on my arm, kneeled beside me, examining the cut bleeding below my birthmark.

"How do you feel?"

"I'm in pain… but that's about it." I rolled my right shoulder, trying to wring out an ache. "Funny thing is… it feels better, now. Is this the affect of vampire blood?"

Jolie looked at me strangely. "The vampire blood is special, but not when it's dormant."

"That doesn't make sense."

"Don't look at me. I don't know."

"Okay," I mumbled.

"I almost forgot," Jolie scratched her forehead. "News like this can spread like wildfire through the Hidden World. It might get pretty rough if you don't keep an eye on your surroundings."

"The Hidden World?"

"The Hidden World is the population of demons living side-by-side with humans… Without human knowledge, of course."

"Even at our school?"

Jolie nodded. "Yeah… there are some. Most don't need schooling. If they use human schools, they generally go to bigger districts. The bigger the school, the larger the selection for… you know…"

"Yeah…"

She looked out the window of the garage door, nodding to herself. "I have to go, Haydn. I can feel the Keres getting closer."

"Wait, I have to ask something…"

"What?"

"If you're a vampire...then why don't you die in the sun?"

She rolled her eyes. "This isn't the time. Now, be quiet while I concentrate."

Jolie snatched up my arm, lapping up the blood still oozing from my wound. She pulled away, shaking out her hair. The next moment she looked a bit bulkier, manlier. She started to look a little like me.

"What...?" I mumbled.

"Most demons have a shape-shifting ability," she mumbled, her voice still her own. "Each one works a bit differently, though. Vampires don't really change shape. We emit powerful chemicals that make our enemies hallucinate and think we're someone else." She cracked open the door, peeked outside. "The Keres, no matter what I do, will think I'm you, for a time."

"Freaky."

"But handy," she said before disappearing out into the night.

After I shut the door behind her, I turned and used the key to unlock the door. I tiptoed to the porch door and locked it quietly. I sighed in relief.

No one woke up. Good, now then—

An arm wrapped around my neck and dragged me backwards. I was in front of Katria, who had shut her door and flipped on the light. She stared at me accusingly.

"Alright, bro, what was that all about?"

How much had she seen?

"Um...what was what all about?"

She shook her golden locks. "Don't even think I didn't see what happened out there! I saw you talking to that girl...Where'd you run off to? What were you doing? And how did she run so fast? How did she pick you up?"

Cornered. But my anger suddenly started to seep between the bars of my conscience. My eyes widened.

"Look, it's none of your fucking business! There are things you don't need to know about. Stay out of it!"

Before I knew it, I was seething with rage. It pooled up in my feet until it started to flood the rest of my being. What had afforded me this anger? Katria wasn't the cause. I hadn't experienced such rage in what felt like a long, long time.

I lifted her up and onto her bed. Anger, a demon that ate away my insides, fueled my actions and filled my voice with opinions that had been, up to that point, very quiet.

"You should just stick to your stupid middle school problems! That's where you belong; middle school! You're naïve and ignorant! You know nothing about my pain or the things I've been through!"

I stormed out of her room, heading straight for the stairs. Chris blocked my path, standing against a wall in front of the stairs. I glowered at him. In return he sent a soothing, gentle gaze in my direction. My anger seemed to die down, the fire fading away. I could hardly remember why I had acted the way I did against Katria.

"You don't need to get so angry, Haydn," he muttered. "Can't you just calmly explain to her? Even if you choose not to tell her, at least take it easy on her."

I sighed, kicking at the air. "I don't know. I just…I guess I don't want her to grow up. I don't want her to go through the things I'm going through."

Chris grinned and chuckled. "I know what you're going through, Haydn. I've been there, done that. But, hey, I might be a bit angry too if I had demons coming after me."

"Actually…Wait, what are you talking about?"

"Isn't it obvious? I know what's going on. I know what the Gaga Girls are."

"But how could you? How would you know?"

Chris patted me on the shoulder. "Uron told me."

"You don't know what I'm going through. So what if Rifu's brother told you what happened!

"Be quiet and just listen. Uron has a twin sister…just like Rifu has a twin. She came after me, but thanks to Uron I was able to escape."

I stared at him, breathing deeply and angrily. "But that was you… Uron wasn't there this time! Now I'm in the middle of a nightmare!"

He snorted. "A nightmare is living out your life knowing you made an unfixable mistake. This can be fixed. It will be."

I threw my hands in the air. "I'm going to bed."

"If you keep up like this, things will only get worse."

"Goodnight, Chris," I grumbled.

*　　*　　*

It was Monday, and I was back at school. However, the Gaga—I mean—Rifu, Jolie, Brenda, and Neferia were nowhere to be found. Of course, everyone was worried about them. If only they knew that they were only food for those four disguised demons. I would laugh at them later.

People eyed me as I strolled down the halls. Everyone knew that I had been invited to the party at Rifu's mansion. No one knew what had happened at that party, though. I sighed, unable to ignore the blatant glaring. I didn't want to get angry. After nearly ripping Katria's head off the other night…

Everyone felt like their whole world was missing. And the weight of their silent accusations exhausted me. I ignored most of them, but they still got on my nerves. There were so many jeers and taunts behind my back. Rumors started flying about how I slept with the Gaga Girls. Others went into grittier details.

Lunch tumbled around slowly. I was hesitant to go, but I walked into the cafeteria and sat down at my usual table. Most of the time there were a few others who would sit with me, but I noticed how they seemed to avoid their usual spots like the plague.

I chuckled slightly to myself, seeing the evacuation of my "table-mates" as a plus for me. I sat back against my plastic chair. The lunch-room was eerily silent today. Only the slight murmurs from small groups of students reverberated in my eardrums. That's why I jumped when I heard the legs of a chair scrape beside me.

"I see you didn't take my advice," he said under his breath, sitting down to eat whatever junk the school was serving.

I sat up and hunched over the table, looking at the boy, contemplating murder. I had almost forgotten that he told me to stay way. Maybe, I should have listened. But how the hell could he have known something bad was going to happen?

"Who the hell are you?"

The boy took a bite of the government-issued meat and smiled. "My name is Gyan Ganesa. Pleased to meet you, Haydn Ladditz."

After he shook my hand, I looked at it and wiped it on my pants. "What do you know about those four? How did you know what was going to happen?"

Gyan took another bite, chewing it thoroughly before swallowing. "Let's say… I've known them for a while. They…"

"Hide among humans, acting like humans, right?"

He chuckled, shaking his head. "Obviously, something went horribly *right*. You wouldn't be able to say that otherwise."

"What do you mean? Nothing went right. I never wanted to be stuck in this kind of situation."

"Oh? But it's the deepest desire that will reap its irony."

"You don't make any sense."

"Like the vampire? I heard she tried to sink her teeth into you…literally."

"How the hell do you know that?" I hissed.

"That I can't say, not just yet." Gyan looked up, grinning. "Looks like you have some company."

I turned, and standing behind me was Sheila. As far as I knew, she was a normal girl who got less than average grades. But she was pretty. Not as pretty as *them*, but pretty, nonetheless.

Gyan picked up his tray, finished with his meal. "I'm done." He gestured with his hand in what seemed like a half-hearted salute. "Good day," he said.

And just as he had come, he was gone. I shook my head. His words were ridiculous. "What the hell does he know? Nothing, he knows absolutely nothing."

"Um, excuse me?"

I had almost forgotten that Sheila was standing there. But my face didn't flush with embarrassment like normal. Instead, I sat back in my seat, stared at the wall, and asked her what she wanted, politely.

"Careful, hanging around me can get you infected by rumors and other contagious high school diseases."

Sheila kind of giggled, her glasses nearly sliding off the end of her nose. Since when did girls laugh at anything I say?

"Can I sit down?"

Since when did normal girls *sit* next to me?

"I suppose. But, I'm telling ya, I'm a biohazard."

"You don't look too hazardous."

"Says you," I chuckled.

Wait, what the hell was happening? So many emotions, none of them too cheerful, had passed through me within the last weekend. Now, all of a sudden, just because one girl was talking to me, I was happy? What black magic was this?

"Um…can I ask you something, Haydn?"

"I suppose."

"Will you go out with me?"

10. Head-splitting Succubus

What was happening? My world, my life, was inverted, reversed, and then divided by two. Was I stuck in a dream where nothing connected? All of a sudden, not even two days after discovering who the Gaga Girls were, I get asked out by a pretty girl like Sheila? Was she a fucking demon, too?

Despite my hesitation, I said yes. That night we went to the movies. Surprisingly, she wanted to see an action flick. At one point during the movie, when it looked like the hero would be sawed in half, she grabbed onto me, as if doing that would save the hero.

After the movie, we ate at Applebee's, her treat, despite my protests. But, unfortunately, it wasn't like I was able to pay for anything. While we waited for our appetizers, I looked at her. She had this cute, round face. Her eyes were blue, a normal shade of blue, just like mine.

"Is there something on my face?" she giggled.

"No…I was…uh…"

"I'm joking, Haydn."

"Oh," I chuckled.

"So, when did you decide to chase girls like Rifu?"

I froze in my chair. Why would she ask something like that? Who asks something like that on their first date? But, she doesn't know about the Gaga Girls.

"They kind of came to me, I guess. I don't see why. I'm nothing special."

"No, I guess not. But, then again, I've always been curious."

"About what?"

She rolled her eyes. "I've been curious about you. You're a *huge* presence in the school, yet, you don't really seem like it."

Is this girl for real? "Are you talking about me, or someone else?"

"Of course I'm talking about you! Who else would I be talking about?"

"There are a lot of other guys…I honestly think they're better than me."

"A bunch of jocks and know-it-alls. Sure, some may be nice, but I've never really been interested in stuff like sports and academics. I'm more of an artist, myself."

Art? Why did she have to be into art? The disturbing sketch inside Rifu's pad crept into my mind, saying *"I'm here, Haydn. Did you miss me?"* I focused on Sheila again. Her platinum blonde, stick-straight hair fell to either side of her face, while her bangs were combed to one side of her forehead.

"And you consider me to be an artist or something?"

She shrugged. "I don't know what you are, that's kinda why I asked you out."

"I'll take that."

We sat through dinner, talking kind of like that. I found out Sheila had been going to Klintwood since kindergarten. But, I knew that already. She did point out how she never really remembered me being so chiseled. I revealed to her my workout routine. She said the sound of it stole the energy from her muscles.

After we finished, I walked her out to her car. She was sixteen. But, even if I was her age, license in hand and behind the wheel of a car, I wouldn't want to drive at night. Especially this night, a night where the wind whipped around the remnants of last week's snow.

"Are you sure you don't want a ride home, Haydn?"

"My step-dad works across the street. His shift ends in about ten minutes. I'll be fine."

She grinned and kissed me on the cheek.

"Goodnight then. See ya tomorrow."

I watched in dumbfounded silence as she drove off into the dancing snow. Only one other girl had kissed me on the cheek. But, I'd rather forget about Jolie than compare her to Sheila. Sheila was a shot at normality after all the weirdness of the weekend.

The wind stopped, cut off by an unseen hand. I felt heavy, my heart thudding like an avalanche in my chest. It was exactly the same as the night before. It wasn't long before I was surrounded by hooded figures. There were eight of them, forming a tight circle around me.

"It didn't take us long to realize how you tricked us," one hissed.

"But, luckily for you, we can't enter buildings crowded with humans. But, now, you're ours."

What was I supposed to do? Jolie wasn't here to rescue me. I remembered her blood. But, did I really have to drink my own blood? It didn't take me long to find out. One of the hooded attackers ran up to me, taking me to the ground. It slashed at me with what I could only call its claws. Blood started to seep from gashes the Keres carved into my hands and arms.

The abnormal weight of this creature, along with the pressure of my own fear, pinned me to the cold concrete. Drops of blood splashed from the vicious attacks onto my face and mouth. I worked my tongue fast, trying to get as much blood as I could. I took one, bitter swallow.

"This is too easy! I don't know why Lady Neferia would send all of us to—"

My fist, swift, deadly, found its way to the Keres' head, a sick thud accompanying its voyage through the air and into the pavement. I stood up, swaying uneasily. Inside, deep inside, I felt a fire. It wiggled out of its core, my core, and trailed along my veins and into every fiber of muscle in my body. Was it anger? Was it Jolie's blood taking effect? No matter what it was, it gave me a power that I had never known before.

"What trick is this?" the grounded Keres hissed.

"No trick," I said simply.

"Are you another demon in disguise? Tell me, who are you?"

"My name's Haydn Ladditz. And I'm going to kick your ass."

The demon took to its feet, its allies swarming me. As if I had done this before, I spread my feet. When one Keres charged me, I ducked down to about its waistline. I smashed the palm of my hand, a technique called a "dragon punch," into the monster's side. It collapsed, and the others came to replace it. I quickly turned and swept another off its feet.

I took a moment to think. When the hell did I learn to fight like this? And where did I get the strength to put down monsters? Something didn't make sense. But, in my moment of thought, I was overpowered and tossed to the ground. One Keres reached out a hand towards my throat, but I kicked it off.

As I stood up, something happened. The parking lot disintegrated, and, suddenly, I was standing in a field surrounded by soldiers with red, horned armor and wicked black swords. I fought each of them off as effortlessly as I had defended myself in the parking lot.

But as the fight seemed to draw to a close, so did my mind.

*   *   *

A voice trickled into my head. This voice was smooth, clear, much like the whistle of a mockingbird. It bent over me, wrapped around me, caressed me. The words elicited from the voice warmed me, as if I had been standing for hours in the cold.

"I love you. I want to stay by your side, no matter what problems you have hidden behind your mask."

*   *   *

I woke up, in one of those stupid gowns, aching in a hospital bed. The stiff mattress didn't help any. Sweat soaked my chest, leaving me sticky and uncomfortable. I wiped my forehead, and then ran my hand back. On the back of my head I felt something stickier, warmer than the sweat. I brought my hand to my face and saw blood.

Gasping in horror, I struggled to my feet. I called out, but took one step and fell to the floor. The pain surged through my body as I collided with the tiles. My right shoulder, the one with my birthmark, started to burn, head throbbing, body torturing itself. I heard a giggle, one that sent me into a funnel of despair. I looked up and there, to my dismay, towered Brenda. Her eyes penetrated my weak gaze as she kneeled down closer to me.

"Well…don't you just look macho?" she lifted my head up with her long fingers, taunting me. "It's hard to believe you're…" She cut herself off, shaking her head.

"Why are you here? Who let you in…?" I gasped in pain as Brenda put a hand on my ribs.

"I let myself in. We're inside *your* head."

Words echoed in my head. *Brenda is a succubus. That means she has the ability to invade your dreams and make you hers.*

"You're a succubus," I muttered.

"Very good, Haydn," she cooed. "I won't let you escape again. You know what I want. Give yourself to…" She cut herself off abruptly. Her face twisted in confusion, her brows knitting tighter and tighter, as if she were in pain.

I gasped. She pushed harder on my ribs, moving her mouth to my ear.

"Listen, I don't have much time. There's more at work here than you might think. Don't leave yourself alone. Jolie…I can sense her inside you. She gave you the vampire's blood. Use it. Escape from me."

In confusion, I dug my hand in the back of my head then stuck it, bloodied, into my mouth, managing to swallow a little blood before Brenda ripped my hand away from me. She was too late. I could already feel the vampire's blood at work. The pain disappeared, all of it, except the burning in my shoulder.

Brenda gasped. I smiled and pushed her off of me and stood up. She grinned and shook her head. "This won't be the last time we see each other."

The next instant I found myself, again, on a hospital bed. I closed my eyes, taking a deep, deep breath. Opening my eyes slowly, I checked to make sure Brenda wasn't anywhere in sight and realized that Mom and Drake were standing over me.

"Are you okay, buddy?" Drake asked.

Mom fidgeted nervously next to him. "Honey?"

"I…I don't know…" I mumbled uneasily, gripping my now wrapped head.

"You've been out of it for a day," Drake mumbled. "Your arms…" he shook his head.

I noticed then how bandaged my arms were. My face couldn't have looked too pretty, either. I wondered what my parents think happened.

"The doctor said a car scraped you."

A car? I would prefer getting hit by a car than fighting demonic minions.

"The doctor said that you should rest. You should be able to return to school by December."

I stared at the white ceiling, taken aback. "Great, now I'm gonna be a week behind in school."

Drake nodded glumly. "Seems that way."

"Do I at least get to go home?"

"Yeah, they said you could go as soon as you woke up. Everything has been resolved. Rest is the only treatment, plus some pain medication."

"Then let's get outta here."

Feeling weak and fatigued, I got up with help from Drake, and we slowly made our way through the hospital. We were halfway to the exit when I heard my name called. I ignored it, not feeling up to social interaction. There was a tap on my shoulder. I turned and there, behind me, was Rifu.

"What happened?"

Drake spoke for me. "He was hit by a train," Drake teased. "Who's this young lady, Haydn?"

"This is Rifu Anerex…" I mumbled, still woozy.

"So, you're Rifu Anerex!" Drake said, obviously pleased. He held out his hand. They shook. "Glad to meet ya."

"So, what are you doing here?" I mumbled weakly.

Rifu blinked. "This *is* the 1st Anerex Hospital. My parents own it, ya know? I came here to entertain kids with terminal illness." Rifu mumbled. Her cheeks were red with false embarrassment, I'm sure.

Mom discreetly examined Rifu, smiling at me briefly before flickering back to Rifu. "That takes quite a bit of caring! Haydn couldn't do a thing like that… he's always too busy working out, you know."

Rifu nodded. "He's told me."

No, I haven't.

I just stood there as Mom and Rifu fraternized over me. My head was throbbing again, and I started to lose my balance. The room spun uncontrollably and I was going to hit the floor. But two hands steadied me. I realized they weren't the big, powerful hands of Drake or the long, slender fingers of Mom. These hands, placed on each shoulder, felt small and delicate yet sturdy at the same time.

I looked over my shoulder and saw Rifu balancing me, her emerald eyes filled with concern, genuine concern. She smiled, her teeth glistening and sparkling. I struggled to smile back. Mom and Drake looked at each other. I could hear them whispering, but I was unable to hear *what* they were whispering.

"You okay?"

"I'll… I'll be better after a week of rest…" I croaked.

Rifu smiled caringly, and I unconsciously realized that she had been walking me out to our car. After my parents unlocked the car, she opened the door and helped me in. She stood there, smiling still. Why was she so concerned about me? And why hadn't she been at school? With so many questions and no time or place to ask them, I felt dizzy, even sitting down.

"See you next week," she mumbled.

"Yeah," *if you're lucky.*

*   *   *

Back at home, bedridden, supper was brought to me and Katria occasionally checked in on me. I hated not being able to move freely. Surprisingly enough, I didn't ache as much as when Neferia attacked me.

Mom poked her head in at one point. Leave it up to a mother to bring up something you'd rather not discuss when you were feeling down.

"How would you feel if your sister came up tomorrow?"

"What?"

"She just wants to see how you're doing."

"Yeah, I bet." Mom left the room, sighing.

I resented Mom for trying to play peacemaker. She knew how much I hated Morgan. To get it off my mind, I tried to sleep, but then thought of Brenda. If I tried to sleep, would she be there? And, what had she been talking about the last time? She could have had me, but then she told me to escape, and how. I decided to watch cartoons. It looked funny, but it made no sense. Have you ever met a sponge that could talk and had a pink sea star for a friend?

"Haydn?" Mom said from the door.

"Yeah?"

"Someone's on the phone for you."

She gave me the phone and retreated down the stairs. I held the phone up to my ear.

"Hello?"

"Haydn? It's Sheila, are you okay?"

"Yeah ... I'll be fine. How did you ...?"

"Jolie told me. I knew I should have given you a ride home."

I was silent a moment. *How did Jolie know?* "When did you talk to her?"

"At school. I'm so, so sorry."

"No, it's fine. Listen, I'm getting another call. Can we talk a little later?"

"I suppose. Hey, do you want to go out? When you get better?"

"Yeah, I'd like that. Next time, though, I think I will let you take me home."

She giggled, warming my insides. *"See you later, hun."*

I clicked the phone over, not even bothering to read the caller I.D. "Hello?"

"Haydn?"

My heart dropped. The voice seeped through the receivers like a deadly, airborne toxin, soaking into my flesh, creeping into my blood, choking my heart.

"Rifu," I mumbled.

"I'm glad you're okay."

"Whatever. I'm sick of this, okay? My first shot at normality, and it was ruined by those Keres freaks!"

"Normality?"

"I haven't exactly had a normal teenage life."

"Is normality more important than innocent lives, Haydn? Is it? Would you trade your life for normality? Would you trade your family's life for normality? And what exactly, Haydn, is normality? Hm? This isn't the time for you to invest deeply into your personal interests."

"You're one to talk. Sheila actually seems interested in me for *me*... Not whatever the hell you find interesting."

"Perhaps, but did I ever say I wasn't interested in you for you? We're getting off-topic, Haydn."

I sighed. "I guess, but, first, let me ask you something. How did Jolie know I was in the hospital? Did you tell her?"

"No, she told me. I asked her to watch over you. She didn't seem to have a problem with that."

I was silent, and then burst with anger. "So, Jolie was *stalking* me while I was on my *very* first date? With a normal girl?"

"Calm down. She was supposed to help you if something happened."

"Yeah, I can see how well that worked." But, as I was about to say something else, I remembered something. "Brenda was in my dreams. She was trying to seduce me."

"Did you kiss her?"

"I used Jolie's blood. Then I woke up."

"Good, because if you had, we wouldn't be having this conversation, your soul would have been trapped in her body forever."

I nodded. "Thanks, I know, but, she was acting weird, as if she'd had a change of heart."

"Doubtful. You seem to misunderstand something, Haydn. You think any one of us would give up? If Jolie and I were after you, you would be dead. It's only because of Jolie and me that you're still alive. We're deadly predators by nature. Humans have made us this way."

I flinched. "You don't have to be so harsh..." I grumbled.

"It just seems like you can never quite grasp the situation."

"I grasp it..."

"*You're just human. All you want is normality, something that is nonexistent.*"

"Whatever! I'm sorry."

"*You have no reason to apologize, Haydn. Anyways, you're coming to Des Moines.*"

"Wait, why?"

"*My sister stole something. It's the only thing that could save you, and your family, at this point.*"

"What do you mean?"

"*Neferia threatens war. We have to kill them.*"

"Um…wow…with what?"

"*I'll explain later.*"

"Okay, but how can I go to Des Moines? I'm stuck in my bed for a week."

"*Lie, okay? It's that simple.*"

"Nothing's ever that simple."

"*Then I'll come up with a lie, okay? We'll go to Des Moines. We have to. Otherwise, you and your family won't be the only ones in danger.*"

"Oh…okay."

"*We'll pick you up in two days.*"

I put the phone down on my night stand and went back to watching cartoons. How on Earth was I going to get past my parents? Well, two days might give them a bit more leniency. Besides, Rifu might come up with a good enough lie that will get me out.

"Bro?" I heard Katria say from my door.

"Come in, Katria."

She came in, holding a two-liter of Sprite, some popcorn, and a DVD. She walked up to me and sat down.

"Mind if we watch a movie together…like old times?"

"Sure," I chuckled, "As long as you don't try to kiss me like old times."

She laughed. "I won't, not while you're sick."

"What movie?"

"*Santa's Slay.* You know, the one starring Goldberg?"

I was a bit hesitant, because *Santa's Slay* was about a demonic Santa Claus who was actually Satan's son. But then again, it was Goldberg.

"Sure, let's watch."

"Yay!"

I watched Katria as she cheerily put the DVD into my player. A sister and brother watching a movie together…that was normal. But, according to Rifu, there's no such thing as "normal." Everything, Rifu, the Keres, Brenda, Jolie, Sheila … it all made my head ache, as if it were about to split.

11. Des Moines

Two days passed. Rifu was coming to my house. We were supposed to go to Des Moines for whatever. What had her sister stolen that could save me and my family? For the most part, I had fought the Keres off just fine by myself, or at least I thought I had. And, despite the sustained injuries, I almost felt ten times better. But, that didn't matter. I just hoped Rifu knew where her sister was. Des Moines was a huge city in Iowa. It was our capital, but nothing compared to Chicago. Still, it was big enough to get lost in.

Rifu was at my door around noon. My Mom answered and what was her initial reaction?

"I'm sorry," she said. "Haydn is still feeling rather weak. He can't go to Des Moines with you today. Maybe next week."

Rifu saw this coming, obviously, because she started to lie.

"Mrs. Ladditz," Rifu smiled generously, "Haydn needs a good day to relax in expert care, don't you think?"

"Expert care?" Mom sounded mildly interested.

"My parents own a private center in Des Moines. It's been proven that when patients stay there, they recover three times as fast as normal. Some people even say they feel younger after they leave."

Mom looked like she was going to buy it for a moment, but then she shook her head. "Sorry, dear, I just don't think Haydn is up to it."

Rifu nodded. "That's alright, just thought I would offer. I want him to get better soon so he can come back to school."

Mom smiled. "Well thank you. Talk to you later."

"No, you won't," Rifu's eyes shined brightly, and Mom seemed to freeze. Rifu grinned and moved past her and into the living room. "Alright, let's go."

"What did you just do?" I mumbled, struggling to my feet.

Rifu helped me up, and then shrugged. "Just a family trick; devils have to find their way around."

I looked at Mom worriedly as we came into the kitchen. "Will she be okay?"

"Yeah, she'll snap out of it after we're gone. But her memory will be altered."

I tilted my head to the side. "Talk about manipulation..."

"In this world, those who can masterfully manipulate others rule at the top."

"I guess so." We got into the Mercedes, and I noticed Jolie was absent. "I thought Jolie was coming?"

"She was called away by the Vampire Counsel."

"Vampire Counsel? This is sounding like a bad manga."

"Demons need government, too. For vampires, it's the Vampire Counsel."

I shook my head. "What about devils?"

"Our grandpa," she chuckled and shook her head. "He's the one calling most of the shots, though Daddy's...I mean, Governor Luci's defied him before."

"Oh, wow. What happened?"

"Me."

I looked away, feeling really awkward. "So, does your grandpa...?"

"What?"

"Does he hate you?"

"No. Actually, he can be really awesome. But he keeps bugging me..."

"About what?"

"Family affairs."

"Oh...I see..."

* * *

The countryside quickly passed us by, an hour gobbled up as fields turned into rows of houses and restaurants and highway motels.

Sooner rather than later, we were in a suburb of Des Moines. Traffic was becoming hectic. People either rushed back to work from lunch or just passed through. It was just another normal day in the capital of Iowa.

"Do you have any idea where your sister is?"

"She likes libraries; the bigger the better."

"Hm…sounds like something else."

Why did I just say that? We both chuckled, so I guess it wasn't terribly awkward. I looked out the window. We were on a ramp now that was set above another road. We were already in the heart of Des Moines. I could see the Wells Fargo Arena a few hundred yards off. Rifu poked me and I turned, her finger pointed to the west. I saw a billboard, one brightly colored with "GRAND RE-OPENING" plastered across the center.

"A library?"

"Yes," she whispered. "And look."

Below the huge words, it said "Accepting Donations: books or money only."

"Wait, why does that matter?"

"The thing she stole? It's a very dangerous book. It's known in the Hidden World as—"

"The Tome of Fire…"

Rifu looked at me, eyebrows knit in surprise. "Um…yeah…how did you know that?"

"I'm not sure."

We sat there a moment, basking in the awkwardness of what I would call a lucky guess, when Rifu cleared her throat.

"Yes, well, it's…not for the hands of anyone lacking the proper knowledge. That book contains magic older than any established religion."

"That's…kind of old…"

"It was made for exactly one purpose: to give whoever held it the power of perfect manipulation."

"Okay, and that means?"

"Have you read *Fahrenheit 451*?" she asked curiously, suddenly.

"Once, earlier this year, but what does that…?"

"For school?"

"Yeah, but, Rifu—"

"Its message is true," Rifu placed a finger on my forehead. "Without books, who would supply knowledge? Truth? Everything could be lies. Normality, for instance. Colors, elements, animals, races…humans wouldn't know." She sat back in her seat, smiling. "It takes an outside force to make sure humans don't destroy themselves.

"But, at the same time, where does that leave me? I'm not human, but that doesn't mean I can't act like one. Demons...we're made out to be these horrible monsters. If you hadn't found out what I was, you would have never guessed otherwise.

"Then I think about something. How do I know I really am a devil? Because my parents told me? How do I know they aren't lying? Their knowledge, whether true or false, constitutes a large anthology. You and I are only small chapters in a larger, more intricate plotline.

"But, these plotlines, what we are, and what we'll be, how are they determined? It takes someone with the power of perfect manipulation to determine that. The government in *Fahrenheit 451* used a form of manipulation. Maybe in their minds, however, they thought their acts were good. But, to you, Haydn, that wouldn't be normal."

I bit my lip. Thoughts filled my head, then exited, then came back. Her words were confusing me. "What are you trying to get at? Humans are self-destructive?"

Rifu looked at me, and then shrugged. "It's happened before, Haydn. Hitler, Stalin, Charles Manson...they ultimately hurt themselves. They tried to take truth and make it into something else. But, what if, by chance, someone took the truth and changed it into something better than a lie?"

"What do you mean?"

"What if I didn't totally destroy the truth? What if I molded it into something that would benefit *everyone*, human and demon alike?"

"I...I don't know. You're...so philosophical. You make me feel stupid."

Rifu rolled her eyes. "It's my upbringing," she sighed wistfully. "As soon as I was able to talk, I was fed so much. Of course, demons have almost an eternity to learn as much as they want."

"And here I was thinking you were just another pretty girl," I chuckled.

She grinned, placing her thumb against my forehead. "At least you're not just another stupid human. You don't want to kill others, do you?"

My lips curled down, my eyes closed and I turned away slowly. I could feel Rifu's eyes on the back of my head. Anger tugged at my lips.

"Some days, there is one person that I would like to meet. Then, kill him."

Rifu took a sharp breath. Did she feel my pain? I hoped so. "Who?"

"My own father," I whispered.

"Why?"

"He left me and my mother alone. Drake came in and helped Mom. He's been a father to me. But Mom's *still* bitter about it, and I am too, more than her. She'd trusted him, and then he just left her."

"Sounds like taking the easy way out," Rifu muttered.

"A shortcut," I mumbled. "I hate shortcuts. No shortcuts."

Rifu put her hand on my shoulder. "Those are strong words, Haydn. Do you truly live by them?"

I turned and looked at her. "Some days…it's hard to tell."

"Do you think you're perfect?" I shook my head without hesitation. She grinned. "No shortcuts. That's perfection…claiming to be perfect is denying your flaws. When you deny your flaws, you ignore your mistakes, and that could inevitably cost you everything. That isn't normal, Haydn. That's self-destructive."

I chuckled and turned away again. She didn't move. Silence for a few moments. Then I felt her arm creep around my side and down to my hand resting on my leg. Her fingers threaded through mine. I felt her sweet breath on the back of my neck.

"But, taking them isn't good either," she whispered.

"I know."

She nodded. "Distrusting everyone, pulling away from everybody except your own family; that's a shortcut. You need someone to help you. You need friends." She squeezed my hand. "Even if it's just one."

I turned my hand over so that our palms met. Her other arm was draped over my left shoulder. This could have been a lie. She could have been seducing me, for all I knew. She made a point, I realized. I trusted hardly anyone.

"I'll trust you," I mumbled.

"Thank you," she whispered.

Ambush

Jolie

If vampires had hearts, mine would be beating wildly. Being chased wasn't something I had planned on when summoned by the Vampire Counsel. But here I was, in the Iowa Events Center, running away from two pursuers. They weren't vampires. In fact, the Vampire Counsel had nothing to do with this.

Lucky me that no one was around today. Nothing was planned at the Events Center today except for a great chase. I zipped in and out of rooms, through hallways, and up and down stairs to escape them. I stopped for a moment to scope out my surroundings.

"Damn it," I mumbled, looking around for an exit. "I have to get to a phone and call for help."

That's when I was struck in the gut, flew through the air, and smacked against a wall, sliding to the ground. My pursuers, a pair of strikingly handsome men, stood over me, grinning toothily at me.

"She's a cute vampire, don't you think, Will?" The one with short, blonde hair and blue eyes said.

"Yes, but Neferia has no time for beauty," the other one, long, brown hair, mused. "But can we really just waste a cute girl like this?"

The other one came up to me, jerking me by the hair. "We're creatures of beauty and seduction, remember? Envy is our sin, lust is our specialty."

The brown-haired one chuckled. "Of course, of course, how could I forget?"

"Besides, we can't let her leave. The devil's sister is luring the boy to that library. I wish we could have dealt with the devil instead of this one. She's much cute—"

I swung a swift kick at the blonde's knee cap. He howled in pain before crashing to the ground. The other one charged me, but I kicked him in a much softer spot. To say the least, he was singing coloratura soprano after that.

"Tell Neferia that she can kiss my ass."

I turned, only to be caught in the face by a swinging tail that sent me spiraling, like a football, through the air, landing me on my back a few feet down the hall. My eyes, after swimming in their sockets, settled on a giant lamia slithering towards me. She stopped behind the two men. One was limping while the other had both hands to his groin.

"She kicked me in the nuts!" he wailed.

"Suck it up," the other wheezed. "She broke off my knee cap."

The lamia grinned, her tail snuck around the two swiftly. "Why don't you both shut up?" Her coils constricted around them. Squeezing and squeezing, their screams escalated until they cut off. Their heads fell back. She dropped them both and glared at me.

"Vampire, eh? I haven't had one before."

I got to my feet and rushed her. "And you never will!"

The lamia swung her tail like a hammer, crushing me against the wall. I fell down, and she swept me up with the debris, bringing the huge, scaly muscle down, slamming me through the ground, into the first floor. I stood up, licked the blood off my lips. How did she catch me so easily?

The lamia clawed through the hole, almost landing on top of me. I rolled back, standing up next to a window.

"Oh contraire my tasty morsel, I think you'll fit quite nicely in my diet!"

She came at me with dangerous speed. Being so large, I knew she couldn't move that fast naturally. But it didn't matter. Grinning, I smashed my hand through the window next to me, my blood staining the glass as it fell to the ground. The lamia encased me in her coils.

"Any last words before you slide down my throat?" she laughed.

"Two, actually," I muttered. My eyes glowed. The bloodstained glass began levitating. They pointed towards the lamia's head. She never noticed them.

I stood up, wiped my blood on the shirts of the men and disposed of them and the lamia. The lamia had reverted to her human form so it was easy to get rid of her. Questions would be asked, especially when they found the damage. But they would *never* find the bodies. Now, to find that library they were talking about…

The Library
Haydn

So many, many books! How many books were in this library? Shelves upon shelves upon shelves…and there were three floors! I'm pretty sure that the only library bigger than this one was the Library of Congress. It was crazy. I was fatigued upon entering.

"You okay?" Rifu asked me, poking me playfully.

"Oh, yeah, I just think I had a hernia."

She chuckled. "Don't worry. I'm sure we'll find Aria in no time."

We started searching the first floor. We didn't find Aria, but want to know what we did find? Historical and factual information; how could there be so many books about history, math, and science? The second floor wasn't any better. It was all about classical English literature and a few fictional pieces. I checked the time and it was already four o'clock.

"Yeah, no time," I mumbled to Rifu.

"Sue me."

"I might," I grumbled.

"We have one last floor. She has to be on the third floor."

"I hope so…" I groaned.

We trudged our way up the third set of stairs, when a voice caught our attention from below.

"Rifu! Haydn!" she called out.

Jolie stood at the bottom of the stairs, heading up towards us. There was a wild look in her eyes.

"Jolie?"

"Why aren't you at the Vampire Counsel?" Rifu asked.

"It was a trap," Jolie gasped. "I was attacked by two men and a lamia."

"A lamia?"

"Are you sure?" Rifu asked.

"What other demon has a giant, snake-like tail?"

Rifu was silent a moment. With a moment's reflection, she chuckled in resolution. "Everything was a trap."

"You're very clever, Rifu."

I turned to the top of the staircase. Aria stood glowering upon us. In one hand she held what I assumed was the Tome of Fire. But that hand held little interest for me. In the other hand she held a chain. That chain trailed out and wrapped around the neck of a blonde-haired girl. Her eyes were blue. Blue like mine.

"Sheila."

12. Perfect Manipulation

"Aria," Rifu gasped. "What are you doing? Why would you kidnap an innocent human?"

Aria glanced at her. "Why else but to kill the other?"

"You're sick, you know that?" I shouted.

Aria lifted her hand, the one with the chain, causing Sheila to jerk in pain. Before I could move, my right arm began to burn. Starting from the shoulder, the pain spread throughout my body. I writhed and almost fell, but Jolie caught me.

"Stop, Aria!" Rifu shouted.

"Why? So *he* can live? Without us, without our family, sister, he wouldn't even *exist*."

The pain intensified, but I bit back the scream that wanted to escape my throat, digging my fingers into the birthmark on my shoulder.

"This is not the place, Aria!"

"You know, don't you? You've had this strange feeling, haven't you? You've felt like you've met him before, but you know you haven't."

"You're nuts! Let Sheila go!" I retorted.

Aria grinned maliciously. "I wasn't going to humiliate you just yet, Haydn Ladditz … if that is your *real* name."

"Shut up!" Jolie hissed. "You're trying to kill an innocent human, just like Brenda and Neferia. You're breaking our law!"

Aria burst out laughing. "And your guilty of ignorance, vampire."

"Hold your tongue!" Jolie replied.

"Aria, give us the book," Rifu mumbled.

Aria broke out into an evil smile that sent shivers down my spine. She held up the gray, leather-bound book. Dangling it, she chuckled.

"Sister, is his life worth so much that you would pursue the secrets of this tome?" She frowned, her eyes burning with hatred. "You know who wrote this book. You know what will happen if this is used by the wrong person."

I looked at Rifu. Her expression was concern-laden, like a wall ridden with bullet holes. But she shook it off, and concern melted into confidence. She held out her hand.

"Hand it over, Aria."

Aria shook her head and stuffed the book away inside her dress. She turned to me.

"I won't let you pursue a naïve fantasy, sister. As the Tome of Fire dictates: the Eternal Flame dominates every domain!"

She tossed Sheila to the floor and took a stance with one foot planted firmly in front of the other. Raising her right hand, tucking the left against her side, Aria's eyes started glowing until they appeared golden. A gust of intense heat burst from Aria's position. It beat against my face, singeing my eyebrows, drying out my eyes, until I looked away.

"Don't take your eyes off her!" Rifu gasped, pulling me to my feet.

In Aria's hand appeared a blue flame. She shifted her weight forward, sliding her right foot forward. She snapped her arm out in our direction, launching the flame like a disk.

"Take him and move!"

Jolie latched onto me and, with hardly any effort, ran across the wall, barely avoiding the fireball. I looked back to Rifu, standing her ground, staring straight at the fireball. We reached the third floor. There was no one else, just the four of us. Jolie dropped me and turned her attention to Aria, who smiled viciously at us.

"My poor, foolish sister, why couldn't she have just listened to me? Of course, she was the only real challenge for me. Jolie…you're a lesser demon. While vampires are powerful…you're nothing like your founder, meaning you're nothing like *me*."

Jolie charged, swinging her hands at Aria like the claws of a dragon. Despite Jolie's angry attempt, Aria simply danced around the haymaker-like assault. Jolie jumped, aiming a kick for the side of Aria's head. I held my breath as Aria grabbed Jolie's leg and grounded her face-first. Another fireball sparked to life in Aria's fist, but Jolie was ready for it. Like a spring, Jolie retracted her legs, coiling, and released, nearly kicking Aria down the staircase. I say nearly because Aria regained her balance instantaneously. Jolie returned to her feet, her fangs revealed in frustration.

"Bearing your fangs? How tasteless of you…"

The next moment, Jolie's rage turned into something of a smirk. She held up her right hand, revealing a book. Aria's eyes quivered in shock.

"How did you get that…?"

"Did you honestly think I was attacking you at my fastest? I'm a vampire. We're known for speed."

Aria backed up, and bumped into Rifu, who stood there, glaring up at her twin. Taken aback, Aria stumbled into Jolie, who wrapped her in a tight, inescapable bear hug.

"Looks like you lose, Aria," Rifu muttered. "You'll be punished for endangering this human," pointing to Sheila, "and for helping Neferia and Brenda to kill Haydn, another human."

At first, I thought, horror or some sort of regret would take over Aria's face, but, where regret should have been, a wry, malevolent smile stood.

"Stop lying to yourself, sister! You claim Haydn to be mortal?"

"Of course! I'm human, after all!"

"Shut your mouth, *slave*!"

"Not this again," I grumbled.

Aria's eyes glowed golden and I suddenly felt my mouth shut. My right arm was trembling, burning. What was happening? Was this Aria's doing?

"Now, Haydn, why don't you go over there and kill your girlfriend?"

"Why would Haydn do that?" Jolie spat. "Haydn isn't some callous killer!"

"Maybe not of his own free will…but under the control of his rightful master…!"

I felt my body moving on its own, standing up, straight and erect, slowly stumbling towards the bound and unconscious Sheila. Jolie was bewildered by my sudden movement.

"Haydn, what are you doing?"

"He's listening! Because he is a—"

Rifu covered her twin's mouth, and then plugged her nose. Demon or not, Aria still had lungs, like any human, and needed to breathe. No, Rifu would never kill Aria, only knock her out. However, I couldn't say the same for myself.

I stood over Sheila. Along with Aria's command, something else echoed in my head, another voice. I remembered this voice from my dreams. It had been there my entire life, but then, as Sheila came to consciousness and saw me standing over her, it seemed that voice came from Sheila herself.

"You came. Of course, I expected you to come. I'm so selfish, Haydn."

Words started pouring from my mouth, despite Rifu's shouts of protest. "I'm sorry. I betrayed you."

She shook her head, standing up, suddenly free of the chains. "Does it matter? We'll be together again, Haydn. Until then, I'll watch over you. Don't worry."

My hands found their way to Sheila's throat…

*   *   *

Darkness…a thick blanket of black ice that kept me motionless. My thoughts, they could wander, as well as my dreams, while my body watched, tortured by its invisible, sovereign chains. A voice floated into my ears. This voice, however, wasn't like the one from before. This voice was heavy, laden with burden.

"I apologize. I never meant for this to happen. You and your mother must escape. We'll meet again, though. You'll see to that, won't you? Yes, yes you will…"

*   *   *

When I woke up, we were in the Mercedes and halfway back to my house. I awoke slowly, as if trying to swim through the murky waters of drunkenness. Rifu sat, silently observing the passing scenery, to my left, while Jolie sat to my right. Neither of them seemed to notice me. I sat up straight, realizing I had been leaning against Rifu's shoulder. Had I been sleeping on her shoulder? For how long?

Then, like a head-on collision with a cement wall, visions of our confrontation with Aria racked my head. Visibly flinching, Rifu and Jolie turned to me, each wearing a grim countenance.

"Are you okay?" Jolie asked.

"What happened to Sheila? What happened to Sheila?"

Jolie shrunk, as if the question were her kryptonite. Rifu, however, wasn't as intimidated.

"You killed her, Haydn."

I turned on Rifu, disbelief forcing itself up in a weak stance around my mind. But, Rifu's words felt true, lacking any tone of sarcasm or wit. I started shaking, my stomach crumpling up in pain. A racking cough erupted from my throat, a dribble of blood snaking out of the corner of my mouth.

"Did I, really?"

Rifu nodded. "A fire...fire leapt from the mark on your shoulder to your fingers, and burnt her to the bone."

"How...how is that possible? I'm human, aren't I? Or is this the work of your blood, Jolie? You...you're lying to me, Rifu, aren't you?"

"Why would I lie to you? I have no reason to! Jolie's blood has nothing to do with this, either. Whatever happened back there...it's a mystery to all of us." But, Rifu's face admitted she knew more than was she was saying.

"Just calm down, please," Jolie whimpered. "If you panic, we won't be able to help you."

"Haven't you helped me enough? Sheila was the first chance I had at a normal life. And what happens? You two...you drag me into this... this demonic nightmare!"

Rifu grabbed me by the collar and pulled me close. "You think we're doing this for fun? *I'm* doing this for the *countless* lives that are in danger because of Neferia's actions." Rifu held up a book, shoving it in my face, as if it were my lifeline. "This book, Haydn, was worth one death. Your *normality* is meaningless next to the lives of others."

"Whose innocent lives? The lives of those in the Hidden World? Because I doubt you mean human lives! Humans...I bet you think your superior to us—"

Rifu smacked me, the bones in her hand popping against my jaw. I started coughing again, blood splashing out of my mouth. Jolie put her arms around me, holding me like a child.

"You don't know a damned thing about me, Haydn! Just because I'm a devil doesn't mean I deserve to be treated like one!"

"Rifu..." Jolie muttered.

Rifu sighed, sat back in her seat, placing the book on her lap. She took out a linen cloth from her dress and handed it to me.

"I'm sorry. It was very rude of me."

"You're...incredibly strong," I coughed, wiping the blood from my mouth and chin. "I'm sorry. All of this...everything's that happened... it's hard for me to take in."

We were silent for a few more minutes as I cleaned myself up. I sat back in my seat, Jolie and Rifu did the same. The awkward silence hung over us like a muffling fog. Jolie spoke up.

"I guess we're in this together, then?"

"Looks that way," Rifu chuckled. "If Haydn will abandon his search for nonexistent things…"

I shrugged. "I guess I have nothing better to do…" We all grinned. I glanced at the book in Rifu's lap. "So, *is* that the Tome of Fire?"

Rifu nodded. "The secrets of this book will help us defeat Neferia."

"Defeat her? Wait, why are we even fighting her?" I replied.

She rolled her eyes. "Did my mention of war pass through your ears like a phantom? Neferia's broken several of our laws. There are certain people who will want war."

"Like who?"

"The lamias, Haydn," Jolie said.

"Why? What have we done to them?"

"Whatever Neferia has told them we've done. Look, Haydn, things aren't exactly stable between my family and theirs."

"Same goes with the vampires. The Vampire Counsel has always viewed the lamias as a threat to this world and the Hidden World."

"Okay, I guess, but how will this book help?"

"This book was written by my grandfather…"

Jolie chuckled. "Good ole granddad…"

I looked between the two of them. "Is there something I'm missing?"

"No, nothing important," Rifu sighed. "This book hosts a plethora of magic we can use to detain Neferia. We can't kill her, however. If we do, then the war will be ignited for sure." She pinched the bridge of her nose, frustrations surfacing.

"What's wrong?"

"Things are becoming really complicated, Haydn. We can't go back to school. People, important people, are getting suspicious. Brenda and Neferia could use that suspicion to their advantage."

"How?"

"People are easily fooled when they're drowning in doubt." Rifu tapped her fingers on the window. "That's why we can't take you back to your house."

"What?" I nearly shouted.

"By now, the news of what happened at the library is probably spreading across Iowa. They'll eventually come back to us, Haydn. They'll eventually come back to you and your family. The Keres won't have to chase you anymore."

"No, I'm going home, Rifu!"

"Do you want to die? Do you know how many connections Aria, Neferia, and Brenda have in the government? You'll disappear, Haydn, and I can't have that."

"Why not?"

"Because…because," Rifu breathed. She leaned in close to me, kissing me on the lips.

I jerked back. Where the hell had that come from? "I'm…I'm sorry…" she mumbled. "You can't get caught. I won't let it happen."

Jolie looked out the window, chuckling. "Lovebirds."

"No, I have to make sure my family stays safe. They could still use them to flush me out."

"Haydn…"

"He's right, Rifu," Jolie mumbled. "Besides, I'm never far away. If something happens, I'll be sure to step in."

Rifu's shoulders dropped in defeat. She sat forward. "Agnate, take us to Haydn's house."

"Right away, Lady Rifu."

Rifu didn't protest, remaining silent as we pulled up to my house. She didn't say anything as the butler, Agnate, helped me out and to my porch door. When we were halfway across the yard, the door flew open and my Mom came out, screaming.

"Get away from my son!"

Agnate, confused, backed away.

Mom put her hands around me, sobbing. Drake emerged from the kitchen, a fight in his stance. "You go on outta here!" he shouted, looking at the butler.

He turned and hopped back into the Mercedes and drove away. Mom and Drake both helped me up and into the house, Mom sobbing and Drake shaking his head. Had they already found out? Were they going to give me to the police?

"Where the hell were you?" Drake growled.

"I-in Des Moines…"

"Why?" Drake shouted. My head lurched. "Stop staring off into space like you're stupid. You're still recovering. You shouldn't be out foolin' around."

"I don't know," I mumbled.

"You don't know? How can you not know?"

My anger started to rise. "Because I said I don't know," I mumbled slowly. "Do you understand?"

Drake stared me in the eyes, then at the door. "You had better shape up your attitude, boy. Otherwise, we're going back to how it was before."

I took a sharp breath and looked at Mom. She nodded. "If you're going to act like you did before, Haydn," she mumbled, "then we have to."

I let out a breath and then pushed past Drake. "Fuck you both!" I shouted, before falling to the ground, exhaustion and pain crippling me.

Drake and Mom helped me up, taking extra care as they helped me to my room. There, they apologized and told me that they only wanted me to tell the truth. They wanted me to communicate with them.

As I heard the pounding on our front door, however, I knew that would be impossible.

13. Re-Outcast

I followed my parents downstairs. A couple of men, big, intimidating men, stood at our door. They knocked on the door again. Drake growled in annoyance.

"We're coming!"

"Dear, calm down," Mom said.

They opened the door. I stayed back far enough to be able to hear the men speak. Each of the men flashed a badge upon Drake's request.

"What do you want?"

"We're looking for Haydn Ladditz. We believe he is a central suspect in a case of involuntary manslaughter."

"M-manslaughter?" Mom gasped. "That can't be right!"

"Can we speak with your son?"

"Not without a lawyer," Drake growled. "Not that he'll need one. Even if it was involuntary, Haydn wouldn't have committed manslaughter!"

"Sir, please don't be difficult. We only want to ask him some questions."

"Not without a lawyer," Drake reminded them.

The two looked at each other right before they both punched Drake, knocking him to the floor. Mom shrieked, and it didn't take me long to realize who was really standing at our doorstep.

"Mr. Ladditz," one man said as he stepped on Drake's chest. "I suggest you come with us if you want your family to live." As he finished those words, the other one grabbed Mom, holding a wickedly-curved knife to her neck.

"You bastards," I stepped forward. What else could I do? There was no way I would be able to fight them off without getting either Drake or Mom killed. "So, you Keres…look like normal humans?"

The one standing on Drake grinned. "How did you know?"

"The wind stopped blowing outside. I don't know how you do it, but it's your calling card."

"Well, perhaps we can show you if you come with us. Otherwise… we'll show some of our…other tricks."

Time seemed to stop for a second, but that second expanded into what felt like ten minutes. In those ten minutes, I heard a voice. This voice was the voice unlike the smooth one that I had heard before. It whispered to me, as if standing next to me.

"They can't truly stop you. You have the power inside to make them beg for their artificial lives. Simply extend your right hand out and touch them."

When the voice disappeared, when time returned to its normal flow, I took in a deep breath, lifting my hands up into the air as a sign of surrender. The Keres on top of Drake stepped off and the one holding Mom dropped her. When they stood in front of me, the voice shouted: "*Now!*"

My hand, at a speed I could never manage, wrapped around one of their shoulders. He grunted. Whatever his thoughts were in that moment, they would never reach his mouth. The spark of flame, the same as Jolie and Rifu described, leapt from my shoulder and landed at my finger tips, instantly igniting the Keres.

The creature let out a ghastly howl as he writhed in the embers that devoured his flesh. Seeing his partner fall before him, the other Keres turned to, perhaps, call for back-up. But, the fury that burned inside my chest, through my body, lashed out, and wrapped my hand around the back of his neck, engulfing him in flames as well.

I watched as the flames consumed both of the creatures. Strangely, as the embers died down, I noticed that the flames hadn't spread farther than their bodies. Moreover, any stray flame that did leap from their burning corpses instantly fizzled out, as if the fire could only exist when in contact with their flesh.

"Haydn…" Mom mumbled.

I helped her to her feet and moved Drake away from the door. I had a feeling that there were more Keres.

"I'm sorry…I…don't know what's happening."

"No, it's okay. Because I *do* know what's happening."

"You do?"

I felt a depression course through me. Tears welled up in my eyes. A girl's face, innocent, round, her golden locks gave her the appearance of a blooming flower. My mind snapped back to reality as I saw the Hades' Bolts flying towards us.

There was no time. There were too many of them. Mom fell to the ground in a heap. Where depression once sat inside my chest, wrath now stood, bearing its fiery fangs in revenge. I stepped out onto the porch, finding the five Keres, once again cloaked, who had shot their deadly arrows at my mother, the only one who apparently knew what was happening to me.

"You sword…is one of anger, and is sparked by the flames of hate and angst. Simply imagine yourself pulling a sword from its sheath resting on your left hip. Then, make them eat the raging fires of your hatred."

Whoever spoke to me I did not recognize, though I had once thought so. But, to whoever the voice belonged, they seemed to know whatever rested inside me better than me. So, in compliance, I rested my right hand on my left hip, pretending there was a sword there, ready to be unsheathed, when the Mercedes sped onto the road and crashed into the yard, bowling over three of the five Keres.

Jolie and Rifu emerged from the car. Jolie's speed, unmatched even by my small display earlier, took her to the throat of one Keres. Her hands, in a swift, scissor-like motion across the monster's neck, beheaded the Keres. Rifu met the last Keres face to face. She planned on facing the monster head-on.

"Haydn, get in the car, now!" Jolie shouted, rushing towards me.

In that split second I took my eyes off Rifu, and by the time I looked back, the Keres had fallen and Rifu was walking towards us, victorious.

"Are you okay?" Rifu asked, uncaring.

"My…mother…" I mumbled.

"What about her?"

"She was shot by the Keres."

Jolie's eyes widened. Rifu looked to the ground, regret tugging at the usual calmness in her countenance. Agnate emerged from the Mercedes, as if reading Rifu's mind.

"Agnate," she said, "take Haydn's mom away from here. And erase the memories of Haydn's step-dad and step-sister."

"What? No! You can't do that! You—"

Rifu mercilessly rammed her fist into my stomach, right below my solar plexus. I coughed up blood all over the ground, my ground, my yard. She didn't seem to care, and, by the way she walked towards the car, I knew she had pulled the punch.

Jolie helped me into the car, leaned me against her shoulder. I was ready to puke, dizzy, head buzzing. Agnate returned and the car took off smoothly. Without any words, I knew we were heading for Anerex Manor, the genesis of this whole conflict.

*   *   *

The estate was the same: large, shiny, but I couldn't stop to admire it today. We quickly filed out of the Mercedes, Jolie and Rifu giving me support. We headed inside and up the stairs. Our advance was halted by a familiar voice.

"Since when did they let criminals run loose?"

Aria stood at the top, grinning like the cat that caught the mouse. I looked away, afraid she might again control me.

"You're the last person we want to see, Aria," Rifu mumbled. "Just go back to whatever hellhole you popped out of."

"I'd only be welcomed with open arms. Grandpa loves me." She turned back to me. "And you, Haydn…you should be in jail for what you did to that innocent girl. Perhaps I should put you there myself."

"You won't touch him!" Rifu shouted.

"Why do you protect him sister? The slave deserves punishment!"

"Go away, Aria!"

Aria stared at me and then back to her sister. Then she stood silent, gazing off into infinity, slowly, like a creeping disease, laughter bubbled up from her stomach and into her chest before bursting out of her mouth.

"Perplexing, but interesting. I know you feel what I feel, Rifu. I know you feel what he is."

Rifu glowered at Aria then turned to me, pushing me towards her room. Aria simply looked after us, reveling in her twin sister's retreat.

"I'm sorry," Rifu whispered dismally, still pushing me down the hall. "But she wasn't going to attack again. She didn't have the advantage."

"I see…."

Questions bubbled inside my head, a dark, eerie cauldron. Who was I, truly? Mom knew something. But, more importantly, what did my birthmark have to do with any of this? And how was a stupid book going to help? When I looked back, straight into Aria's eyes, I saw a burning hatred that emulated the sun in ferocity. But Rifu kept pushing me.

We hurried to the garden. There, we found Perse, tending to the flowers.

"Mom—I mean Mother," Rifu called, waving.

Her mother turned and smiled. Then she saw me and frowned.

"Haydn."

"Ma'am."

"Rifu…" she mumbled.

"It's okay…we can handle this."

"Have you told him, yet?"

She shook her head slowly. "No…but…he doesn't need to know."

"He does need to know, dear." Perse sighed. "Telling him he doesn't need to know is like saying death is the best option. Death is never a good option, Rifu. Humans have tried time and time again to justify killings. If you put a mask on a killer then he becomes a masked killer; murder is murder. *Remember* that."

I visibly flinched at the edge in her words. Though her scorn wasn't directed at me, I felt the full force of her motherly proverb sink into my chest like a hook.

"Look, with the Tome of Fire we can—"

"The Tome of Fire? You would use *that*? For what purpose?"

"To seal away Neferia, mother! And to break Haydn's…" Rifu suddenly cut herself off, as if narrowly avoiding a terrible head-on collision with a semi-truck. "Look, just trust me. I can handle this myself."

"Perhaps, Rifu, but remember what I've told you. And you, as well, Haydn; murder *is* murder."

"We're off to my room," Rifu grumbled, pulling Jolie and me along.

Rifu and Jolie sat on Rifu's bed. I took the chair at Rifu's desk. She groaned as I pulled up to the bed.

"We just keep sinking, Jolie," she mumbled.

"Yeah, tell me about it."

As if they had room to talk. Their lives weren't flipped upside down. They still had family, while my mother was dead, and my first girlfriend had been turned to ashes.

"Fuck you both," I muttered.

"Sorry, Haydn, but I hardly know you," Rifu giggled. "Maybe if you told us some of your dark secrets…"

"I have no dark secrets."

"Really, you're going to lie to a devil? How stupid do you think I am?"

I sighed. "Is this really the time to be joking? I'm responsible for the deaths of two people."

"Death is an easy subject to poke fun at. Or, so it goes."

"How Vonnegut of you," I mumbled.

My eyes fell to the floor. This was certainly a new side to Rifu. Maybe, all demons were as aggressive. Strangely enough, I didn't mind it.

"You must have some idea."

"Perhaps, but why don't you enlighten us?"

"Almost ten years ago, I went on a trip with my parents," I started, already disturbed by the flood of memories. "We went to the Omaha Zoo in Nebraska. That day, I was 'volunteered' by my older sister to feed a boa constrictor… Literally."

Jolie looked away, biting her lower lip. As blood started flowing from her pale lips, Rifu placed a hand on her shoulder.

"Is something wrong?" Rifu asked.

"I think… I think I should go," she whispered. She stood up and turned, shooting out the door.

Rifu looked after her and then back to me, as if she was solving a puzzle.

"Well, what do we do now?" I asked.

Rifu pursed her lips. She moved closer to me and sat down. She looked me in the eyes. Those emeralds… most men would pay attention to a girl's boobs or butt, but there was nothing more dazzling on Rifu's body. Her eyes, like an oasis in a desert, gave me an unusual comfort.

"Haydn," she whispered, "You know how I said death is easy to make fun of?"

I raised an eyebrow at this. "Yeah, you just said that a few moments ago."

She looked towards a blank canvas set up parallel to the bed. "I didn't feel that way a few years ago. What's more is that I was foolish enough to believe everyone was good. But some humans… can be so *demoniac*."

I really didn't know how to respond. Was she really opening up to me? Why would she? I had barely given her my trust.

"I'm sorry," she said suddenly, "I probably don't make a lot of sense."

"No, you're alright."

"It's … I want to tell you something. You told me one of your darkest memories. It's time I traded you one of mine."

Rifu got up and walked over to her desk. She got on her knees and pulled out a canvas from under the desk. The colors of the painting were pallid, but I could make out the dejected atmosphere; a wretched girl held onto the husk of a boy, blood streaming down her cheeks.

"You drew this?"

"I drew this, after… I killed someone."

I looked at her, wide-eyed. "What?"

14. Memories
Rifu

"It was three years ago. It seems like forever now. I thought it was a dream, but it turned out to be a nightmare, but I prevented it before it could sprout. I was only a sixth grader. I didn't know any better, even if I was a demon.

"I sat in my first period class. Half of the sixth graders had that class first period. If they didn't, then they had it with a different teacher. I didn't really pay attention. My nose was stuck in a book. My hair was up in a ponytail. A blue sweatshirt and jeans hugged my developing features.

"Even back then, guys were staring at me. They didn't stare at me as often, but they still stared. It would start to get worse in about a year, but until then I was pretty much normal. I wasn't really interested in things like love. Love was a thing I read about in books. I never expected what was about to happen.

"Our white-haired teacher took the front of the room, calling us to attention by whacking the chalkboard with her meter stick. She smiled upon us all, as if her presence was a blessing.

"'Boys, girls, we have a new student here today. He's from Florida. Please, if you don't have anything nice to say, then don't say anything.'

"The door opened, and in walked a tall, dark-haired, caramel-skinned boy. His nose was small and his lips were thin, but he made it look good, at least, to me anyways. My heart throbbed in my chest, and that rarely happened, considering who I am.

"'This is Armando Diaz. Be courteous and help him around.'

"'Hello,' he mumbled.

"He looked around and stopped on me. He smiled. At me. I was instantly entranced.

"Later in the day, I went to my locker and bumped into someone. After I picked up my book and looked up, I found Armando, reading the same book.

"'Oh, sorry,' he muttered, 'I wasn't watching where I was going. I'm stuck so far inside this book.'

"'You...read Orwell?' I asked suspiciously.

"'Yeah, *Animal Farm* is my favorite. I'm confused about some of the symbols, though.'

"Most would brand him as a nerd, no, *alien*, if they knew he read classic novels for leisure. I read books because of the art. Then, an idea igniting inside my mind, I smiled.

"'I could help you. We could go to Gutekunst after school.'

"'Gutekunst?' he mumbled confusedly.

"I giggled. 'I'm sorry, it's the public library. How about we just walk there after school?'

"He nodded, smiling. 'That'd be cool.'

"*Score.*

"I hid my excitement well, turning and walking in the opposite direction, even though I forgot what I originally went to my locker for. I didn't care about all that, though. I was going to walk with this boy. My attraction to this stranger was no less than vexing, however. I had just met him and already had this strong desire to know *everything* about Armando. That afternoon was going to be great.

"Or, so I had thought.

"Gutekunst used to be a house. It was big, red, and made of brick. A wooden walkway that doubled as a patio stretched around half of the old building. It was a pretty cool place to hang out at, whether you needed a book or a place to...well, you get the idea.

"After school, I met Armando out front. We walked up to the library and sat outside on the rails of the patio. He wanted to know who I was, much like I wanted to know him.

"'My name is Rifu Anerex,' I mumbled. 'My Daddy's running for governor.'

"'Wow,' he whistled, grinning. 'Politics…I bet you're rich.'

"I shrugged. 'A little bit,' I fibbed. 'Most of our money comes from my grandpa.'

"'Who's your grandpa?'

"'Oh…um…you wouldn't know him. He does a lot of…underground work.'

"'Like a…miner? Or an oil worker?'

"'Yeah, something like that.'

"He grinned, staring up to the clouds. 'I wonder, is your grandpa proud of your dad?'

"'Actually, he wanted Daddy to stay in the family business, but Daddy fell in love with my mom.'

"Armando nodded. 'I know how that feels.'

"I blushed slightly. 'Really? Who did *you* fall in love with?'

"'The girl next to me,' he declared nonchalantly.

"My face started to burn. I looked at him with a shy grin. 'Then, is it okay if I show you something?'

"He smiled. 'Go ahead,' as if he already knew what he was going to see.

"I took his hand and led him away from the library. We went down a street and turned right. Another right, and then left until we came to a wall of trees. We squeezed through the cracks in the wall and emerged out into a clearing. In front of us sat an abandoned gazebo behind a large, untouched snowy expanse of land. I pulled him towards the gazebo.

"'Isn't it so beautiful?' I gasped. 'I love this place.'

"Armando nodded and smiled. 'It's a great place. No one will see us either.'

"I turned to him and tilted my head. 'What do you mean?'

"Then my heart sank, my eyes burned. Three, no, five feelings mixed into my head. They ranged anywhere from lust to regret. No, none of them came from Armando. They came from others. I turned around. Five high school boys stood behind me in a crowd.

"'Good, Armando,' one said. He looked stupid, but was athletic. He was the kind of person that would spit on someone for the fun of it. But I felt like I recognized him from somewhere. 'Now, guys, hold her down for my little brother.'

"Armando grabbed me from behind as three others latched onto me, forcing me to my knees. I looked up at the boy standing before me. His name was Miller. I couldn't remember his first name, but I did remember him trying to ask me out. It was kind of sweet, because he offered me chocolates and flowers. But, as I said before, love didn't interest me. He was unceremoniously rejected.

"'Remember me?'

As he stood there, my mind painted visions of clothes in the snow; bare flesh writhing on the ground. Heated pants echoed in my ears; his screams of pleasure and my screams of terror. His hand was against my cheek; blood stained the snow.

"'You disgust me,' I coughed.

"He reached out his hand towards me. I grabbed it and, without thinking, broke his wrist. He yelped in pain, the other guys tried to get a better grip on me, but they weren't going to overpower me. I dropped them each to the ground. I stood up against older Miller, who was about two times taller than me. That didn't matter, though, to me, or to any devil. I lifted my hand, and a yowl of unexpected agony escaped Miller's lips. Younger Miller had, wisely, retreated. Armando, however, had fallen onto his back.

"'What the hell are you?'

"'What are you talking about?' I said, sitting on top of him. 'I'm just a stupid girl. Oh, wait, no I'm not.'

"He stared at me, bewilderment plastered on his face. His mouth opened to speak, but nothing would ever escape. My hand wrapped around his neck, restricting his air. I bent down low and stuck my lips to his.

"*Good… the kiss of death…*

"I pulled away, his lifeless body under me. He was pale, crumpled, and lifeless. Tears swelled in my eyes. What had I done?"

In the Present
Haydn

I sat there in silence. Ice crept up inside me, freezing my veins, my lungs. It froze everything. I couldn't breathe. On the outside I was on fire. My right arm trembled. Anger nestled inside my icy chest. All the ingredients were there: tragedy, hatred, and betrayal.

"That's why…you didn't kill me," I mumbled grimly.

"Partly, but don't pity me. I don't want your pity." She turned away. "Armando was forgotten, but remembered, even if I did erase the memories of those other boys. Because of *his* selfishness, it's hard for me not to generalize. It was all because I wanted something that was an illusion, Haydn. He never loved me, but I thought I loved him. That caused an unnecessary death. Something I never want to repeat." She looked at me. "Now, ask yourself, do you truly want normality?"

What *did* I want? I wanted to live. I wanted to be normal, but Rifu said normality didn't exist, and chasing it would end me up like Armando. At one point, I had wanted my family to be safe. But, my mother was dead. Drake and Katria wouldn't remember me, thanks to Rifu.

"Are you okay?" Rifu mumbled.

"I don't know…my head's so murky right now."

"I understand. I want you to know that you can step away after everything is over. We may not be able to revive your mother, but we can erase your memories and…Then you can forget about us; demons, vampires, succubae…just forget about the Hidden World altogether. You'll have your…normality."

"But it won't be the same. I'll know somehow, Rifu. Without you…"

I looked to the ground. What had I just said? Rifu was a demon. Did I just admit something? It was blasphemy. But…did I really feel that way?

Rifu slowly put her arms around me. She whispered something in my ear. My heart spiked. A cool breeze ran up my back. I started to thaw on the inside. She let go.

But I didn't want her to let go. And, at the same time, I wondered why she even put her arms around me in the first place. What did she feel deep inside her own chest? She probably knew already how I felt.

"We have one dilemma left, Haydn. We have to set a trap for Brenda. By using Brenda, we'll be able to get to Neferia. Any ideas?"

Pursing my lips, I sat back against the chair. How would we reel in a succubus?

"Well," I chuckled, "we could say I'm willing to become her slave."

"That doesn't sound half-bad."

"What? Wait a moment…"

She chuckled. "It was your idea, Haydn. Brenda might believe you if you feign submission."

"Yeah, that's the problem. What if she doesn't believe me? It won't work."

She brushed a lock of blazing red from her face. "Have some confidence in yourself, Haydn. Even Jesus Christ faced doubt, but he still did what had to be done."

"But he died!"

Rifu nodded. "Then came back from the dead and ascended into Heaven." She threw her hair over a shoulder and smiled. "There will be no problems."

"Okay, say we do convince her, then what?"

"Then you leave things to me, Jolie, and the Tome of Fire."

The Tome of Fire…I had nearly forgotten about it. What magical secrets were etched into its pages? I was intensely curious.

"As I said before," Rifu said, having felt my curiosity, "the Tome has some very dangerous magic in it. I plan on relying on the less harmful spells."

"What kind of spells are we talking about?"

"Sealing spells, slavery seals, and…"

"Slavery seal?"

Rifu stopped dead in her tracks. Slowly, she nodded and hesitantly responded. "A slavery seal is what makes someone a slave to any demon family." I touched my right shoulder. "That isn't a slavery seal," Rifu quickly mumbled. She was hiding something.

"Then how come Aria was able to control me?"

"I…"

Rifu straightened. Something flashed across her face; fear. She stood and pulled me to my feet. Hurriedly, without a word, she opened her closet and shoved me inside.

"Clear your mind, Haydn," she whispered, "and don't come out until I tell you to."

She shut the door in my face, literally closing the door for any sort of objection. I cleared my mind as much as possible, though, and focused my ears on what was happening outside. I heard Rifu sit on her bed. From the rustling, I would say she was pulling her art pad over to her. Then, the door opened.

"Ah, my niece!"

"Hey, Uncle Charon."

The man's voice was thin, wispy, like that of a frail old man. But, I could tell by the heavy footsteps, Rifu's uncle was not frail, and was not an old man.

"Do you have any idea why there are so many policemen outside? They're talking to your mother now. It seems like they're looking for that boy…"

"Oh? I don't know why."

A moment of silence preceded Charon's reply. "Well, they say he committed murder." Then, like switching channels on a television, Rifu's uncle switched topics. "Do you still play guitar?"

"Not really. I have too much going on at school."

"Please," he scoffed, "you don't need a human education to succeed in this world! You're already ten times wittier than the average lawyer, and perhaps ten times faster than an Olympic sprinter! Why waste your time? Besides, you grandfather loved to hear you play."

"Maybe I'll pick it up again."

"Do you still have it here? In your closet, perhaps?"

Oh crap. Does he know I'm here?

"No, it's in storage," Rifu replied calmly.

Another silence. Then, "Well, I suppose I should leave now. Seems like the police will be storming your room any moment, I don't know why, though."

"Yeah…that is kind of strange…"

"Enjoy your day, Rifu."

He was gone. It wasn't long, though, before a dozen footsteps flooded Rifu's room. Demands were thrown around, calmly at first, but Rifu's knowing disposition caused a full sweep of her room. When they found me, I was instantly in cuffs. Rifu was screaming for them to let me go. She swore they would all be fired before the day was over, screamed I should have hope. The men chuckled, regarding her threats as empty.

Her threats empty or not, didn't change the situation. There was one member of the squadron that spewed legal babble at me as they dragged me out of the manor. Involuntary manslaughter…mentally ill…minor…asylum…What I got from the jumble of legal jargon was that I wasn't going to jail. And, even if I did, I had a feeling I wouldn't be there for long.

Hope died.

15. Asylum
Rifu

What was going on?

I crept down a long, dark hallway. Shortly after watching Haydn being taken away, the power went out. Daddy had just gotten out of another family meeting with Grandpa and Uncle Charon. I was never told what they talked about. I knew that Daddy was never happy with the meetings. They always boiled down to shout matches between him and Grandpa. Then the power went out, and Daddy asked me to turn on the generator. And there I was.

My cell phone was tucked away in my jean pocket. I could call Jolie or Haydn if something were to happen. Haydn…I wondered if he was okay.

I rounded a corner and came to a stone staircase descending into darkness. Memories from my childhood days painted themselves against my eyes. Even though I was evil incarnate, a devil, I was scared of the dark when I was younger. Now, I felt the darkness seeping through my pale skin and soaked into my blood, snaking its way into my heart.

Find the generator room and turn on the power. That was all Daddy said when the lights went out. He sounded kind of worried, but it wasn't my place to question him.

Down into the darkness I went, feeling the wall with a cautious hand. Devils couldn't see in the dark. Where was Jolie when I needed her? One false step and down the steps I went, crashing gracefully at the bottom of the stairs.

"Damn," I hissed, sitting up. "I hate Daddy for putting the generator room in the basement! I can't see an inch in front of my nose."

The darkness seemed alive, writhing, pulsating. I found it hard to breathe. I stood up slowly, swinging out my arms to try and grab something, anything. Finally, I clasped my hands around a circular object. My fingers examined the metallic sphere. A wheel...no, it wasn't a circle. It was a single rod...with a sphere on top. It was a lever. I pulled it. A cranking, groaning, whirring noise shook the room, and on flashed the lights.

"Phew," I whistled.

"Sister."

I turned to find Aria standing against the wall opposite to where I stood. Her eyes were searching the ceiling, hands tucked behind her back. She didn't look at me while she spoke.

"You do realize what you're doing, right?"

"Um, turning the power back on?"

Her eyes regarded me sharply. "You know what I'm talking about. That *slave* you insist on protecting: Grandpa would have a field day with you...for more than one reason."

"I don't know why he would. He's not a *true* slave."

"So," she grinned, "you admit to something of his slavery, then?"

"How can I not? You manipulated him into killing that girl. But, I think I'm already figuring that little trick out."

"What do you mean?"

I shook my head. "Never mind you."

She stepped away from the wall. Her eyes never left my face. "How can you sit here and deny everything? Haydn is what he is! Can't you see that? Let's turn him over to Grandpa, or better yet, kill him!"

"Why? His death is unnecessary..."

"It's necessary! Haydn must pay for his father's crimes! And if you won't take him down, then Grandpa surely will."

"I know how Grandpa acts. That's why no one is going to tell him."

Aria shook her head. "You know it's not that easy, sister. Grandpa doesn't need to be told."

"I know that Uncle Charon could get in the way...or you. But I hope you wouldn't."

"In the way of what?"

"My plan..." at that moment, my phone rang. I glanced at my pocket with a sigh. "We'll finish this later."

She turned, without another word, and ascended the stairs. I retrieved my phone from my pocket, Jolie's number illuminating the tiny screen. I answered.

"Rifu?"

"Yeah."

"Where's Haydn?"

"He was just taken away be several policemen."

"You sound rather calm about it."

"I have my reasons, Jolie."

"Reasons?"

"Let's talk about this later. Get over here, now."

Into the Depths
Haydn

It didn't take long to get to the asylum. And didn't it just look so invit-
ing? I could hear the screams already from the insane patients, all
the crazies.

I wondered, as the police walked me from the car to my room, just
how many people were there because it was their own fault. Most were
there because of a genetic disease or major injury, but I kept wondering
if there were any cases like mine. Not exactly similar, no, I doubt there
would be any other restrained for using mysterious powers to burn his
girlfriend to a crisp.

Inside was almost as bland as the outside; plenty of white for everyone and outlandish, smiling nurses. Everyone seemed to be ignoring
the screaming patient being dragged through the lobby. How could
they miss him? He was screaming that his friend was a vampire. Oh,
wow, how coincidental.

We stepped up to the main counter, met by a Geisha. Wow! I hadn't
known we'd gone to Japan. She looked just like the rest of the nurses.
She smiled too much. Her tone was too friendly. She was *way* too pale.
I would have to say she was dead, but maybe only her brain was dead.

"Welcome to the Aria Rehab and Recovery! You must be Mr.
Ladditz! We've been waiting for you! I'm sure you'll recover quickly
under our top-notch care."

This woman was just a little too excitable. She moved out from
behind the counter. Another Geisha took her place, her smile just as
annoying and misplaced. My Geisha stepped in front of us and bid
us to follow her through a maze of halls and walls of different, yet
similar, doors.

I wasn't surprised when we got to my room. It was white, what a
shock! Actually, the desk lady almost disappeared when she stepped
into the room. I was forced down on the bed as the ghost lady began
discussing procedures and blah-de-blah with the policemen. What did
it matter? They looked like they hardly cared.

The woman approached me then and handed me a schedule and she smiled gently. "Welcome to the Aria Rehabilitation center for the disabled and mentally unstable."

As she walked off, I started laughing. Now, I was going to go insane. White walls, seclusion, white darkness...an *asylum*. I shook my head, and sat down on the white-sheeted bed. I stared into the wall across from me. I kept staring, staring, until it seemed like I would black out and be enveloped in darkness. I went unconscious, and when I woke up, I wasn't in the white room anymore.

The Golem

Rifu

Jolie met me outside of my manor. Her expression was just how I felt; anxious. I turned and led her inside and we quickly retreated to the garden where Mommy was quietly tending to her plants. I had told her what had happened, including how I threatened to fire the policemen, with laughable results.

"Haydn's probably been taken to the rehab center outside of Marshalltown."

"You mean the *asylum*?" Jolie quipped.

"I'm not the one who labeled it *rehab center*."

"Why would they resort to such extremes to catch Haydn? I mean, don't they realize that your father could simply pull a certain string and…"

"I know, Jolie. It's because they were *paid* to."

"Neferia?"

"Probably."

Mommy gasped, her eyes going wide. "I…I felt him…" she mumbled.

"What? What do you mean, Mother?"

Mommy shook her head. "He's…on the ferry. Not his body, or soul, but his mind is on the ferry. His soul and body are…"

"In the mental facility…" I turned to Jolie. "Jolie, I think you should go to the rehab center and get his body while…"

"Sister, you seemed to have this planned out pretty well."

We all snapped around, seeing Aria standing against the hedge, a grim smile on her face. "Haydn has many bullet holes riddling his past. But, in my opinion, honestly, I think you probably have them memorized. What with your composure…"

"You did this!" I shouted. "Why did you have to believe Neferia and Brenda in the first place?"

Aria frowned. "Stop taking the spotlight from yourself. Stop feigning innocence, sister. You aren't as ignorant as you're making yourself out to be."

Jolie shook her head. "What *she* does is none of your business! You don't even go to our school! You don't know who Haydn Ladditz is!"

"And you would?" Aria's grin turned malicious. "I believe you do, Jolie, you creepy, dark, vicious stalker!"

Jolie staggered, as if someone stabbed her through her stomach. "What…what are you talking about? I only watch him to make sure nothing hurts him."

"Oh? And how long have you been doing that? Hm? A few years? A decade?"

I turned towards Jolie. Her eyes were to the ground. She bit down on her lower lip. Aria burst out into wicked, crazy laughter.

"You poor, poor, poor vampire girl! Vampires are empty… Especially you!"

"Aria!" Mommy snapped.

"Shut up!" Her voice sounded warped as she screamed. "Vampires are empty, hopeless shells of demons that are required to drink the lifeblood of other creatures to survive! Without humans, you would perish! You're almost as bad as the humans!"

I had heard enough. With a swift swing, my palm met with Aria's left cheek, sending her to the ground. Blood oozed from her cracked grin. She looked up at me. Something about her face seemed so familiar, yet so different.

"Dear sister…are you saying you'd put a filthy human slave before your family? Of course you would." She bared her teeth. Her eyes changed color to a glowing yellow. "I guess, then, you must die!"

Something wrapped tightly around my abdomen, almost squeezing the life out of me. I yelped in pain, my vision blurring a little. The next moment there was a high-pitched screech and a shower of blood. When my vision cleared I saw a tall figure with long, silver hair standing over a crumpled body.

"Uron!" I shouted. Then I looked to the body beneath him. It was Aria, her neck slashed open. But, the next moment, the body deflated, as if someone had popped a balloon.

Jolie stepped over to the "skin" of Aria. She picked it up, rubbed it. Then she turned to me. "It's clay…"

"It wasn't actually Aria," Uron said as he turned to me. "I found Aria unconscious and tied up in her room. I revived her, and she told me what had happened to her." Uron studied me a moment. "But, I suppose you already knew that."

"What?" I gasped.

He shook his head. "Never mind you. Lamias have the uncanny ability to copy the powers of whomever they encounter. There's no telling the arsenal of talents and powers that Neferia has stashed away. This is one of them...the ability to create a skin that looks like someone else. Much like the skin vampires wear to protect themselves from the sun. Then she created a golem, one in her image, and slid the skin over like a glove."

Jolie stumbled backwards, Mommy catching her. "What exactly are we facing?" Mommy mumbled.

Uron shook his head. "An age-old threat that can no longer be overlooked; Neferia tipped off Uncle about your friend. Now, I'm afraid he's going to do some...unsavory things with his body before turning him over to Grandpa."

"What do you mean...unsavory things?" Jolie mumbled.

"That much, I don't know."

16. The Ferryman
Morgan

It'd been a little over a year. Ever since that last fight with Haydn, I never thought about coming to visit him. I remember I called Mom last week and said I'd be up to see him, but I never did. I didn't know what would happen. As far as I knew he still hated me, just like he hated Dad. But I wasn't our father, I was his sister. And, apparently, they couldn't get a hold of Mom or Drake, so they would have me come and sign the papers of his admittance into the rehab center.

I tumbled down the highway in my Ford pick-up truck. It wasn't hard to find the rehab center. It was one of the biggest buildings just outside of Marshalltown; plenty of space to create a nice, haunting location for patients.

I pulled into the guest parking lot in the front of the building. I looked up at the titanic letters extruding from the front. "Aria Rehabilitation Center." My heart began to sink. Was it my fault he was here?

Without another thought, I stepped out of my truck and turned to grab a cardboard pizza box. Inside was a pepperoni pizza…Haydn's favorite, last time I checked. I closed my door and turned to walk up to the entrance.

The Ferry
Haydn

When I woke up, I wasn't in the asylum anymore. Everything was black with a reddish tint. I was standing on the deck of a ghastly skiff. From its sides hung decayed remains of outlandish creatures. Back and forth the small boat slowly rocked and groaned. I wondered how I came to be on this nightmarish vessel.

"Where am I?"

Then there was a frightening laugh. I slowly turned to my right. A man with medium-length, silver hair stood staring at me. He looked like Rifu's father, but his hair was too long. I took a few steps back.

"So," he chuckled, "you're the boy?"

My face went hot and I looked away. "You…you're Charon, Rifu's uncle. I recognize your voice."

The man laughed, shaking his head. "Good memory, Haydn Gabriel Ladditz. Or, at least that's what you call yourself."

My eyes went wide. "How do you know that? First Aria, and now, you…I've never told anyone *that* secret. No one should know!"

"Oh, but I do. Haydn, would you mind telling me what that mark on your arm is?"

"My birthmark?"

The man's cracked grin turned into a childish, disappointed frown as he tilted his head at me. "Really? Is that what you believe it is?"

"What is it supposed to be?"

He threw his arms up in the air. "Give him a *hint*! Aria has been preaching it to you this entire time! It's a slavery seal! Or, at least, that's what she thinks it is. In actuality, Haydn, the seal is meant for so much more. Unfortunately, it's incomplete."

"Incomplete?"

"You see, that seal is the window for your power. Oh, I see my words are confusing you. The way your eyebrows knit up…the way your mouth flounders, searching for words. Well, Haydn, that mark is more than a window to your power. It's also a window to your past… your *true* past."

"True past?"

"Maybe I'll tell you…or, maybe I'll let your father tell you."

My knees locked up. Inside my chest, a lick of fire brushed against my heart. "My father…what does he have to do with this?"

"I'll tell you," his grin grew like the moon shifting through its lunar faces, "but first, I would like to have fun with you." He threw up his right hand and a small riff opened up in the air. Through the riff I could see the rehab center, as if I were looking through someone's eyes. "Look familiar?" Charon chuckled. "Because it's the same room you're staying in."

"What? But…I'm right here."

"Your body and soul are there. But your conscience, your mind, is right here with me, meaning that anyone with the ability, like me, can easily take control of your body."

"What are you planning?"

Haydn?

I stopped breathing. I turned towards the riff. Through it, I could see Morgan staring directly at the riff. I turned back to Charon.

"What…are you doing?"

Charon burst out into maniacal laughter. "Your power is fueled by rage, hatred, and vengeance. I know how much you despise your sister…she's the one who lit the flame. She pushed you to where you are now. The anger, the hate, it's all *her* fault. Through her, you'll be able to look deep inside and see my words are truth."

"What are you going to do?"

The ferryman's grin grew wider and wider. "She has such a pretty face…I would enjoy escorting her across the River Styx…but first, I want to have fun with her; oh, so much fun for scarring her young, innocent, little brother."

I continued to stare at the tear in space. Morgan…she had been the start. She made me afraid of everything. I couldn't trust anyone. I had no friends. It was her fault. It was time she paid for what she had done.

"Do it," I mumbled.

Charon looked at me with a vicious smile. "If you so wish, Child of the Dark Hunter."

I ignored what he said and stood there watching as Morgan interacted with "me."

Closure

Morgan

He rested on the white bed, staring blankly into my face. I was trying to figure out what he was staring at. He was starting to make me feel so awkward. I guess I deserved more than awkwardness, if it was really my fault he was here. All those years ago…

Every time I thought about it now I would start sobbing. Nothing could change what was done, though. I held out the pizza for him to see.

"I brought some pizza. Why don't we sit and talk?"

I was probably the last person he wanted to see. I felt like we were playing hide and seek. I couldn't seem to faze him, even when I mentioned pizza. Last time I checked, Haydn would always perk up to pizza. Then I let out a large sigh. I quietly moved to a chair and pulled it up to the bed, and sat down.

"So, it finally happened? My little brother snapped?" I mumbled. "Haydn…" I looked directly at him. "What happened? Why are you in *this* place?"

He looked away, in shame, I thought. But he didn't have embarrassment on his face. He was grinning. What could he be up to? I shook my head and turned towards the desk.

"A little boring here, don'cha think?" Still, no response from him. "You know, Chris called me up the other day and told me what happened. Said how you started going back to your old ways. But… murder?"

"Yeah," he grumbled.

That was progress. "I feel like… I'm kind of at fault."

"Why? Because you are?"

I was taken aback by his acidic tone. What had happened to Haydn? He stood up and grinned.

"Morgan," he croaked, "have you… enjoyed your life?"

I stared at him wide-eyed. "What… what are you talking about?"

"I'm just wondering… if it'll be okay… to kill you…" he murmured.

I nodded slowly. I stood up, stepping backwards towards the entrance. When I turned, there he was again. I turned back around, and there was no one there. Just about then, Haydn wrapped his hands around my neck and threw me onto the bed.

"You slut," he growled. "You stupid, careless, evil, jealous bitch!"

"Haydn…" I coughed.

He staggered towards me, an evil smile permanently printed on his face. He came up beside me and sat down on the bed. His eyes seemed gentle for a moment, then his hands slithered around my neck again.

"Die…"

My head started ringing. The two bags in my chest called lungs started burning and scratching as if I was breathing in nails. My head started to stop thinking. My vision was going dark. I wasn't going to make it…

But…I guess…I…deserve…it…

17. From Slavery Come All
Haydn

At first, I was excited. I relished in the thought of killing my sister. Especially at that moment, when the fire of vengeance roared inside my heart. But, despite the fire, I didn't feel any better. In fact, it burned. Even though my mind wasn't there, I could feel her throat, slowing pulse, and draining life against my palms, burning, sizzling.

That's when the excitement faded away. That's when my hatred melted into fear; taking frustration out on others…instead of dealing with them…that's the worst shortcut of all. Suddenly, I felt like everything was my fault. I knew I couldn't let Charon's fun continue.

As Morgan faded out, I looked over at the Ferryman, who was thoroughly enjoying himself. Screaming, I threw myself at him. He didn't notice until I sent us both crashing to the ground. I curled up my right fist and threw it into his face, a sickening thud as my fist landed.

"I won't let you kill what family I have left!"

I cocked my other fist to throw, and when I threw it, he caught it as if it were nothing. Then he simply threw me away towards the edge of the ship. I almost slipped off, but was able to grip onto the edge.

"Insolent mortal," he spat. "You can stay there for the rest of the ride! Be grateful that I was ordered not to dispose of you." Turning back to the riff, he cocked his head to the side when the riff had blackened out. "What is this?"

"Uncle!"

I managed to pull myself up to my chest. Rifu stood with her mother at the helm of the craft. The ferryman grinned.

"Dear niece, welcome to my home! It's been so long since your last visit."

"Don't act like everything's fine," Perse snapped.

Charon scowled at the white-haired woman. "If I wanted you to speak, wench, I would have demanded it."

Wench?

"Watch your mouth!" Rifu shouted. "Don't ever talk to my mother that way."

"You protect someone who would pollute your pure, satanic blood?"

"She *is* my flesh and blood. She's closer to me than you!" Rifu said.

"So, what am I? A monster?"

"I never said that, but you did."

He shook his head, an eruption of laughter booming from his mouth. "Rifu…do you honestly think you could live amongst humans all your life? They are no better than *slaves*, like Haydn! *They* even know that. Ever since the beginning of their existence, they have enslaved their brethren. Why shouldn't we do the same to them?"

Rifu glanced at me and then back to her uncle. "Shut up. You don't know anything about the humans I know."

Charon looked to me. "You mean him? What's human about him, Dear? You know he's as demon as you and me."

I nearly lost my grip. What did he say? My arms burned, weak from sudden fatigue.

"And, Rifu, don't pretend like you don't know that. I've felt you've known the truth ever since that day in your father's study. You've known who he is for quite a while." All expression disappeared from the man's face, as if his face had been blank since birth. "But, why would you need to know something like that? What is it that you're hiding inside your mind, Rifu?"

As Charon rambled, I managed to pull myself up and over the edge of the ship. I stifled my breaths as I stood up. Charon wasn't watching me as closely.

"If you know I knew what Haydn was, then you should know what I'm thinking." Rifu chuckled.

"But I don't. So, instead of playing this game, I'm going to probe your brain and see what I can find!"

"In your dreams!"

I moved to Charon's side and slung my elbow back, landing a serious, sickening blow to his rib cage. As he gasped, I slipped one of my legs behind his and tripped him. He stumbled backwards and over the edge of the ship. My lungs burnt, my arms were on fire, but I felt accomplished. I stood up and looked over to Rifu.

She didn't look at me. Guilt was plastered across her lips like tape. I walked towards her slowly, and was suddenly received with an iron-clamp hug. She quickly planted her lips on my cheek. I felt a flutter in my chest.

"How touching."

I whirled around to find Charon standing on the deck, unharmed and royally pissed.

"I am sure my father would love to hear how his granddaughter is in love with the son of his traitorous servant."

"You don't dare speak to that monster about this," Perse shouted.

"He already knows, Perse. Who do you think sent me? My father only wishes to reunite son with father."

"What do you mean?" I growled.

"Don't worry, you'll find out soon enough. Your father would love to see you, though. The Dark Hunter reuniting with his son…"

"Dark Hunter? What do you mean?"

"That is your father's title as a servant. He's had the name for millennia."

"I don't believe you!"

"What is your name?"

"Haydn."

"Your *surname.*"

"Ladditz."

"Liar," he growled. "Tell me the surname you were granted at birth." He pointed a bony finger at me. "Reveal your true surname; the one of your father!"

My jaw dropped.

"Your father had that name for a long time. He gave it to you when you were first born over a hundred years ago."

"What?"

He broke out laughing, nearly doubling over. "Indeed, Haydn Nikolaou…"

He knows… my real name.

"What are you talking about, Uncle?"

Charon broke out into a fit of laughter. "Rifu, there's so much about this boy you don't know. Even with the vast knowledge you possess, you don't know *everything*. And, the fact is…Haydn's family has been involved with devils more than once. First, it was his father, and then it was his brother, and then Haydn himself twice before."

Twice before? Me?

"What did you do to Chris?" I clenched my fists. "Tell me, how the hell is he involved in all of this?"

Charon stifled his laughter, but not by much. "I did nothing. It's what your father did."

"Uncle, what are you babbling about?"

"Rifu, this boy's father…tried to protect his first son. He could never know, however, that his wife's second son would become a short-lived slave."

"What do you mean short-lived?" I mumbled.

Charon chuckled.

"That can't be…" Rifu mumbled.

"Boy, search the darkest depths of your heart," Charon commanded. "You will find it to be true. It's the deathly contract your father signed millennia ago that binds you in fate with our family. Your memories… I can tell just by the look in your eyes that you have seen fragmented pictures of your life before."

The visions…are memories? I felt his words were true. But, so many things swirled around in my head, and, at that point, I felt that a blatant lie could be reality.

"I…don't remember coming into contact with devils before," I muttered.

"How wrong you are…" he sneered. "It doesn't matter. You've been a very ill-behaved slave. It's time for you punishment."

He lifted his left hand up, a dark aura gathering in his palm. The darkness turned into a spiny material that stretched out in two directions, forming a wicked pole. From one end of the pole, a blade curved outwards, appearing sharp enough to cut through solid concrete.

"We have to get out of here!" I shouted.

"We can't, Mother has to charge her energies before we can teleport again! Quick, Haydn, use the vampire blood!"

"Don't listen to her, Haydn." I looked up and around, hearing that deep, familiar voice again. *"The power isn't within any foreign agent…it's inside of you."*

I remembered the instructions the voice had given me earlier, taking my right hand and placing it on my left hip. There, energy of my own gathered and turned into a bright flame. From this fire I pulled a sword, a katana-shaped weapon, into existence, sparks falling from the blade.

"Haydn," Rifu mumbled.

Charon grinned. "That is proof enough of your chains, Haydn! No mere mortal has those talents!"

I steadied the sword in my hand, as if I knew how to use one. "How do you know so much about me? How do I even know if you're telling the truth?"

"Die mortal!" Charon cried, ignoring my question.

I rolled, clearing a vicious slash from Charon's scythe. Then I stopped to realize something; I *rolled* out of the way. When the hell could I do that?

I charged, swinging the blade gracefully, skillfully, as if I had been born with one in my hand. As my blows did little to harm Charon, however, I realized how outmatched I was against the demonic ferryman. I started to get frustrated. I wanted answers, vengeance. The anger was rising within. And he knew it.

"Angry?" he chortled. "Good, accept it."

"Don't listen to him!" Rifu shouted.

"Listen to me! Let the anger wrap around your heart! Become one with your hatred towards me, towards my words, towards my existence!"

"Shut the hell up!"

My angry blade came crashing down hard on the steel of his scythe. He swung in a deep arch, nearly slicing me open from the waist up. Stumbling backwards, I heard a scream.

"Haydn! Help!"

I turned, but only Rifu and Perse stood there, watching me with concern-laden eyes. As I turned back to Charon, I was struck by déjà vu, a sick, dizzying sensation that brought me to a knee.

"Haydn!" Rifu shouted.

"Well, it seems like Haydn is remembering … I can sense it." Charon lunged for me. "But too late for that, now!"

Without second thought, I stabbed the sword through his chest. He gasped, black blood spraying over the deck like a mist, Charon falling back into a pool of blackness, as did I.

"You're free, Haydn … " the girl said.

18. Black and White

There was laughter everywhere, echoing like a continuous hail.

Slave… lies… family… century… keys… devil… doll… hunter…

Then, I stood alone inside a room made of wood. There was a fire blazing, the heat making me sweat. The luscious aroma of spiced meats and pungent cheeses filled my nostrils. Suddenly, I felt safe and secure. To my side was a girl with golden hair. She smiled at me.

"About time you woke up."

"Sorry, I really needed a nap."

The girl held up a handkerchief. "For you," she said, blushing.

I took the cloth into my hand. One side was black, while the other was white with black lettering. My mouth twisted in confusion as I looked back to the girl.

"Black and white should always go together, don't you think?"

Then, everything was ripped away, like a veil, as my eyes finally ripped themselves open. Once my eyes adjusted, I took in my surroundings. It was a library about the size of a tennis court. On each of the walls, save for one corner where a door stood, there was a bookcase overloaded with books. I was resting on a plush, red couch. Across from me, a lone candle shared a round, wooden table with stacks of papers and books.

I sat up, dazed. Where was I? What had happened? Shards of glassy visions stabbed at my mind. My heart flooded with grief, regret, and confusion. I looked around once more, sighing, as if expelling the air from my body would rid me of the voices, the visions.

I stared into the fire of the candle, and shockingly I started to see myself. Flashes of the past started to play out in the flame, as if it were the screen and my brain was the projector. I saw all the way back to the beginning. Where was I? Who was I? Who knew? All my "false" normality and comfort was up in flames.

The door creaked open and Rifu silently slid inside. Slowly, she maneuvered herself to the couch, as if I would strike her at any moment. Cautiously, she sat down next to me, struggling to smile.

"So, how are you doing?" she asked, almost generically.

"Fine, I guess," I mumbled bitterly.

Rifu's eyes shifted to the floor, then to the candle. It was as if she were watching something as well. As if her brain was a projector, too. Then, she slid her hand over mine.

"I guess I don't really know much about you, after all."

"Stop...I don't want to hear this," I growled.

"Haydn, a dead rat could tell you're feeling horrible. I don't need some demonic ability to know that."

"Stop pointing it out." I pulled my hand away, crossing my arms. "It's hard enough trying to deal with all this supernatural bullshit outside of my head...but inside?"

"Just move on. Okay? Things can be fixed."

"What about made-up things like normality? Huh? You can't fix something that doesn't exist in the first place."

Rifu chuckled. "We're like polar opposites, Haydn. But, at the same time, we're not."

"It doesn't work that way."

She grinned, looking back to me. "It could, if you want it to. My father's always told me that anything's possible if you want it. He wanted a semi-normal life, one away from the 'family tradition.' He wanted to be happy."

"I thought you said there was no such thing as 'normal?'"

"Normal, Haydn, is something that doesn't exist, because everyone experiences things differently... normality suggests a singular form through which we all experience things. Normal, however, is whatever makes you happy and comfortable."

"Are you happy? With this life? Being a demon?"

"I used to hate this life. That's why I made friends with people like Brenda and Neferia. I didn't know what I was getting myself into, especially after I met you."

"I can't be that special," I whispered. "I don't even know who I am."

"You're Haydn, that's all that matters. You don't need someone to explain to *you* who *you* are."

"Whatever, Rifu!" I stood up, my inner anger stirring. "I remember things…things that I did, but couldn't have done! This birthmark…my family…my mom…my father…Sheila…"

"Calm down, Haydn."

Rifu reached out, gently pulled me back to the couch, and then nestled her head against my chest. "Remember what you said? You said you would trust me. I also gave my trust to you."

"I can hardly trust myself, Rifu, considering I seem to hardly know anything about myself anymore. And…you…you seem like you're hiding so much from me…"

"Haydn…"

"I don't know. I just have so much stuff sticking to the inside of my skull."

"Then let it out. I'm listening."

"Do…do you think black and white should go together?"

"That's a funny question."

"I think they should, but Morgan…" I looked at Rifu, tears creeping into my eyes. "Is she okay? Did I kill her?"

"She's fine, Haydn. But we had to erase her memories before she found out about your mother."

My lungs quivered. I hunched over, as if caving in on myself.

"Black and white…Like Yin and Yang…"

She lifted my head up. We were face to face, her arm wrapping around my head. I could hear her breathing slow, while my heart began to race. Rifu started singing.

"I can't live without your love, and I can't die.
Still I'm standing in the rain, when daylight dies."

Her emerald eyes were brighter than I had ever seen them before. My heart spiked an unhealthy number up in the two-hundreds.

"I want to be by your side. I want you by mine."

"I…"

"Don't talk…" Rifu trailed off as her nose touched mine.

Before I knew it, our lips were melding. Our differences, my problems, and the world melted away. She was gentle, her lips caressing mine, massaging them carefully. Then she flung her arms around me, pushing me down onto the couch. She kissed harder, almost crushing herself against me. At first, she was graceful, dreamy. But, then, she was convulsing like something out of a nightmare. I started to suffocate. I tried to clench my mouth shut, but she opened it with ease. I felt my life slipping away. This wasn't a normal kiss. I somehow managed to push her away, gasping for air. I stared at her in bewilderment.

She wore a pleased grin, a touch of blush painted her soft face. She wrapped her arms around me and pulled us close. We didn't kiss this time. She curled into my body. Black and white.

"Haydn, I hope you don't mind," she whispered. "You're mine now. I'm sorry. I should have asked you first before I…"

"Before what?"

"I drained a little bit of your soul. And then put some of my own into you. I only want to protect you. Binding me to you seemed the easiest way to do it."

At first I was scared. What did she mean? I was in the palm of her hand, that's what it meant. Even if she was a devil, she had turned into a friend, even if I didn't think of her that way at first. Then, it seemed, she was so much more.

I wrapped my arms around her, nestling my chin in the side of her neck.

"I forgive you," I mumbled breathlessly, still dazed.

"Even if Jolie has the same feelings for you?"

"I don't know what it is about her, but I get a strange feeling every time I look into her eyes. Every time I see her smile…"

"Don't worry about it. You have too much on your plate as it is. We still have to deal with Brenda. And, somehow, Jolie and I were able to convince her to go on a date with you."

"Wait, what do you mean?"

She curled a lock of hair around her finger nervously. "It was simple, really. Combining my ability to shape shift and Jolie's doppelganger illusion, we made Brenda think she was talking to you."

"When did you talk to Brenda?"

"Last week, while you were unconscious," she sighed.

"How long was I unconscious?"

"About two weeks, why?"

"What day is it?"

"December twenty-third. It would have been hard to manage, but at least you would have been safe."

I almost shouted, pushing her off of me. "You…you were going to go ahead and put yourself in danger, weren't you?"

She was slightly shocked. "Haydn…I just didn't want…"

I shook my head and looked away. "I don't want to hear it. Now, I'll take things over. I'll end this, all of it."

"Haydn…"

The door opened, and Jolie crossed the short distance towards us. She plopped the Tome of Fire down on the couch between Rifu and me. Jolie looked at us briefly before opening up the book to a dog-eared page.

"Look here," Jolie muttered hastily, almost inaudible to my ears.

Rifu took the book and skimmed it, then her eyes twitched, and she quickly re-read it. I could see little notes scribbled in the margins of the book. The contents of the book itself were in a foreign language. Rifu cussed lowly. Her eyes flickered to me and then back down to the book. She closed it and motioned for Jolie to take a chair. Jolie pulled up the nearest chair and sat down promptly, her eyes avoiding Rifu and me. Rifu wrapped her arms across her chest, sighing.

"Alright," Rifu finally started. "Let's explain something." She closed the Tome. "The spell we're going to do is very simple, yet very danger-ous. We're going to break your seal."

I pulled up my brow in confusion. "My seal? Do you mean my birthmark?"

"Yes." She waved her hand towards the closed spell book. "You see, after some reading, Jolie found out how Aria controlled you. It's certainly not because you're bound to us. You see, every seal imagined originated from my grandfather. Now, each seal has a separate purpose, but they can easily substitute for another."

"That means…she could easily substitute my birthmark for a slavery seal?"

Rifu nodded. "And that's exactly what she did."

"So, what's the plan?"

"We use the power of your seal to put a temporary slavery seal on Neferia," Jolie explained. "Force her to call off her Keres, and then hand her back over to the lamias. Problem is, however, that there's a hefty cost."

"What is it?"

"Brenda has to die," Rifu mumbled.

"What? Why?"

"The spell requires the life of a demon."

"I thought we couldn't kill anyone?"

"Unfortunately, Haydn, the lamias have demanded Neferia's return. If we don't kill Brenda, then we will have war."

"What about Brenda's family?"

"Succubae are nomads, Haydn," Jolie interjected. "Even if one family is upset, the whole clan won't do anything."

That was exactly what I *didn't* want. Death was already a good acquaintance of mine; I didn't want to keep making regular trips to see how he was doing. But, I had to think about *everyone*, like Rifu said, and stop being self-centered.

"What do we do, then?"

"You have to drink her blood," Jolie said matter-of-factly.

"You say that like it's a normal thing to do."

"It is for me…"

"Anyways, how do I convince her to let me drink her blood?"

"Well, succubae are very vain," Rifu chirped. "You could convince her somehow. I'm sure she'll agree."

I regarded the information warily. Many lives rode upon the success of this plan. Katria's face flashed through my mind as well. Even if she would never remember me, I couldn't fail. I stood up to walk around the room, stretching out my cramped muscles.

"Well, nonetheless, it should be an interesting conversation-starter."

"Yeah, right," I grumbled.

"We're going to imbue the magic into you now. Tomorrow, when Brenda's blood touches your lips, your seal will open, like a floodgate, and we'll be able to temporary seal Neferia. But, be warned, if she were to somehow escape, you would only have until the end of the year to live."

"Why?"

"The cost of the spell is a life, whether it is the demon whose blood you drank or your own."

"Can we do it later? I don't feel like going on knowing that if I drank someone else's blood on accident…"

Rifu sighed. "I suppose."

"The only immediate problem now," Jolie declared, "is that fuzz on your face. It has to come off…" Jolie grinned impishly at me.

"Hm…true, though succubae usually don't care…" Jolie glared at Rifu. Rifu winked at her mischievously. "Then again, we should play it safe!"

"Are you serious? Lives are hanging in the balance and…no…not happening. I'm especially not letting two *demons* shave me. That's a disaster waiting to happen."

Jolie smiled. "It won't be a problem, trust me."

"We'll have that beard off your face before you feel the razor," Rifu chuckled.

This was so embarrassing. I turned and made a beeline for the door. They beat me there.

"Come on, Haydn…" cooed Jolie.

"You need to look good for Brenda," teased Rifu.

I shook my head and tried to wheel around to get away, but they already had a hold of my arms. They hauled me away like I was nothing. It didn't surprise me that no matter how hard I struggled I couldn't get away. Didn't they know that beards and men were like black and white? They shouldn't be separated!

19. Christmas Sacrifice

Christmas Eve. Last-minute shopping, spending quality time with your family, thanking God for everything you have received, and the birth of Jesus Christ. A tranquil and traditional occasion; no one would expect anything to go awry. If a murder took place, it would definitely be noticed. For example, if the victim were, say, the daughter of a very wealthy family, someone is bound to hear something about the death.

Everyone was wallowing in peace and happiness. Oh wait, did I forget to mention that I, Haydn Ladditz, wasn't?

One month before, I met the Gaga Girls face to face. Then, I was in euphoria. My delight climaxed when I received an invitation to stay the night at the Anerex estate with the four girls. A month later, I was standing in the cold streets of Marshalltown looking to take one of my enemies out on a date. What was wrong with this picture? Everything. I was dressed in a nice pair of black dress pants and a matching vest. Over the vest was a warm dress jacket. I felt like I was going to prom. Jolie and Rifu had spent the night before preparing. We needed that preparation.

But, before going to Marshalltown, I was enchanted with the magic from the Tome of Fire. Rifu mumbled a verse of Latin words, a shining light washed over me, brushing against my skin like smooth silk in the wind. From that point on, I had to remember to let only Brenda's blood touch my lips. Not so hard to remember, right?

Silently, I waited for Brenda. She was going to pick me up. As much as I was against being trapped in a car with a succubus, I had no choice. No matter what trick she pulled, I had to remain strong and stay awake. If I fell asleep, then she would have me.

For half an hour, I thought she wasn't going to show up. I was ready to walk to the nearest pay phone and call up Rifu and Jolie, but, then, a black, monstrous Hummer rolled up in front of me. Who the hell drives a Hummer in winter weather? The driver got out and grinned at me.

"Haydn Ladditz, Brenda is waiting."

Her face struck a chord of familiarity inside my body as she tipped her hat. But, I ignored that as I slipped into the Hummer.

"Hello, Haydn," Brenda whispered.

I turned to her and grinned. "Hey... Brenda."

"So, you decided you couldn't run."

"Yeah."

Well, what else could I say? Jolie had said that succubae were vain. I tried some flattery.

"Your hot body was stuck in my mind ever since I first met you."

"Oh? Go on," she sighed.

I wasn't good with compliments. Damn, should have used a different excuse.

"Your hair..."

"What about it?"

"It's like... sapphire... thread..."

She giggled weakly. "I do try to take care of it. What about the rest of my body?"

"It... it... it..."

What the hell do I say now?

Brenda motioned me to stop, a low giggle escaping her lips. "I understand. It's okay. I know there so many ways you could describe my body, it's just overwhelming you."

"Yeah," *We'll go with that.* "You're a masterpiece drawn by no human." *Where the hell did that come from?*

"Oh, come here."

I slowly scooted closer to her. She reached for a button that rolled up a window separating us from her driver. Then she turned back to me, her face drooping into the grimmest expression.

"Haydn, drop the crap."

Whoa, what?

"What... do you...?"

"You can stop trying to suck up to me. Look, I know you may think I'm trying to kill you, eat your soul or whatever, but I'm not."

"What?"

"Look, I know this may sound weird, but the truth is that our driver here isn't my driver. She isn't even in my family. She's a servant to the lamias. She's Neferia's slave. Neferia has been spying on all of us, lying to all of us."

"And why all of sudden are you telling me this?"

"Ever since…that time in your dream…I've felt like you shook her control…somehow."

"Okay…why should I believe you?"

She gripped my jacket by its collar and pulled me into her face. "Stare into my eyes. Notice anything different?"

Afraid of being hypnotized, I wrenched my eyes shut. But, after a few moments, I opened them and saw *her* eyes. And I *did* notice something very different about them. They were so bright and clear, like the sky.

I jerked away. "Yeah, you have beautiful eyes, so what?"

"I know I do…but that's not the point! Think back to when you first met us. A month ago, in the hallway, think about our eyes."

I did and I realized something. Jolie's eyes…when I saw them that day, they were a color I couldn't quite describe. Then, the night she visited me, I could clearly see they were crimson. I realized, also, that it was the same with Rifu. Her emerald eyes had been murky that day. But when I was with her last, they were so bright.

"Your eyes…they're brighter now than on that day."

"Except for Neferia's," Brenda hissed. "It's because she had us hypnotized!"

"Slow down, what?"

"Lamias have the ability to mimic the powers of others. And guess what? They can also modify them to fit their needs. Kind of how a snake without a rattle modifies leaves or a pine cone to make predators or humans think it's a rattlesnake."

"So, you're saying she hypnotized you, Jolie, and Rifu?"

"Yes," she sighed. "Something bad is going to happen…"

The Hummer jerked to a stop. The driver turned around, her eyes locked onto us. She cocked her arm back and busted through the window.

"That'll be enough, Brenda," the driver laughed. "Neferia is waiting for you both inside the cathedral."

"Cathedral?"

"A cathedral's an odd place…"

"That doesn't matter, but you won't be drinking Brenda's blood tonight, Haydn."

Brenda looked at me, eyebrows knit up in confusion.

"Yeah…I was…um…going to kill you."

"Well…I don't blame you, honestly…"

"Enough chit-chat," the driver scowled. "Get out, or I'll force you out."

"You look just like a human, what are you going to do?"

The next moment I was staring down the sharp point of a bolt. It was attached to a mutated, fleshy bow made from the driver's arm.

"That…wasn't there before."

"That's because I'm not human. I'm a servant to the demons of this world. I'm a Keres, love."

I felt like I couldn't breathe. She was a Keres? The beings that had chased me were humans? No, she wasn't human. Humans couldn't make crossbows materialize from their flesh. What the hell was a Keres?

"Now, get out of the car."

Then, I thought about something. When I was shot by a Hades' Bolt before, and was completely unaffected. Charon had said I was a demon…even if I didn't believe it.

"Your arrow won't affect me? Why should listen to you?"

The driver shook her head. "Even demons can't survive shots to the heart, dumbass."

Whoops…

*   *   *

We had been taken to an abandoned church practically in the middle of nowhere. It was huge, Gothic, with spirals and flying buttresses reaching desperately for the sky. In front of the cathedral, a Mercedes sat with a cracked windshield and broken side view-mirrors.

Rifu's car…that could only mean…

The Keres opened the large double doors of the cathedral, pointing for both of us to proceed inside. Candles were lit on either side of a long aisle. At the head of the aisle was an altar that sat under a titanic cross hanging from the ceiling. Standing at the altar were Jolie, Rifu, and Neferia. The white-haired Neferia turned to us, her grey eyes glowing bright.

"Ah, Haydn Ladditz and poor, poor, traitorous Brenda, I welcome you."

"Neferia, what do you want?" I shouted.

"Blunt and to the point; very well, I'll compensate you. My motives are very, very simple. Have you ever heard of the legend of Lamia? She was a queen with immense beauty. She was so beautiful that a man who claimed to be Zeus fell in love with her. He swept Lamia off her feet and promised to marry her. Then, he revealed who he actually was. He was a servant to Lucifer."

"Lucifer?"

Neferia turned on me, suddenly in front of me, and backhanded me into the ground. "Don't interrupt me!" She cleared her throat. "Lucifer had been looking for a wife to wed his son. He took Lamia, presenting her to his son. But his son told him that he was tired of his arranged marriages, his plans on destroying the world. He had chosen love in a slave Lucifer owned and, in turn, disowned Lucifer. The Fallen One was beside himself, taking his anger out on Lamia by killing her children and turning her into a snake-like creature."

"What the hell does this have to do with us?"

Neferia wrapped her hands around my throat, lifting me up above her head. "The fact is, Haydn, it has everything to do with this entire group!" She threw me across the room and into a bench, giving way to the floor.

Rifu jumped forward. "Stop, Neferia! If you hurt anyone, kill anyone, kill me!"

Neferia started chuckling. "Oh, Rifu, poor naïve, Rifu…this spans back way before your existence was even a concept! No, no there is so much you don't understand, even if you think you know everything. But I know…I *do* know *everything*."

"What do you mean?" Jolie said.

"Shut up, you remnant!"

"Remnant," Jolie hollowly repeated.

I struggled to my feet, my ribs and back aching from the fall. My legs almost gave out. Luckily, there was a wall to support me. Though my lungs felt punctured, I kept breathing. My eyes locked onto Neferia, fury set deep into my core.

"What are you talking about? I have nothing to do with your damn family!"

"But you do. You are the son of the man who called himself Zeus! You are the son of the devil's servant!"

Charon's words clicked and linked, like a chain, to Neferia's words. Everything made better sense now. My father…he had stolen Lamia away. He was a tool of Lucifer, Rifu's grandfather. But…how exactly was Lucifer involved? And Rifu and Jolie…

Rifu made her move then. With agility unmatched, she sped across the floor, stopping behind Neferia, throwing a fist that connected with the base of Neferia's neck. The lamia spiraled straight through the decaying wall, the old cathedral groaning in pain.

There was a brief pause before Neferia returned, her icy hand wrapping around Rifu's throat before she even reached her. She held Rifu high, grey eyes pinning her in place.

"*You* are the reason I am cursed! You *are* the reason why I must devour souls and bodies. Your grandfather forever plagued my family with anger and death!"

Jolie tackled Neferia, plowing her into the floor. After falling, free of Neferia's grip, Rifu gasped for air. Rifu looked to me and shouted.

"Haydn, use that sword!"

I nodded. Focusing, I placed my right hand on my left hip. Instantly, I felt the ache melt away as a fire spread from my core out into my limbs. I pulled my hand away, the katana-shaped blade appearing as it did before.

Jolie stood up and backed away from Neferia, who now stood with fury engraved on her face. Power seemed to radiate from her, and I almost felt more scared of her than I had before. Almost. Anger overwhelmed my other emotions. My number one goal at that moment was to kill Neferia, even if I had been told not to.

"Do you really want Brenda to die?" Neferia chuckled.

I turned around, while Jolie and Rifu looked at me weird. Brenda was at the mercy of the Keres, a bolt pointed to Brenda's head. The poison wouldn't affect her, but the blast to the head would.

I don't want anyone except Neferia to die…Wait, what's wrong with me? Why would I want anyone to die? Neferia can't die. But she's manipulated us all. So much pain…and she's been the one pulling the strings this whole time.

"Snap out of it!" Jolie shouted. "Brenda is under Neferia's control! That's why she's not fighting back!"

I shook my head. "I'll take out the Keres! You two take care of Neferia."

I charged the Keres, swinging the sword in a low arch. Still clasped to Brenda, the Keres dodged me as if she were an illusion. I threw the sword like a harpoon, aiming for the Keres. She dropped Brenda and fled to the rafters, the sword falling harmlessly. I quickly picked up Brenda and snapped her out of her trance.

"Brenda, summon your abilities and *do something*!"

It seemed as if a switch had been turned on. Brenda stood up and turned towards the Keres who, then, made a nose dive for us. Brenda lifted up her arm, and it transformed into a crossbow, just like the Keres's bow. She fired a flurry of bolts at the Keres, each one dunking into the creature's flesh. The driver fell to the floor screaming. It was as she crumpled that her hair changed colors, her eyes becoming recognizable before crumpling up into dust.

"How is it possible?"

"What is it Haydn?" Rifu said, before Neferia smashed her into the ground. Neferia's laugh rang like a haunting melody in my ear.

"She was a good slave, but not irreplaceable. But, to you, however, that might be a different story."

I turned with, what had to have been, for Neferia's smile dropped away, unimaginable fury in my face. It wasn't hard to recognize the face of the dying Keres. In fact, it wasn't her first time dying.

"So, Sheila was also part of your plan?" I spat.

Neferia's smile returned with a vengeance. "Indeed, she was."

"But there was a skeleton! How do you explain that?" Jolie said.

"Well, the original Sheila wasn't as cooperative as I thought she would be…at least, not with me. My stomach, however, was another story."

I turned to Brenda. "And her? Is she also another puppet?" Brenda looked down to her arm, again normal.

Neferia started laughing. She kicked Rifu away and tossed an oncoming Jolie into the altar.

"She isn't a succubus, Haydn, that's just a fabricated lie. It's a cover. She never was a succubus. But, you've figured that out already."

Brenda stopped moving. I scowled.

"A Keres," Neferia moaned, "a servant to true demons. Poor girl thought she was a true demon this whole time. Oh, look, she's crying!"

Slowly, Brenda slumped to her knees, her makeup running as the warm tears flowed down her face.

"Neferia, you've done enough," I growled. "It's time you die."

"No Haydn!" Rifu shouted.

Neferia cackled. "Yes, kill me! And when you do, this world will be consumed by war! My plans…the manipulation…the killing of your mother, *his* wife, Haydn, has all led to the cusp of something far greater!"

I paused, considering Neferia's words. "You killed my mom… because she was my father's wife?"

"To kill off *his* family; your father, wherever the bastard is, will know what is like to lose his children!"

I lost all sense of right and wrong. My emotions were gone. All that was left was a ruthless killer. With seemingly one step, I stood in front of Neferia; sword aimed to decapitate her. But, at the last moment, she changed, morphed, and Neferia was no longer standing before me. The girl, the girl with the blonde hair, stood before me, wearing a white blouse, holding onto the handkerchief.

"How... do you know...?"

The girl smiled. To me, then, she wasn't Neferia, but someone else, someone I had met before. Someone I had shared ideals with. She was someone I had shared my love with. My arm burned as I stood there, head pounding at the pain, sword disappearing from my loss of concentration.

"I'm the girl you couldn't help, Haydn. Your father took you and your mother and ran. While others suffered, you survived and were given a second chance at life. Now, I'm going to take out my grievances upon your soul."

Jolie charged in from the side, taking Neferia through the hole in the wall. I stood there, shaken, unable to help. Rifu walked up to me, brought me close to her. I frowned, gripping my right shoulder.

"Is... Neferia really...?"

"No, she's lying, Haydn. But, Haydn, you can't let whatever happened in the past hold onto you. Let go of it. Let go of your anger. There could be a chance we don't make it out of this. I just wanted to say that I love you."

"What?"

Rifu smiled. "Trust me. And trust others." She wrapped her arms around me.

Subtly setting into my head, Rifu's words dissolved my anger. I was still angry at Neferia for her manipulation, but I felt like I was in control, the fire in my arm dying away.

"I love you too, Rifu."

We turned and chased after Jolie. We found her outside. The sun was beginning to set, and snow clouds were gathering over us, as if the angels were watching this very battle.

"Neferia, pay for your lies!" Jolie shouted.

They were moving at humanly impossible speeds. They matched each other punch for punch, kick for kick. Neferia was still in human form, having dropped the guise of that girl. They danced in the sunset,

Jolie throwing a haymaker, trying to take off Neferia's head. The white-haired villainess ducked with a grin.

"Do I lie? How do you know? Has your family recorded their history day by excruciating day?"

"Of course, and I've read it all!"

Jolie aimed a kick for the ducked Neferia, just missing her as Neferia rolled away, standing up on all fours.

"You probably read what they *wanted* you to read. How do you *know* what they tell you isn't a lie?"

"Because they're my parents!"

Neferia blocked a wild punch thrown by Jolie. With her caught off guard, Neferia wrapped an icy claw around Jolie's pale throat. She squeezed a little.

"Oh, how wrong you actually are."

"How…would…you know…?"

"I only pretend to be a fifteen year old girl. My name isn't Neferia, either. But you'll never have the privilege of knowing my real name." She squeezed tighter. "I've been around longer than you think, little girl."

That's when Rifu and I stepped in. She took Neferia's left and I ran up from behind. The lamia dropped her vampire victim and turned to swing at Rifu, catching her on the left shoulder. I cocked my fist for a blow to her head, but once again, hesitation set in. Neferia *did* look like a fifteen year old girl, and while I looked at her…

Help me.

"Poor, poor, pathetic Haydn," she hissed, kicking me in the ribcage.

I soared through the air, grinding into the ground almost twenty feet away. The pain wasn't as intense as it should have been, but it still gnawed at me. I wanted to cough up blood, to cough something up, but nothing came up. I wouldn't last through many other blows like that one.

"You're as foolish as Jolie." Rifu swung at her again, only to find her wrist caught in Neferia's hand. "And you, devil-girl, are the same. Naïve…ignorant…I bet you think your mommy and daddy met when they were young and happy."

Rifu escaped her grip, unleashing a head-splitting kick to Neferia's side. Though she stumbled back, it seemed the white-haired girl had barely been tickled. She stood straight, a grin on her lips, a scowl in her eyes.

"Dear, dear Rifu, don't make me have to devour you. I only planned on eating Haydn, but I have plenty of room if you insist." Jolie finally struggled to her feet, letting out a few racking coughs. "And if I eat you two, of course I would have to complete the set!"

This wasn't good. I saw the doubt on Rifu's face, the defeat in Jolie's eyes. There was hopelessness sprouting in my heart as well. What could we do? It didn't seem like we could do much.

Neferia's hands somehow found their way to Rifu's throat, gripping tighter and tighter as she hoisted her into the air. My heart squirmed in my chest, and my mind started to fizzle. The blood in my veins raged like a hurricane as my anger fueled every breath I took.

"Now, die," Neferia muttered.

There was a low groaning noise, and if I hadn't known better, I would have thought it was Rifu's life being squeezed from her body. It was coming from inside the cathedral. There was a loud snap and a rumble. The wall near us exploded as a large, metallic cross flew through the air towards Neferia and Rifu.

The cross crashed with a screech. At first my jaw dropped, then my heart. I scrambled to my feet and ran towards the cross. It had embedded into the ground, down much too deep to see any bodies. Then I heard coughing and ran around the cross. Jolie sat there, her arms around Rifu, sitting in Jolie's lap.

"Haydn," she muttered.

"How did *that* miss?"

"Jolie…saved me…"

Jolie looked away with a grin. She helped Rifu to her feet. I stared at Rifu stupidly, fear setting deep in my veins. I looked over to the cathedral. Out of the large wound emerged Brenda, her face red and stained with makeup.

"She…deserved that…"

I smiled and turned to Rifu. We stared at each other for the longest time. My lips twitched, and then my eyes started to burn. A salty tear silently crept down my cheek. Rifu grinned.

"Rifu…I thought you were going to die."

She giggled. "I thought so too."

"I…" I sniffled. "If it hadn't been for Jolie…I wouldn't have been able to save you…"

Rifu shook her head. "It's okay. At least you're alive."

I stepped towards her as she came to me. Our arms wrapped around each other, and without hesitation, we locked our lips. Jolie sighed dreamily before turning away in embarrassment. Brenda stood against the rubble of the cathedral wall while Rifu and I made out. When we finally pulled away, it was with a smile of pure delight.

Two things happened then. The ground started to shake, and my body was encased in a heat which intensified. It began to course through my veins, burn my heart, and reduce me to ashes as I fell to my knees.

"Haydn?" Rifu gasped.

Brenda got up from her spot against the wall and moved towards us. I managed to catch a glimpse of the fear and anxiety on her face before her hand morphed into the crossbow. The titanic cross groaned. It was slowly tilting away from the cathedral, and eventually landed with an earth-trembling impact.

The pain intensified. I could hardly keep a breath in my lungs. Fires were engulfing every fiber of my being. I couldn't do anything but huddle and cower in pain. Rifu stood up.

Hiss.

No, it couldn't be, could it? I didn't know what was happening. All I could hear and feel was the pain shifting through my body. But I could hear Jolie shout something, and I understood it perfectly.

"Neferia!"

I managed to turn and look at Neferia, unscathed by the attack. From her waist up she was human with small patches of scales cascading from her shoulders down her arms, while below her waist was serpentine. In total, she was at least forty feet long. Her tail was about as thick as a tree trunk, grey and rock-hard.

She chuckled. "You thought I was going to let you go? No, I won't die until I have vengeance!"

She charged me, the ground shaking beneath her weight. No matter how much I willed myself to move, it hurt too much to try and escape. Rifu sailed by, scooping me up before Neferia smashed the ground with her tail. Rifu set me down nearly fifty feet away.

"What's the matter?" she whispered.

"The…pain…"

Jolie and Brenda charged Neferia. They were repelled by a lazy swish of Neferia's tail. If she could muster that much power, than she certainly was a force to be reckoned with. We should've gotten out of there, but I couldn't move. The fire was burning and burning; the smoke was clouding my vision. The embers smoldered my voice.

The large tail sliced down upon me like a guillotine, but Rifu was a step of ahead of Neferia and, stepping in front of me, caught the lamia's tail. Rifu forced Neferia back. The lamia froze, and at first I thought she was scared. Then a plume of flames shot up my spine, and my cry rang loud.

Neferia chuckled at this. "Something wrong, Haydn? You look like you could use a little Christmas cheer." The grin on her face grew wider. "I *knew* about your plan this whole time. But I didn't think it would backfire!"

"But," Rifu growled, "Haydn never drank any blood!"

Neferia broke out into a fit of maniacal laughter. The pain escalated with each laugh. My ears began to ring, making it had to focus in on what Neferia said next.

"On the contrary, dear Rifu, you kissed Haydn. The spell … well … it's being completed as we speak."

Rifu wrenched her jaw shut, biting her lip, blood trickling from the corner of her mouth. "When … had I started bleeding?"

"When my hands were around your throat, Rifu, gently, but deeply, I sliced the corner of your mouth. In a few minutes, his power will be unleashed. Then, he'll either die or have to kill you." She shook her head. "But, it's not like you're going to survive that long. I plan on filling my belly before then."

Her coils struck, wrapping up Rifu, who squealed in fright. Neferia continued to coil around her, squeezing tighter, and tighter, and tighter. The fire only kept raging inside me, preventing me from helping Rifu. Neferia slithered next to Rifu, her tongue tracing circles on her cheeks. She grinned evilly at me and then looked back to her prey.

"Devil … a rare treat. And to think, you thought you would be spending eternity in a dream of love. No, love doesn't exist at all!"

Something happened. The fire began burning again, but this time it didn't hurt. My heart pounded like a war drum in my chest. I noticed my senses had become sharper. Everything around me was so vivid. Without much effort, I could hear a small bird fluttering in the snow almost two miles away.

"Goodbye, devil spawn!" Neferia began to stretch her jaw open to stuff Rifu inside, but Rifu's head would never grace her maw.

Neferia crumpled. Rifu fell out from between her coils. At first, she looked around wildly, like an animal, but then noticed me, kicking Neferia in the side of the head. Neferia fell to her back, bewildered at my sudden assault.

"Damn you, Dark Hunter's son!"

The sword appeared in my hand, a flurry of sparks. I looked deep into Neferia's eyes and saw my reflection. At one time, I believed that the boy in the mirror wasn't me. But as I gazed at my reflection in the eyes of Neferia, I felt like myself, and not an outcast.

"I'll kill you, Neferia. I swear to God!"

Neferia slithered, bolting across the ground and sprang up behind me. She knocked me forward with a head-butt and slapped me with her tail. Despite the new fire inside of me, Neferia would be no easy foe.

Turning on my right heel, I lunged, sword aimed for any part of Neferia. She, like a ghost, side-stepped and moved passed me, retorting with an elbow to my back. I fell to my knees. Like sweeping dust from the floor, Neferia scraped her tail across the ground, rolling me along with it.

She raised her tail high, ready to drop it on me, but I stood and slashed with my sword. Hissing in pain, Neferia swung her tail around to my right, sweeping me against the wall of the abandoned church. Without hesitation, Neferia rushed me, clawing my arms and chest with sharpened nails. I howled as the cuts burned in the cold air.

Rifu joined me, running at Neferia from behind. She kicked the serpentine woman in her lower back, causing Neferia to stumble forward. Jolie stood next to me suddenly and whispered to me.

"You have to use the slavery seal spell. Otherwise we won't make it out alive!"

"Are you kidding me? She doesn't deserve to live!"

"Haydn!"

"Forget it, she's dead!"

I gripped my sword with both hands and ran forth. Occupied by Rifu, Neferia didn't notice as I swiped at her side. Blood blanketed the grass along with Neferia's roar as I stood beside Rifu.

"What are you doing?" Rifu muttered. "We can't kill her!"

"After all that she has done, Rifu, you would grant her mercy?"

"Remember what my mother said, Haydn, murder *is* murder, no matter who dies."

"This isn't murder, it's a favor," I ran forward, the helpless Neferia bent over, holding her gushing side. "I'm doing the world a favor!"

Rifu watched in horror as Neferia crumpled to the ground. She saw the blood dripping from my blade as I stood away from Neferia's body, her head rolling across the ground. I didn't want to look at it. I felt sick then. The fire having fueled my rage was dead. And after a few moments, I dropped my sword, along with my heart, as the truth set in. Rifu stepped over the lamia's remains to stand next to me.

"Haydn … ?"

I pulled away from her.

"Wait, Haydn …"

"Don't come near me."

"What?"

"Don't...come...anywhere near me."

"What's wrong, Haydn?"

"The spell," I mumbled.

"I don't understand..."

"Don't play dumb!" I snapped. "Unless I kill you, I'm going to die! I'm scared, Rifu."

"Haydn, don't talk like that!"

"It's true, though! And, above all, I don't want to kill you! I can't!"

There was a long, uncomfortable silence. I began to pace away from Neferia's corpse. Her blood soaked into my hands, as if it were cursing me.

"Kill me."

I slowly turned around, looking to Rifu.

"No," I murmured.

"If I die," Rifu replied, "then you won't."

"No!" I shouted.

"Haydn, you—"

"I'm not going to put your life before mine!"

She stood there, her face caked with dirt, sweat, and blood. Her eyes were wet with tears. Slowly, reaching out her hand, she moved towards me.

"Haydn...I *want* you to kill me. I want you to have the rest of my soul!"

"I told you already that I *won't*."

"Please, I'm giving you my life! Take it!"

My body quaked under her dark, evil resolution. Stumbling backwards, I turned and ran. I didn't have to look back to see her tears hit the ground with the snow of the Christmas Sacrifice.

20. Get Out Alive

The soles of my shoes slammed hard against the ground. I had so much ground to cover. I had to get away. But where was I going? My speed, strength, and endurance had increased tenfold. Exhaustion seemed impossible. Trees watched me as I ran past them. They looked so familiar. I stopped. I was in the timber near my house. Why did I go there? Of all the places to run to, why did I have to run towards my family, the people who wouldn't remember me? I had to get out of there.

I gasped, falling to my knees. A wet, deep, sluggish pain slowly snaked into my chest. What was going to happen? When I died? I only had about a week left. Jolie had said I would die at the end of the year. What was I supposed to do? Run. Rifu would die for my selfish life otherwise. I wouldn't let her do that. And I couldn't go back home.

There was always the possibility of suicide. It could all end then, I thought. No one would have to sacrifice anything. I would be paying for my own mistakes.

"I would be paying for my sins," I whispered.

What sins?

I looked up. My eyes scanned the quiet forest. Two birds silently skipped from branch to branch. The snowfall sounded like an avalanche to my ears. Who had spoken? Maybe, it was just my conscience.

"I have so many. My anger; my wrath…Wrath's the deadliest sin of all."

Your anger is a curse, yes, but not your sin.

"Who are you?" *Am I going insane?*

You wouldn't know me now. A falsified image, you see.

"Can you at least give me your name?"

If I did, what good would that do you? You're not meant to give in so easily.

"What do you mean?"

Take her life. Rifu will never die.

"Wait, what do you mean she won't die?"

She will never die. Trust me.

"What do you mean? Tell me, please! Is there a way I can spare her life?" There was no response. "Tell me!"

I slumped over, all my will to live draining from my flesh.

*   *   *

I heard something, a familiar, resonant sound full of care and concern. The sound grew inside my head. How little it had been originally. But I felt as if the sound had grown a body and was touching me, shaking me. I recognized the sound.

"Mister…what happened to you?" the sound said.

I opened my eyes slowly to see *her* there. Her hair was bundled under a blue snow cap; she was in a light-blue winter coat. I could smell how new it was; a Christmas present. Her eyes were filled with worry.

"Are you okay?" Her face lit up when she saw my eyes open without a word. She pulled me up into a sitting position.

I looked upon her in silence. I wanted to leak out all the emotions trapped inside. It was too much for me to take. I hugged her, silent. She froze under my touch and then trembled, almost thrashing against me. I squeezed tighter, desperate to keep her at my side. I wanted her to stay here, but I knew she couldn't. She would never remember me.

Her body felt weaker. Then, she slumped against me. Panicked, I moved her over to a tree. I examined her for a moment, and before I even touched her forehead, I could tell she had a fever. Had she been searching for me all the whole time? No, that was impossible. She didn't remember.

"Katria…why are you here?"

My step-sister looked up at me weakly. "How do you know my name?

"I was…guessing," I mumbled. "I apologize. Are you okay?"

"I…feel sick…"

"I'll take you home."

"How do you know…?"

"Just forget about it."

*   *   *

I stood outside my house. Well, it used to be my house. Seeing it then pained me like nothing else. It didn't take but a few moments of standing there before Drake and Morgan rushed outside, taking Katria inside. Drake thanked me and invited me in. Any other person would have felt happy and warm. All I could feel was numbness. They brought me inside, wrapped me up in a blanket, and sat me at the table.

"Where are you from?" Morgan asked.

I was a little hesitant to answer. "Around here."

"Really? I've never seen you before."

"I'm… running away."

Well, it was the truth.

"From who? If someone's chasing you," Drake interjected.

"No, I'm pretty sure they aren't chasing me."

"Did you run away from home?"

"A long time ago."

This was only intensifying the pain. If only I could tell the truth. But I knew I couldn't. Then, I noticed something. A question bubbled up inside of me, and I turned to Drake.

"Excuse me for asking, but do you know a boy named Chris Ladditz?"

"Um, no, why? Is he your brother?"

"Yeah…"

I shook my head. Charon's laughing face slowly lit up in my head. How had Chris been involved with demons? He had mentioned something before, but I didn't take him seriously. Charon's words stuck in my heart like a cold knife.

"Are you okay?"

I stood up, throwing off the blanket. The family stared at me as I threw on my shoes and headed towards the door. Drake jumped up to stop me from getting away.

"Where are you going?"

"I can't stay here." I growled.

"At least stay for the night!" Morgan shouted.

My fist found its way through the glass of the sliding door. I stepped through it, unharmed, without a scratch. I turned back at my former family, glaring at them.

"Your eyes…they're golden…" Drake stammered. "Who are you?"

I looked to the ground. "I am no one but a forgotten outcast." And, once again, I was off.

*   *   *

I was bulleting across highways and over fences and under bridges so fast people probably mistook me for a low-flying bird. I had no place in this world. There was nowhere to go. And Rifu…she had once said I was special. Was I so *special* that I couldn't touch others?

I stopped. Where was I? I was standing on a highway wedged between two soy bean fields. It branched off into several directions. I was surprised that there weren't more cars out. I saw a few, but they didn't matter.

I turned north and started running again, the highway quickly disappeared behind me. I was never coming back. Soon, it would all be over. Then…what would happen? It seemed almost too easy. In fact, it *was* too easy.

I leapt over a frozen river when *it* hit. I took a nosedive hard into the ice. Pain slashed through my body. I looked down and saw the blood flowing evenly from a gash carved into my leg. Before I could even lift my head, claws were at my throat. I glanced at the claws, a sharp breath escaping my lungs as I recognized the very familiar hands.

"Jolie?"

"Haydn," she replied flatly.

We stayed there, frozen, waiting for the other to make the first move. Time seemed to slow down. I wanted to ask her what she wanted, but I couldn't form the words. Something told me she wanted to say something, but never removed her hands. Finally, she broke the drawn-out silence.

"Why are you running?"

"Isn't it obvious? I *can't* kill Rifu…I won't be so selfish as to let her die for me."

Jolie's claws eased up. She circled around and stood in front of me. Her eyes were wide with relief but her brow was furrowed in anger. The smack of her open palm against my cheek echoed down the frozen river and through the nearby trees. Tears silently streamed down her face.

"Would you shut up?" Her gaze was drilling deep into my soul, and it felt like nothing was safe and secret anymore. "What would you know about selfishness? You have nothing to be guilty about! You think you're being so selfish by letting Rifu sacrifice herself? You're being selfish by *not* letting her die for you! It's the greatest thing she could do for you, and you reject it! It's the most disgusting thing you could do!

"It doesn't matter she won't be around…she wants to sacrifice herself for you. You don't realize how much she's suffered ever since that night! She's had *nightmares* about you, Haydn and can't explain why! She wants you to be safe, yet she doesn't know if you are or not. She can't tell because you keep running! You hide yourself and then lock everyone else outside! Did you ever stop and contemplate how that might affect everyone else? Did you?

"Yet you keep running, even when she offers the greatest thing she has; her life, her *soul*. She wants you to live on and be happy. She has nothing left except an empty empire and envious eyes." Jolie shook her head. "I'm not saying this because I want you to come to me if she dies, because it's the opposite. I don't want you if you're going to keep running like this. I *hate* you. Learn that, because it won't change. I gave you a chance, but you made a decision that wasn't right or wrong. Then you made a wrong decision; you ran away, and so it's too late. Now go back, and allow Rifu to complete herself! Don't be selfish, please, don't be so damn selfish!"

I stood there trembling, but not with anger. I was trembling with grief, with guilt, with greed. I didn't want Rifu to end her life for me. But Rifu had already been betrayed by love once. Would this just reignite that buried wound? Would I just be the fuel to a fire that would inevitably engulf the human populace, much like my father before me? If it would make Rifu happy, to know that I took her soul, then I would do it, grievingly.

"But tell me this one thing. Why would you give up so easily? Rifu said that you had feelings for me." I eyed her carefully, scrutinizing her reaction.

Jolie looked into my eyes deeper, frustration fading from her face. Cupping my face in her hands, she stroked my hair and pulled me close, and then draped her arms around my neck, her forehead against mine.

"It was one day…I'll always remember it just like it happened. No amount of magic could ever warp the things that occurred that day. I couldn't control myself, please understand. Hate me if you want. Please, understand, I was only a little girl."

21. Before — Jolie

"Most were shocked when a seven year old could outdo them. In most cases, that was me. Everyone said I was talented. Strangers said I was a musical prodigy and a gifted athlete. But, to me, nothing was a gift. I paid for my great talents. Vampires always do.

"How did such great creatures like us become so scared of lower beings like humans? We were a minority, yes, but we still deserved to be on top. Why would our elders say otherwise? They controlled the government and swayed the military, but never effectively integrated our race into human society. We could make humans and demons equal. But no one saw what I saw. Living in luxury, no matter what secrets were kept, was their only agenda.

"There were few who did care about a future. Father was, and is, one of them. So, he encouraged me to excel in my classes. Without fail, I stumped and astounded teachers at every turnaround. They always wondered how I was skilled in almost everything. Vampires, along with most demons, don't sleep. We have all the time in the world to master the trivial affairs of early childhood. But when my teachers insisted I was too advanced for their classes, my parents would argue otherwise. Maturity didn't come through knowledge, they said. It only comes through experience. So, I stayed and was the subject to gossip both flattering and crude.

"Some said I was exceptionally cute for my age. My haters claimed I had fake hair and thought I was too pale. These things didn't matter to me. No form of prodding and poking did any harm to my personality. But every stone wall has its weakness. Mine was in my voice. Or my lack of a voice, I should say. Up to an hour after birth, a vampire is very weak and very vulnerable. An enemy of my father had hired a nurse to kill me. The assassin took me away to strangle me, but I was saved by a friend of Father's. It wasn't until they examined me carefully that they discovered I would never speak.

"After the incident, Father's friend invited him to stay at his manor in Iowa until we were safe from our enemies. Father agreed, and we immediately moved in. Father invested in second skins since most days could be rather sunny. Second skins were a genius invention brought about by vampires who loved the sun but didn't want to get killed by it. With our second skins in place, Father hoped we would be able to live out our lives peacefully. Of course, Father couldn't hide forever. We had our own manor built. And soon after, Father ran for senator.

"No one knew who Father was at first, but he was an intense, charismatic speaker and accomplished the tasks set before him. He was improving the economy so much faster than any other, even if the governor would turn down most of Father's plans. But after seeing some of his work, expert economists from D.C. requested Father's assistance. He wasn't home much after that.

"I was ecstatic to find out, one summer afternoon, that Father would be returning for almost three weeks. Unable to remember the last time we had together, my usual grimace was replaced by a wide smile. Mother was also very pleased with Father's return. His usual visits weren't very long; a weekend at most. This time would be different, and because of that, Mother and I were filled with an energy that I just can't describe.

"The moment he stepped into our home, I knew he had something particular planned. He wore a playful smile that radiated the true beauty of vampires.

"He said to me: 'Honey, do you like zoos?'

"I had never been to a zoo before. Father was always worried about my safety. There was no time to consider such a thing. That's why I loved them.

"'Well, then, how about we go to Omaha for a few days?'

"He handed me a brochure advertising the Omaha Zoo. It was down on the southeastern border of Iowa and Nebraska. Seeing live animals was an exciting idea. Nodding vigorously, I took the brochure and absorbed every detail about the place. For the first time in my short, short life, I actually felt like a normal little girl. Going to a zoo like any other family was truly something.

"'Good, we're going tomorrow, so pack your bag tonight!'

"I grinned and dashed off to pack my suitcase.

"One luxury I had, which could also be a curse at times, was that I was an only child. When my parents were around, I usually garnered their undivided attention. When they weren't…well…the only company I had was a pestering traditionalist. Traditionalist vampires believed in living within our capital city, the City of Snow, and the regions surrounding it, instead of occupying the human world. She constantly begged Mother for my hand in marriage to her stupid son. Mother would tell her to ask Father. He would leave it up to me. I would shake my head no. She would leave. It was a routine, like a girl who walked into a candy shop to look at her favorite candy but, unable to buy it, would leave. I felt like she viewed me that way; a piece of candy for her son to devour. But I digress.

"We left early for the zoo, and I was acting erratically. Mother threatened chaining me to the seat several times. But nothing would contain me. I was ready for something dreadfully amazing.

"After arriving, my parents let me out, unknowingly opening the floodgate. Out of confinement, I set my sights upon an unknowing populace. My feet carried me towards the entrance. Closer and closer I drew towards my destination, when I saw someone else running. Was someone planning on attacking me? I slowed, my vampire instincts nearly taking over, and I wheeled to face my attacker. As my attacker stumbled to the ground, however, I quickly realized I foolish I was. A small boy with dark brown hair sat at my feet. He had deep, blue eyes and a round face with a cute, flat nose.

"I was awestruck. But by what? He was nothing special. Yet I felt so attracted to him. Not in any serious way, but something was there. And apparently there was something about me he liked. Why was he staring at me so intently? He opened his mouth.

"'You have pretty eyes.'

"I didn't know what to think at first. It wasn't the first time someone had complimented my eyes. But I was trapped by his compliment, as if someone had caught me in a tightly knit net.

"'Aw…'

"'Your son is such a young gentleman,' Father said.

"'Why thank you…your daughter is quite lovely,' the boy's mother replied, flattery powdering her voice.

"'Thank you.'

"'How old is he?' Mother asked.

"'He's only five, but we teach him the best we can!' the father said proudly.

"'You've done very well so far, then,' replied Father approvingly.

"'She's seven years old, only two years apart!' Mother took out a camera and slid us close together. My face got hot. It felt as if I were hanging over an active volcano. 'Do you mind if I get a picture?'

"I did.

"His mother took out her camera. 'As long as I can get one, too!'

"Mother hesitated a bit and then finally shook her head. She knew that we wouldn't appear on normal film. Our skin, even our second skin, reflected light in a way that would make us invisible on normal film. 'Here, this is a special-made camera. It prints the pictures right away; much cheaper than a disposable camera.'

"His mother's face sagged in disappointment. Finally, she nodded in agreement and moved back to allow Mother to get a clear shot.

"'Say, cheese!'

"The camera snapped and even after the pictures printed out, I was still standing so close to the boy. Maybe too close. He didn't look at me, he was listening in on our parents, but I couldn't keep my eyes off of him.

"As Mother bantered with the boy's parents, I noticed the beating of the boy's innocent heart. It was as if I could see the blood racing through his tiny body. My icy fingers reached out to encircle his warm wrist. I would lift his wrist up and lick his arm. I would memorize the texture of his soft, youthful skin as I savored him. Then, without warning, I would move up his arm, my nose buried deep into his skin as I followed the path of the blood racing through his body. Then I would reach his neck.

"I pulled away. My canines ached. Feeling with my tongue, I found my needle-sharp canines were sticking out farther than usual. Was I finally becoming a mature vampire?

"'Come along,' Mother murmured to me as her and Father started to walk away.

"I quickly followed, but not without looking back at the boy. What else could I do but smile and wave? My lips formed a smile that was awkward because of my fangs, however, and I quickly turned around in retreat. What was I doing? He was only human, nothing more.

"Later, I was alone, sitting on a stone wall not far from the entrance of the rainforest. Father had forgotten something in the car and left to get it. Mother got caught up in conversation, so I snuck off. A lot of people looked at me strangely, especially this one group of middle school kids. The boys were especially staring at me, while the girls gave me a nasty glare, as if I had kicked their puppy. Maybe it was because the boys were paying more attention to me than them? Who knew?

"Surveying the crowd, I was surprised no one had asked me to get down. Maybe they thought my parents were nearby, or maybe they just didn't care about a lone girl like me. Someone did care, though.

"'Why are you so high?'

"I looked down, and my mouth formed a small smile. At the bottom of the wall looking up at me was that small boy. His eyes reflected the sun so innocently. Without thinking, I patted the spot next to me.

"'I can't climb up there,' he replied.

"I tilted my head to the side. Well, I did have long arms for my age, and it wasn't that tall of a wall. After holding out my hand to him, he looked at it hesitantly. Would he trust me, a stranger, to get him up there safely? He jumped for my hand. Next thing he knew, he was sitting beside me. He stared into the crowd.

"'How did you do that?'

"I grinned, running my index finger and thumb across my mouth. Obviously he had been expecting some kind of verbal response.

"'Why won't you say anything?'

"How was I supposed to explain I was mute, when I couldn't talk? I pointed to my throat then shook my head.

"'What?'

"I scratched my head. This was going to be trickier than I thought. I opened my mouth. After pointing down my throat, I tried to talk, but all that came out was a gurgling noise.

"'You can't talk?'

"I nodded. His arms were around me before I could object. There was no problem with his hug. He had just taken me by surprise.

"'I'm so sowwy,' he mumbled.

"How was I supposed to respond? Up until this point, I thought most people other than Mother and Father only cared about my beauty. Who cared if I couldn't talk? They never stopped to think about the things I wouldn't be able to say. My heart always sank to the darkest of places when I thought about the possibilities. The boy lifted his head up.

"'Haydn!' someone called out. That had to be his name. He looked at me with sad puppy-dog eyes as I wrapped my arms around him.

"'I have to go…'

"No he didn't, not if he stayed with me. But I knew better than that. I had to let him go. We were still young. We would probably meet again. He smiled at me goofily.

"'I'll see you again,' as if echoing my mind, he mumbled, 'won't I?'

"I smiled bitterly. Why did there always have to be something to separate us from the things that mattered most? While no one was looking, I held him tight and jumped from the top of the wall. After we landed safely, I slowly let go of him before disappearing into the crowd.

"A little later, I had circled through the crowd several times. Mother wasn't where I had left her. Had she gone looking for me? I stood to wait for her. That's when I bumped into a group of girls. It was the same group of three from before. One of them got up in my face. That's when it started.

"There were three of them and one of me. Despite being a vampire, I felt uncomfortable. This one girl had her ears pierced and wore five layers of make-up. Who wore that much make-up at her age? She towered over me. Why was I so nervous? She jabbed my shoulder with her bony fingers.

"'Why, don't you look like a little princess in your pretty white dress?'

"One of her friends nudged her a little bit. 'Come on, leave her alone…'

"'Shut up!'

"She pushed me to the ground, causing the skirt of my dress to rip. I stared at it in a stupor. Mother had made the dress from scratch for my seventh birthday. The girl laughed so obnoxiously that I snapped. After leaping to my feet, I peeled my lips back in a snarl, a loud growl rumbling from my throat. The three girls froze and became pale as snow. Their leader started shrieking in panic. She pointed at me accusingly. I put my hand to my mouth, my fangs protruding farther than before. They started to ache. I was now a full-fledged vampire.

"I couldn't close my mouth, it hurt too much. The girls kept screaming and screaming. People started gathering around and stared at me. My ears rang. My knees were about to buckle under the crowds' eyes. And as if things couldn't get worse, two words pierced my head.

"'My *baby*!'

"Recognizing the voice of the cry, I quickly bolted from my spot and ran inside the rainforest. If I were human, cold sweat would've be running down my face. There was a crowd gathered outside the snake cage. I knew I could never force my way through the crowd without getting noticed, so I crawled under them. And when I finally got to the other side, I froze to my spot.

"It was the boy, Haydn, caught in the maw of a deadly boa constrictor. His eyes were dull and his body had stopped squirming as the large serpent slipped its mouth over him. Why didn't anybody do something? Were they going to let this boy die? I wouldn't.

"Time almost stopped as the snake brought Haydn in up to his shoulders. I ran by the animal tamer and snatched a sharp knife hanging from his belt. My vampire power of illusion camouflaged me as I acted. With knife in hand, I lunged for the boa, plunging the blade deep into the snake's flesh. Struggling, I pulled back to slice the snake's head from its body. When it stopped swallowing the boy, I made my retreat.

"As soon as I was outside, I dropped to my knees, caught in the pain of my own tears. I could feel it. Haydn's fear had rushed into me as I cut him free. It still resonated throughout my being. And worst of all it was *my* fault. I learned later that the shrieks of those girls had startled the hungry snake and it lunged at him.

"My parents discovered me shortly, along with my torn dress. They tried to comfort me, but I knew that it would never be enough. They could wash the tears from my dress, but they would never be able to wash the guilt from my non-existent heart.

"After that, I followed the boy. I moved to his school and watched him in the hallways. I watched him while he worked out, while he walked home, and while he slept. He would never come that close to death again.

"But I…don't know why…but I…

"Am I really alive?

"Who am I?"

Purpose

Haydn

Jolie fell to the ground, and I followed her.

"Jolie, what's wrong?"

She shook her head. "I just can't remember…"

"Remember what?"

After a moment of silence, she let me help her to her feet. We stood there, and she was staring up into the sky. When she looked back down at me, she smiled.

"Oh, Haydn, I'm so sorry."

"It's not your fault, Jolie." I reached out to comfort her, but she pulled away.

"Don't you hate me?" she whispered her voice so low it was almost inaudible. "I almost got you killed, and yet you try to comfort me?"

"What's the point of hating you? If it hadn't been for you, I wouldn't be here." I smiled, tilting my head to the side. "It was the first time you saved me. And it wasn't the last."

"But if it hadn't been for me," she groaned, "then you wouldn't have been put in this situation!"

"It's in the past, Jolie. Besides, you aren't the main cause."

"You make it sound so simple, Haydn."

"I don't know how simple things are going to be after this. I just don't know, Jolie. Where am I supposed to go?"

"I guess that's for you to decide, Haydn. You make you, Haydn, not your situation."

Jolie sighed and turned away from me. I turned to leave. I had a lot of ground to cover, but I stopped and looked back over my shoulder. "Jolie…how can you talk now? You were mute when we met. How can you speak now?"

"That's what I don't remember," she muttered.

"I'm sorry for digging up the past," I chuckled.

I was gone then, off in the direction opposite of the bleeding sky. Whether I wanted to or not, I had to end this. It was clear that I had to do this. What would I do if I didn't? My soul would become the property of Hell.

So, I was off to kill Rifu.

22. Brother's Word

As I closed in on Anerex Manor, so did my rib cage around my heart. Maybe, I was making the wrong decision. But Jolie's voice whispered at the back of my head. She kept telling me to not be selfish. I still didn't understand what she meant. Did I really understand what I was doing?

But after Rifu's gone, I would be left alone. I couldn't go home. Short of breath, I slowed to a walk. My head was spinning out of control. Why would Jolie encourage me to kill her best friend? Nothing fit together, like a puzzle with all the wrong pieces. I crashed to the ground. Shuddering sobs overtook me. Drake would be wondering why I wasn't stronger. He wouldn't have let me cry like this. But he wasn't there. He would never be there ever again. It was just me, and my grim resolution.

The bleeding sun was clotted by the clouds. Murky as night, and I felt safe and secure for a single moment. If Rifu and I could have met in a different lifetime, then could we have had a future? Probably not; she would have made me soul food.

After finally gaining control over myself, I stood up and started running again. A few minutes later I stumbled into a cornfield. I was less than four miles at most from Rifu's mansion. Anxiety's vines crept up my spine and encased Courage, sapping my willpower and feeding my fear. My legs refused to move.

"Keep going."

I arched my neck so I could see my mystery motivator. I gasped in pain as I got to my feet. My eyes and ears had to be lying to me. Why would *he* be standing in the middle of a cornfield?

"Chris," I muttered.

"Don't stop. She's *waiting* for *you*."

I stared at Chris in disbelief. It wasn't him. No, he couldn't know about Rifu. I had a deep feeling inside that Chris never knew.

"Who the hell are you? You're not Chris! You're not my brother!"

He sighed. "Haydn, do you know how much you remind me of him? It hurts to look at you."

"Who are you?"

"I apologize for lying to you. For lying to your family, I knew it was wrong. But you must understand that I did it for your own good."

"Shut up!"

There was a loud snap. *Crack.* The person who stood before me now didn't even come close to resembling Chris, if you could call it that. Before me was a mass of flesh and bone, shuffling around. Within a few moments, a tall, lean yet muscular man stood before me. He had long, white hair with green eyes hidden behind a veil of bangs. His jaw was hard, tensed, and his hands were slender, yet they looked powerful.

"I am Uron Anerex," he said. His voice was graver and deeper than it had been. "Chris might have mentioned me at least once."

"You mean *you* mentioned yourself."

Uron grimaced, rubbing his temples. "Yes, I was disguised as your brother. For most of the time you have known him, it was actually me."

I didn't flinch. I didn't cringe. The fire of wrath clawed against my ribcage.

"What happened to Chris?" Even as I said it, I felt I had a decent idea as to what had become of Chris.

Uron looked at me with a softened gaze. His features became less intimidating, and he smiled like Chris always did when we were together. No, it was his smile. Not Chris's smile.

"I guess I should begin with explaining your birthmark."

"It sealed my powers, right? But, who gave it to me?"

He nodded. "Your father, actually. You see, your father originally received a mark similar to that one as a symbol of his servitude. He served under my grandfather as his Dark Hunter."

"What did he hunt?"

"People, relics, souls, whatever my grandfather hungered for. But enough about *my* family history. Seven years ago, Chris and I were best friends. There was nothing we didn't do together. We were inseparable. He, unlike you, did not possess the mark of your father, at first. Eventually, Chris moved away, at least, that's what everyone saw." He frowned. "It was a black and cold reality."

"What happened to him?"

"I invited Chris to my home a little after graduation. He had gotten his first tattoo. On his left arm, the same arm as your father's, he had your birthmark replicated. My grandfather had been visiting at the time. He saw Chris's tattoo. Thinking it was the seal of your father, he sought to claim Chris as another servant. Fortunately for Chris, Grandfather couldn't touch our friends due to our father. But, it wasn't over. My twin sister took great interest in Chris. She wanted him badly, and she would do anything to have him. But my sister was never great with words, so she decided to take him forcefully. She tried to get my father's help. When he told her no..." he trailed off into silence. I could see the pain in his eyes... as if he were reliving the events. "She wanted him. Not just his soul, but she wanted his body and love. She wanted everything that had to do with him." Uron glanced at me, his eyes full of hatred, not towards me, but towards his sister. "She went to my grandfather.

"Our grandfather bypassed our father and went straight to Chris in his sleep. He convinced him to give his life, soul, and body to my sister. What she didn't know was, with the mark Chris had, if he pledged himself to any member of our family, he would become Grandfather's property as well. I couldn't let that happen. I spared him an eternity of suffering."

Instantly, my hand was wrapped around Uron's throat. "You bastard!"

As if he were made of sand, Uron somehow slipped through of my grip and moved away from me.

"Please, forgive me, Haydn. I didn't want Chris to suffer. I would rather know he was at peace in Heaven than kissing Satan's feet until the end of time!"

Pinching the bridge of my nose, I didn't say anything. Tears started to push against my eyelids. I wanted to cry. All my life I had always been involved with demons. They were always pulling at my strings.

"After that, I tried to run away, only to be caught by guilt. It was my fault that Chris was gone. All I could do was to try to compensate you and your family. I found your house, I found you, and I became Chris. Or, I tried to become Chris. I've tried for seven years. I knew it was going to come to this point. I wanted to warn you, to guide you. But you were too young. Three years beforehand you had almost died. You probably wouldn't have believed me anyways." He chuckled, shaking his head. "I'm sorry for the lie I've planted into your heart. I only wanted you to be happy."

Lies…there seemed were a lot of them, especially inside my heart. What if I were just one big lie? I released a shuddering sigh, the cold winter air transmuting it into vapor before my eyes.

"At least…" I gulped. "At least you didn't hide it *forever*…but…it still hurts, you know?"

"I apologize. You don't know how much it hurts me as well."

"It's kind of ironic. It's almost a similar situation with…well, you know…"

"Irony is not the villain here, unfortunately. Fate is just too cruel to those entangled in the affairs of God."

I shook my head. "I don't want to do it. But, at the same time I have to. How could I let her suffer through life? I can't let her be enslaved by her own guilt."

Uron chuckled. "It's very important to my sister. Rifu loves you."

"How do you know?"

"I have the same abilities as her. I know how she feels. When your name is mentioned, her emotions spike."

"Maybe…"

"I can tell. She blames herself for your problems. I have a feeling that giving her life to you, in her mind, is the least she could do."

"But it's the greatest thing she could do for me."

"She thinks otherwise."

I rubbed my brow, sighing. My gaze fell to the ground. "So…when Chris—I mean, when you said he had to meet with…um…you…"

"I was actually meeting with my family. There's a lot of unrest in the Anerex family. Father, especially, believes in the tension between us and other families."

"Like the lamias."

"Yes. Father has been trying to resolve the issues between our families for some time. We had believed we were close to an agreement. Then it was discovered that a rogue lamia had been slain in Des Moines."

"Jolie," I gasped.

He nodded. "They were willing to look the other way, considering that particular lamia was an exile. But after recent events…"

I remembered Neferia's bloody head. "It's my fault. I killed Neferia."

"Neferia was driven into a blind, insane rage after she discovered our families' negotiations."

"And she tried to attack us. My father…it's his fault. He's at the center of it. If he hadn't abducted Queen La—"

Uron shook his head. "You're overly mistaken, Haydn."

"If it's not *his* fault, then who deserves the blame?"

"This is not the time to worry about that. You don't have much time, and Rifu's patience is wearing thin."

"No, I want to know about my father! I want to know about these memories…these visions I keep having! He's linked to them isn't he? My mother knew…Charon said they were my memories…"

Uron shook his head. "You don't know how many blessings you have. Do not take them for granted. Jolie will be waiting for you, despite how you think she may feel."

"Stay out of my head!"

He turned away, a deep growl rumbling from his throat. "Haydn, there are still a lot of things you don't know. Even though it may seem you're losing something, it may only be taking on a different form. Like snow to rain."

I turned to leave, unable to bear anymore of his words. His voice stopped me.

"Forgive me, Haydn. I shouldn't have burdened you like this. But you'll understand soon. I will keep watch over your family. And I still love you like a brother. Chris is proud of how far you've come."

I wheeled around to face Uron again, but he was gone. My eyes searched the field, then the sky. The sun wasn't even halfway over the horizon. I left that place without another distraction. The Anerex estate was only a few miles down the road from the field. I took my time.

23. I Will Not Die

The large door loomed overhead, a grim reaper awaiting its next victim. While I stared at it, memories of the zoo snaked into my mind. My fear slithered up and down my back and encircled my waist. Even though my heart was crying for me to stop, my feet wouldn't. Before I knew it, I was at Rifu's front door.

Finding the door ajar, I wondered if she was expecting me. Then I wondered how Rifu's parents felt about the situation. They would probably try to stop me. I slipped through the doorway, my eyes darting from one corner of the colossal lobby to the other. There were no signs of life. No lights were on except for the fireplace. What if Rifu had taken back her offer? What if she ran away? I wouldn't blame her. I had almost run away.

She was here somewhere. Why would she leave a fire burning? A fire doesn't just light itself. I moved cautiously towards the fireplace and looked over the small gathering area. Noticing the couch, I approached it. On the middle cushion was a small book. I picked it up and instantly recognized it.

"Rifu's diary," I mumbled.

I flipped the small book open. It opened to a page containing an envelope. It was from Rifu, of course, and it contained a key and a note. Unfolding the note, a braced myself. It was her handwriting.

And at the bottom of the note was her neat, tidy signature. Just like in the invitation.

Haydn,

I know you'll come. You'll probably notice that no one's here. I don't know where they are, but the house is ours, otherwise. This time, it's your turn to be "it." Your decision to run hurt me. I won't forgive you easily. And though you may possess the key to my grave, I promise you this: I will not die easily.

Rifu

An ominous sensation swirled inside of me, creeping up my throat. Beads of sweat started to roll down my face. I wiped them away. Why was I scared? I stood up and looked at the flame. My initial visit here had been wondrous at first. Now, agony reflected in everything I saw. Rifu hadn't told me her whereabouts, but she didn't have to. I knew exactly where she was. Without another moment, my feet were slowly carrying me in the direction of the greenhouse.

As I walked, I felt as if everything was watching me. The shadows danced around me, laughing at my paranoia. My thoughts were interrupted when I heard a creaking noise from the floorboards. As soon as I took another step, a crackling noise reached my ears, like flames devouring wood.

I whipped around to face the creeping licks of blue fire enveloping the hallway entrance. Where had the flame come from? Could it have sprung from the fireplace? It didn't matter. I was a demon, right? The fire shouldn't bother me. At that moment, a wicked tongue of flame caught my arm. I howled and reeled back in pain.

It's not normal fire. It's hellfire. It can burn anything, including demons.

"Who said that?" I shouted.

Unless you want to become ashes, I suggest you make it to the greenhouse.

I followed the voice's advice and made for the greenhouse. But something didn't make sense. Why would Rifu's family let their mansion burn down? They had left so much behind. But that was trivial. Rifu was my main priority right now.

I found the glass doors and threw them open, catching them before they shattered against the outside walls. Once inside, I slowly pulled the doors back in and closed them. I turned around, shoveling in breaths while I looked at my hands.

"My reflexes are amazing." If only they didn't cost a life.

I looked up to the greenhouse. All of the flowers had wilted. Dead plants littered the ground and cursed the scorched trees striving to survive. My skin crawled. Everything was so twisted compared to before. Ashes were still falling to the ground. I laid my eyes on what was left of the maze: a browned, crumpled remnant of Perse's gardening mastery. What had happened here? I set my eyes towards Rifu's door on the other side of the large greenhouse. It seemed larger than before. That's when I realized I had been slowly walking towards it after I entered.

Rifu's door stood before me, a Kraken in the way of my Andromeda. My soul would never come clean, I thought. My hands would be permanently blackened from Rifu's blood.

I stretched a trembling hand out towards the doorknob. I thought I couldn't reach it. It was as if there was a wall of icy gel between me and the door. But I finally placed my hand on the doorknob, and it wouldn't turn. I took my shaking hand away and put my other one in its place. I pictured Rifu's smiling face in my head. But that made me ache all over. I forced the knob to turn, forced the door open, stepped inside, and shut the door.

"It took you long enough."

I caught my breath. She was sitting on her bed, guitar in her lap, fingers slowly plucking at the strings, and eerie melody dancing in the air. Not even for a moment did she look at me. I would have turned to stone if she had.

"I ran almost halfway across the state," I replied.

"Why were you halfway across the state?"

"I didn't know what to do."

"And your point is?"

"I was trying to decide whether I wanted to take the shortcut or take the hard way."

"Oh, really?" she mumbled. "What was the shortcut?"

"Killing myself," I mumbled.

"How do you know that wasn't the hard way?"

"Because you would suffer and I would rest in peace!"

She looked up. Her eyes were bloodshot. Tears started to peak out from the corners of her eyes.

"And what about you?" she mumbled. "Aren't you going to suffer when I'm gone?" Her words stabbed me in the chest.

"I didn't mean it like that! Please...it's hard to think about. I don't want to think about it!"

"And what happens when it comes to pass? What are you going to do?"

I stayed silent.

"It's okay, if you don't have an answer yet, Haydn." She stood up, placing the guitar on her bed, and slowly stepped towards me. "You have some time to think on it."

"What do you mean?"

She twirled away from me.

"Didn't you read my message? I said I wouldn't die easily." Then she was in my face, grinning fiercely. "And I meant it." She shoved me into the door. Before I could respond she was lifting her arms. In each hand a lick of blue flame blossomed into an azure fireball. "And if you don't fight, you'll die!"

The flames barreled towards me. I snapped my head forward, and I fell backwards in a mess of flame and wood. The heat was intense as I scrambled to my feet, barely dodging another deadly flame. Rifu charged me and socked me in the gut. Her fists wreaked havoc on my body, landing a blow on what felt like every square inch of flesh. Her foot found my chin, a sick crack as I spiraled into the air.

She can fight like this?

I smacked the ground. My breath and soul seemed to leave my body. This was torture. I didn't want to kill her, let alone fight her!

"Get up!"

I coughed. Rifu stood over me, her bare foot on my chest.

"Are you really giving up? Do you really want to die?" She shook her head. "Are you taking the easy way out? Taking the shortcut?"

She pressed down on my chest. If I had been normal, the pressure alone would have killed me. She let up and then cocked her fist back.

"I'll be glad to oblige you, pathetic dog!"

I swung my leg, sweeping her off her feet. My feet were planted firmly on the ground seconds later. I stared at Rifu until she got back to her feet. How was I supposed to fight her?

"Are you just going to stand there?" she growled. "First you run away, now you don't have the gall to take what's yours?"

"This isn't fair, Rifu!"

"What isn't fair is that you rejected more than my body, more than my heart...you rejected my *soul*! And on top of that, *you* would have *died*! Where would I be? What would I do then?"

"I didn't want you to die! I *love* you!" My chest heaved in pain. I wrapped my arms around my rib cage. "I don't want to kill you. Isn't the guy supposed to give his life for the girl he loves?" I started sobbing. "I don't want you dead."

She had heard enough. Without another word she rushed me. I closed my eyes and expected her fist to meet my face, or to be set on fire. Yet there was nothing except my sobbing. I was crying like a baby and after a few moments I opened my eyes. Her eyes met mine. I gasped and fell back. Tears were rolling down her cheeks.

"How do you think I feel? Did you think I wanted you dead? I love you, too." She wrapped her arms around me. "I was so angry that you ran. My mind went to a dark, dark place. I felt like I could never forgive myself if you died."

I clutched her to my body. "I don't know if I'll be able to let you go."

Rifu pulled away and looked at me. "You have to move on, Haydn. But I want you to remember the short amount of time we had. Even though it was so short, it was so sweet."

I grabbed her and pulled her back towards me. "But what am I supposed to do? This will be goodbye, forever. I don't want that. I want to be with you forever."

She sighed and smiled. "Nothing's…forever, Haydn. Keep that in mind. Everything…is…We could meet…" she started to sob before collapsing against me.

I put my hand on the back of her head. Silent tears crept down my cheeks. We sat there, her mansion burning around us. The greenhouse, no matter how hot the flames got, kept us safe. I thanked God for that. This would be my last moment with Rifu. I didn't want it ruined.

"Haydn," Rifu whispered.

"Yeah?"

"Can you tell me something…before I go?"

"Anything."

"Charon and Neferia both said that Ladditz wasn't your real name. They called you by another name?"

I nodded. "Yeah. Ladditz is the last name I took after Chris. He hated our father as much me."

"Can you tell me…your real name again? Please? I forgot it. And I don't want to forget you."

In the silence, in those last few moments, everything seemed to be a dream. Everything around me seemed to be an iridescent chimera of higher meaning. In that last moment, it truly felt like saying my real name through my own lips would be enough to keep Rifu alive.

"My real name is Haydn Gabriel Nikolaou."

"It has a ring to it. I wish I could have taken that name in the future."

"I wish you could have shared it with me."

"I can't stay much longer. If I do, I might not want to leave you."

"Then I'll die."

"We've been through this before."

I nodded. A shuddering sigh escaped my lips. "How do I do this?"

We stood up, and she got on the tips of her toes. She started closing her eyes. Her mouth closed in on mine.

"You form your lips like this… and we… will become one…"

Our lips met. I closed my eyes.

Epilogue: When Daylight Dies
Jolie

"Are you sure you want him here, Jolie?" Father asked me.

I nodded impatiently. "He has nowhere else to go. Were you even listening to me?"

"He's dangerous. The lamias are going to be after him…"

"He also killed Rifu. He probably won't be getting over that anytime soon. I found him standing outside of the Anerex mansion. He doesn't have a family to go back to, Father. He has pneumonia because he was standing in the rain with…" I shuddered.

"Rain? But, it's winter."

"The whole mansion was burning. And it wasn't regular fire. The flames were blue."

"It had to have been hellfire."

"Hellfire?"

"It can burn through anything; even demon flesh."

He seemed to be thinking something over. To me, Haydn's well-being was my top priority.

"Please, just let him stay." At that point, I felt like I was speaking for more than one person. Father didn't like telling me no. He never liked to displease his little girl.

"He can stay. I just hope you've made the right decision."

I wrapped my arms around him. "I feel like it's the only thing I can do."

"As long as you're sure, Jolie," he mumbled.

His face was twisted in uncertainty. I pecked him on the cheek, rushed out of the study and bolted down the hall. I dodged servants like I was in an obstacle course. I stopped in front of the study Rifu and I hid Haydn in a month before. There he was again, trying to cope with … well … a lot. I felt personally responsible, of course. But my pain felt doubled. I had a strange obsession for Haydn. Ever since that day ten years ago, it seemed like.

I cracked the door and poked my head in. He was up. That was good. But he didn't look at me. His eyes were watching the crackling flame. Nothing seemed salvageable from this shipwreck.

"You okay?" as I plopped down next to him on the couch.

He didn't respond.

"Are you going to speak to me within the next century? Or am I going to have to learn how to read minds?"

He flashed me a warning glance. I knew this wasn't going to be easy.

"So…" I changed the subject. "Do you feel good enough to go out and do something? I heard there's this killer band from California in Des Moines tonight."

No response. He just stared into the fire like it was the only thing he had left. I sighed.

"Please talk to me, Haydn."

He looked me in the eyes. They were red and swollen. He pushed me away without a word. He was getting on my nerves.

"Were you and Rifu close?" he asked.

I almost jumped off the couch. He sounded like someone had shaved his vocal cords with a rusty razorblade.

"Yeah, we were pretty close. We've known each other since we were young."

"How young?"

"I was about six. She was four."

"That is a long time. But, not as long as I feel old, not as long as I feel sad … and it doesn't seem like you're as sad as I am."

Ouch. "That's kind of harsh, Haydn. You shouldn't be so hard on yourself."

"And why not? If it hadn't been for me, then she wouldn't be dead."

"You really have to learn to stop tacking the blame on yourself," as if I had room to talk. "Neferia had just as much to do with her death, if not more."

He didn't respond. I sighed.

"Fine, sit here and mope for the rest of your miserable, goddamned life! That won't bring Rifu back!"

"It was hard, you know?" He looked into the fire. "Fire was everywhere. I wanted to get out of it. And I didn't want to leave her in there. So I carried her body out into the cold before I lost the last of my strength. Then she went limp. It started snowing hard, but the heat from the flames…turned it into rain." He started coughing. "I don't know how I'm going to live without her."

I wanted to say that he didn't have to live without her. That she was always with him. But that was just some coping mechanism humans had developed. That wouldn't work with him. He knew she was gone. But for some reason, I didn't want to believe she was gone.

Instead of trying to cope, instead of trying to cover up the truth of the pain, my mind created an alternative solution.

A song started playing in my head. I remembered way back when I first heard it. Rifu and I transcribed the song by ear. I sang it, Rifu played the guitar. The music was melodic and eerie, but strangely comforting. I felt alien, remembering those days. It felt like I wasn't even there. I took a deep breath. I imagined Rifu's voice channeling into my own, and just let go.

Still I count the days and nights since I survived.
This lonely abyss is the place I've learned to hide.
But the memories conflict with the story I keep in my mind.
Then reality comes over me like darkness to blind.
I can't live without your love, and I can't die.
Still I'm standing in the rain, when daylight dies.

About the Author

When asked to talk about himself, Blaine Blade responded:

"Penning stories has always been close to my heart. Cats play a close second. Of course, writing doesn't take up all my time. I'm a local rock-star. At least, I'd like to think I am. I play guitar in a band, and write music every once in a while. And when my parents aren't teasing and torturing me, my girlfriend cleverly picks up where they leave off. My dog, Case, is always there to make sure I get a sloppy kiss for my efforts.

"My mind is like a museum of ideas…if I didn't write most of them down…well, that's another story idea altogether, isn't it? When writing, though, I try to stick to what I would like to read. Action, dark back-plots, teenage dilemmas, and a hint of poetic romance to make everything look pretty! In future works, including the second Eternal Flame Trilogy book, plan to see plenty of those things from me."

CPSIA information can be obtained at www.ICGtesting.com
Printed in the USA
LVOW041837010412

275523LV00001B/28/P